The Secret Ingredient to Falling in Love

The Secret Ingredient to Falling in Love

Molly Kendall

Cover illustration and cover design by Molly Socks.
Instagram: mollysocksdesign
Website: www.mollysocks.design/

Library of Congress Control Number: 2022906136

Publishers Cataloging-in-Publication Data
The Secret Ingredient to Falling in Love;
by Molly Kendall
328 pages cm.

ISBNs

Paperback: 978-1-7363062-4-6
Hardcover: 978-1-7363062-5-3
Ebook: 978-1-7363062-6-0

Printed in the United States of America

acknowledgements

First, I want to say that this book would not be possible without the millions of wonderful readers on *Wattpad* who have been supporting me from day one. This book was the start of my writing career, and I cannot express how much love I have for this story, flaws and all (and Lord knows there were MANY). If it weren't for the help of my amazing editor, Christiana, I would have been too embarrassed to release this book. Now, I am very excited to present the new and improved story, with characters you love—or will grow to.

Second, I want to say thank you to my very dear friends - Erin, Rabiya, and Eryn. Gals, this book literally would not exist if it weren't for your constant excitement and love. Thank you for being so sweet, and for loving me despite my stupidity. This one's for you!

Lastly, shout out to my family, who have been so supportive as I branch out a new leaf, and my Rebel Team, for being so awesome. These adults have been my role models, and I love you all dearly. *You know who you are.*

__chapter one__

Sarah

"Sarah!"

I brace myself for impact as Gina, my best friend, comes flying over. She throws her tall frame into my short one, almost knocking us both over in the process. Her long, dark, curly hair smothers my face as she crushes me into her chest.

"Gina, you're crushing me!"

"Oh, oops!" She laughs as she removes herself. I straighten my sweater, blushing at all the weird looks from the other kids. *Oh no, first day back to school and I've already attracted too much attention for my liking.* I take a moment to assess her style. Black leggings with a flowy, pastel pink off-the-shoulder sweater that compliments her golden brown skin paired with black flats and her long, brown hair in a low pony-tail. Gina has always had a sense of style that's simultaneously cute and comfortable. Her motto is to always look great, but always be ready for a flash mob. As a dancer, she is adamant about

1

practicing any moment she can spare. "I love your outfit! Super cute." She fawns over me. "And you didn't even need my help!"

I blush and glance down at my outfit. A red cable-knit sweater, washed-out jeans, and red Converse to match. The sweater is a little tight, hugging my larger figure. I was worried it would be too tight, but decided to brave it anyway since my mom picked it out for me last Christmas. My hair, red and shoulder-length, naturally curls at the ends. My eyes travel down my body again, catching on the ways the sweater exposes my large hips. Glancing over at Gina, I can't help but admire her slender frame. Built from years of dancing, Gina is about half my size. Granted, my bigger frame is natural for my short stature and bone structure, but that doesn't stop the insults people throw my way...

Gina nudges my shoulder with hers. "So how was your weekend? We didn't get a chance to call each other like I promised." She winces as she realizes her mistake. "My bad."

I release a dramatic sigh. "I know, I know. You were too busy enjoying your last weekend of freedom in Florida with your aunt to call your best friend." Flicking a strand of hair over my shoulder for extra flair, I finally glance over to gauge her reaction.

She shoots me a deadpan look before lightly punching me in the shoulder, "Whatever." She rolls her eyes, her lips forming a grin. "Seriously, what did you end up getting into?"

Her smile is contagious as I launch into telling her about my weekend. "I got a surprise visit from my parents. They weren't supposed to be home for another two weeks, but they happened to be nearby as they headed to their next event so they decided to stop home to see me." I glance back towards the school building, trying to hide my frown. "Unfortunately, they left early Sunday morning, so I didn't get to see them for long." I shrug and hike my bag further up onto my shoulder. My parents are constantly out of town, which leaves me alone at the house for weeks, sometimes even months, on end. Their business, *Jonesing For It*, is a traveling food truck that goes across the country to cater events like large weddings, concerts, Comic-Con, and other really awesome places. They started out as a small diner here in town doing simple fan-based meals. People really started picking up on it; between parents begging for us to cater, venues requesting that we travel to them, and a massive following on social media due to lots of great reviews—by the time I started high school, they decided it was time to expand. Their love for fan-based meals got them a permanent welcome at Comic-Con; other large events are fan-based as well. *My favorite memory is of a completely Marvel-themed wedding—costumes and all.* They get to experience so many new things and meet loads of interesting people. It makes me happy that they're living out their dream of sharing their recipes with the world, but it also makes me sad that I can't be a part of it yet.

"I feel so bad for you, S. I hate for my mom to be gone more than a day. I can't imagine weeks at a time." She nudges my shoulder and gives me an encouraging smile. "But hey, you're doing really good on your own. Miss Independent over here." She starts softly singing "Miss Independent" by Kelly Clarkson.

I snicker as she quickly forgets the lyrics, our smiles growing as we glance at each other and giggle. "Really, don't worry about it. I'm happy for the time we do get together." Even still, my heart pangs at the thought of them being gone again as we make our way up the school stairs.

"Is it just me, or is it really exciting to be going back to school?" she asks, averting my attention from my temporary sadness to the bustling students around us. *Senior year.* It's hard to believe that soon we'll be off to college.

I shake my head. "I'm excited for the Home Ec program they're having this year. Finally we'll be able to work properly, other than just reading about recipes." A few years ago, the school board had decided to cut the class due to insufficient funding. However, students petitioned for the class to be reinstated this year. A bake-off fundraiser, started by yours truly, helped raise enough money to get the necessary equipment to start.

"Ugh, yes! Glad I'm not the only one who's excited." Gina nudges me. "Couldn't have happened if it weren't for your and your parents' grand baking plan!" I smile at the memory. The bake sale really wouldn't have worked without my parents' agreement to sponsor it—helping me get a ton of students to participate in making fan-based cupcakes and then letting the customers vote on the best by way of donations.

She shoots me a large grin and runs ahead of me to the school doors. I can't help but laugh at the irony. While everyone else around us is groaning about being back in school, we're both equally excited to be here. I say a silent prayer before pushing through the large doors.

Gina beats me to the administration office, leaving me to walk in alone. As I push through the large door, a slash of fear shivers through me at the sight of the administrative aid, years of memories surfacing instantly upon seeing her face. Then, there beside her, I catch sight of a new boy. I give him a once over. Dark brown, slicked-back hair. Comfortable black tee showing off his muscled biceps, paired with light washed jeans and black Converse. *This boy is a looker, for sure.* He casually leans against the desk, while the receptionist shamelessly bats her eyes at him and adjusts her sweater so her name tag—which says SAMANTHA—is positioned just perfectly over her chest. My eyes flicker over to see his reaction, only to find his dark green eyes already staring at me.

Gina whispers, "Oh my cheese fries," while I stand there awkwardly shifting on my feet, trying to understand why he's looking at me. My palms grow sweaty under his piercing gaze. *Is my hair out of place? Do I have something on my shirt?*

Nervously, I wave at him before I approach the desk. Samantha glares at me and the boy turns back to his papers.

"Uh, hi. I'm here for my schedule."

I scratch my neck, the boy still standing not even a yard away from me. Samantha still scowls at me.

"And?" she snaps.

"I kinda need it for my classes..." Samantha scoffs at my response, opening her mouth before Gina conveniently cuts her off.

"And mine too!" Gina pops up next to me, also providing a much-appreciated buffer between me and the boy's gaze. "Gina Robertson."

Samantha rolls her eyes again and taps away on her computer. As we're waiting, the boy makes his way towards the door, but not before giving us one last glance. I swear I saw him giving me a small smile.

"Sarah, your outfit looks *especially* comfy today. What's the new style, hobo?" Samantha smirks as she holds our papers hostage, waiting for me to give her the satisfaction of a reaction. I frown and clamp my mouth shut, my body immediately tensing.

"At least she has a style. What's your excuse?" Gina snaps back. She raises her eyebrow and holds her hand out for the papers. Samantha sneers at us then tosses the papers on the desk, quickly storming away into the office behind her. Gina shouts a sarcastic "Thank you!" after her before she pulls us out of the office then down the halls to our lockers.

"Well, that went worse than expected." She shoots me a knowing look. "Are you okay?"

I shrug off her concern, too ashamed to admit my hurt. "Yeah, I'm okay. I wanted to avoid her as long as possible...apparently God had other plans." Gina gives me a small hug.

"Well, don't listen to her. She's just jealous. Anyways..." She clears her throat, then glances down at her papers. "Okay, I have locker number 210. Which one do you have?" She looks down the hallway with determination, then turns to me.

I look down at my papers and realize that I have my least favorite class first and my most favorite last. *Well, better to end the day happy, I guess.*

"I'm 216."

"Yay! So we'll be close to each other!" She claps her hands, bouncing up and down in her spot.

I playfully roll my eyes at her then look back at my paper, "What classes do you have?"

"I don't know; let's compare." We put our papers side by side. Gina doesn't have any classes with me before P.E. Or after, for that matter.

"Well, looks like I'll be ending the day in luxury. Not." She groans and drops her hand.

"Come on. English isn't that bad. I quite like it." I grin up at her and hold back a laugh when she huffs and crosses her arms.

"Of course you do! You read so much your eyes will explode," she says. I look at my schedule. I start my day with math (*ugh*) and end it with Home Ec.

"Aww, looks like we'll only have P.E. together this year!" Gina throws her hands up and cries out. I laugh at her antics and shake my head.

I raise an eyebrow. "We'll have lunch together too, you know."

"Urgh, I know, but it's just not the same." She frowns, mocking the motion of banging her head onto my shoulder. "This year is going to be boring."

The shrill warning bell breaks us out of our conversation. We wave to each other before walking off to our classes, excited to get them started.

I get to my class a few minutes before the main bell, which means I mostly get to choose my seat. I head to the back row, not wanting to sit up front with the teacher. Being up front gets you volunteered to do *a lot* of things, things you do not even want to be doing. *Thank goodness too; last year was torture.* Now, I've never been one for a lot of attention. Being an only child, having one solid friend growing up, and only getting to spend time with my parents every few weeks has left me to become best friends with myself. I prefer my personal bubble, and when that bubble is disrupted by something or someone, I flounder. Which is precisely what happened last year when Mr. Hanover called me to the front of the room to solve an equation. I was so nervous, I couldn't get my answer out. The class laughed at me for weeks, and Mr. Hanover–thinking that I simply wasn't "paying enough attention" in class to know the answer–repeated it to ensure I learned my lesson. *Again, last year was torture.*

The class starts five minutes later. Ten minutes into Ms. Spencer's rundown of the syllabus, the boy from the office walks in.

"Glad you could finally make it, Mr. Mills." Ms. Spencer jokes lightly, a small smile on her face.

"Yeah, I'm not." He rolls his eyes and scans the rest of the classroom.

She frowns immediately and straightens up her stance. "Since it's your first day here, I'll let that attitude slide. Please take a seat by...Miss Jones. Miss Jones, please raise your hand."

I slowly raise my hand as the boy's eyes land on me. When he recognizes me, he smirks slightly before making his way to the seat right beside me, plopping down rather loudly. The teacher continues on with her lesson, while I silently look around the room, trying to avoid eye contact with Mr. Mills, whoever he is.

The girls are all staring at the boy, giving him heart eyes and trying to show their stuff, and I do *not* mean their homework. I look over at the boy to see his reaction to all the staring, only to find him already staring at me. I whip around to the front where the teacher is talking, when someone taps my shoulder. Repeatedly. I shrug off the finger and try to ignore it the best I can, but it gets harder every time. Finally, I meet the boy's stubborn smirk as he leans over.

"Hey. I'm Zander. What's your name, gorgeous?"

I blush, then look away, too embarrassed to answer. I've never been complimented like that before, at least not by a boy my age. *Don't stutter. Please don't stutter.* I repeat the mental mantra as I turn back, "Um, Sarah." Our eyes meet, sending a whole new wave of embarrassed heat through me. It's odd to have so much attention from one boy, namely because it's such a new feeling. *Why do I feel so embarrassed? It's just my name!*

"A beautiful name for a beautiful girl."

"I uh—guess you could say that." I tuck a piece of stray hair behind my ear, fidgeting with the back of my earring to distract myself. My eyes roam over his features a second time today. Dark green eyes, sharp jaw, hair perfectly slicked back. It almost reminds me of the guys from *Grease.* Now that I'm up close, I see a faint scar marring the top corner of his lip. *I wonder what that was from? What's his story?*

"Can I see your schedule?" He raised an eyebrow expectantly, making me blush brighter. His intent gaze is really doing a number on my self-consciousness. *Has he noticed the two pimples on my cheek?*

"Um, sure." I hand it over and turn back to the teacher, who is now typing on her computer while the other students chat.

"Hey, we also have Home Ec together. And English. What a coincidence." He smiles at me and returns my schedule to me. *We have what?!* "Looks like we'll be seeing a lot of each other, then."

I try to keep calm. "Oh, that's cool, I guess." My eyes dart to the front of the room. Our conversation dies there.

Soon, the bell rings signaling the end of class. The boy—I mean, Zander—and I get up to leave. As I reach for my bag, my foot unexpectedly catches on the strap. I yelp as I trip and bump my nose directly against Zander's firm chest. His arm flies out to catch me, forcing me against his chest even more. My cheeks go ablaze as I scramble out of his hold, squeaking a quick "Sorry" under my breath as I hurry out the door, trying to get to my locker before the other kids fill the hallways.

Finally at the safety of my locker, I get my books out for my next class while my mind replays what just happened. His scent is trapped in my nose, remnants of cinnamon and pine mixing together. He smells like a walk in the woods. I walk towards my English class, squeezing around everyone and mentally begging them not to notice my still tinted cheeks.

His easy charm is somewhat off-putting. His compliments swirl around in my head, and I don't know what to make of them. Out of all the girls in this school, why does he want to talk to me? He is certainly attractive enough to score any one of them.

My thoughts shift to how last year went. Students picking on me throughout the year, all of the unwanted attention. I certainly don't want a guy that all the girls fawn over to be focusing on *me*. That's just a recipe for a jealous disaster. *No, thank you.* It'd be best to just stay away and lay low this year.

__chapter two__

Sarah

Pop!

"Haha! Eat my plastic!"

Gina shoots Nerf gun bullets at me from around the corner of the hallway. I ninja-roll behind the couch to reload.

"You can't escape this time. Just admit defeat and let me pick the movie tonight!" Gina yells, the sound of plastic clicking into place signaling her reload.

"No way! You'll pick another sad movie." I sneak through the kitchen and go up to where she stands in the hall, looking for me in the living room.

"How would you know? Let me pick!" She has yet to notice me, so I take my chance.

"Maybe next time." I aim the gun at her. She turns around quickly as I fire one dart at her forehead, hitting the target we both have taped to our heads.

"Dang it, Sarah!" Gina sighs, dropping her gun to the floor.

"Haha! *Captain America* it is!" I dance around in victory.

"I guess I'll get the popcorn." Gina laughs at my stupidity, shaking her head.

An hour later, Gina braids my hair while the movie plays in the background of my bedroom. We're both wrapped up in blankets, snacks scattered across the comforter.

"Steve Rogers is so cute," she says, tying off my braid. "Speaking of cute, did you notice how the new guy was looking at you?" Gina sighs dreamily and mockingly swoons into my lap before scrambling to sit up in front of me.

"I doubt he was looking at me. He was probably looking at you, and all your hotness." I laugh and section off Gina's hair.

"Oh no, honey. He was definitely looking at you!" Scoffing, I finish braiding Gina's hair.

"Don't scoff at me! You know it's true!"

"Meh, it doesn't really matter." Laughing, I roll over and close my eyes, trying to avoid any further discussion. There's no way I'm telling her about our conversation in math class.

"Pfft, to you, it doesn't!" Gina scoffs, rolling over too.

"Yes, that is true! Goodnight, G, love you."

"Love you more, S."

We both fall into silence, drifting into dreamland. I think about the mystery boy.

Was he really staring at me? He couldn't have been, could he?

Before I realize it, Gina's yelling at me to wake up. Rushing around to get ready is not the best thing to do in the morning, but I do it anyway. I run downstairs into the kitchen, tripping on a few steps on the way. "Oh good, there's still bacon left!"

Gina laughs at me, getting up from her chair. "Hurry up and eat, we're gonna be late."

"I only live ten minutes away. Besides, this coming from the girl who is notorious for always being late." I smirk, dodging the bacon she launches at my head.

After we wash our bacon down with orange juice, we rush out to her car and speed off to school, probably breaking the law on the way.

We arrive at school with a few minutes to spare. I hop out of the car, my eyes scanning the mostly empty student parking lot. I catch myself searching for a certain someone before I realize Gina has yet to get out. I poke my head through the open window. "What're you doing? Hurry up!" She jumps at my voice, dropping whatever was in her hand. I hurry to her side of the car and yank open the door.

"Goodness, woman! Let me finish putting on my mascara!" Tucking the wand back into the tube, she jumps out of the car. She slams the door and we hurry our way to our classes.

Gina, I guess you could say, would be your somewhat typical girly girl. She loves to shop, do make-up, and fan-girl over hot guys. Bubbly, talkative, and friendly, she's the perfect recipe for "popular girl." Yet she's still a total nerd in school and a total goofball. She's the perfect mix between cute and awesome, without letting it affect her social standing.

I, on the other hand, am not. I'm not well versed in the world of make-up, I can't even curl my hair without help, and most of my outfits are comfort-oriented, but Gina also has her hand in my sense of style. It's not that I hate being a girly girl. It's just that I literally suck at it. And if I were to start now, it definitely would not go unnoticed. I much prefer to stick my head in my books and skate through the semester unscathed.

Gina's my only friend, and when she joined this school two years ago, I didn't fit in as well as the other kids. Being alone so often, I grew comfortable in silence, and my books were my closest friends. They let me live out adventures without actually leaving my comfort zone. Gina was the preppy, nerdy girl at the back of the classroom, who, much like myself, didn't fit in. So we easily connected and became best friends.

"Okay, see you later!" Gina yells at me while running off to her first class. *Yet another day in paradise.*

It's time for Home Ec. Everyone else has been slowly trickling in, and I have yet to see Zander. *Maybe he's sick or something.*

"Alright class," Mr. Barnes says. "Today we'll be making a simple omelet. Take out your fry—"

Zander bursts into class. "Sorry I'm late," he says. "I was held up."

"Very well, then. You're just in time for making omelets. Please take a seat next to...Miss Jones! Please raise your hand!"

I raise my hand, blushing furiously. *You have got to be kidding me.*

Zander makes his way towards me. His hair is ruffled now, like he ran his hands through it one too many times. His eyes seem dimmer, sadder compared to when I last saw him. But even with that, he looks good. I bet this guy could pull off any look if he tried. He looks over at me, smiling stiffly as he takes his seat, but then his desolate mood seems to change in an instant.

"Guess we're partners now." Then he winks at me. The audacity!

"Yeah, I guess so." We take out our frying pans. A small smile forms as I think of the many ingredients my dad loves to add to his omelets. Garlic powder, onion powder, salt, pepper, parsley, and bits of ham. I always tell him he makes things complex, and he always says, *"Complexity is unique, and what are we if not unique?"* With a small laugh to myself, I crack the eggs into the bowl and start mixing them when I hear a very loud and obnoxious *SPLAT.*

"Oops." Zander looks over at me with egg all over his hands and shells in the pan.

"What happened?!" I whisper yell as I hurry over and start wiping up the egg mixture. The washcloth doesn't absorb the mess. I keep pushing the goop around. Zander stands out of my way, egg still all over his hands. All the other students have flipped their eggs. Some are sliding them on their plates.

His demeanor darkens. "I was distracted." My brain tries to process his words. *What happened before class?* Out of the corner of my eye, I see Mr. Barnes coming our way, a fork in his hand.

I am going to fail this class before it even starts.

Panicked, I flip the omelet, egg shells and all. *It'll just have to do.* I quickly put some cheese in the middle and then put it on a plate, pushing it to the edge of the table for Mr. Barnes.

Zander smiles and softly whispers, "Calm down. It'll be alright."

"Easy for you to say," I growl, my chest tight. He doesn't understand how important this is to me, even if it is just an omelet. This class is my start to something greater, and had I had the proper chance I would have used my parents' recipe.

But it's too late. Mr. Barnes has reached our table, ready to taste our omelet. He takes the first bite and grimaces. I wince.

"The omelet is cooked well, but, maybe next time, try not adding egg shells." Everyone laughs at us. Just like the failed omelet, my skin sizzles from embarrassment. He walks away, dismissing the class on the way back up to his desk. My frustration reignites as the laughter fills the room. I clench my fists by my side.

"Sorry, Sarah." Zander picks up my bag and hands it to me, chuckling like the rest of the class. Our eyes meet, his widening once he fully takes in my stature. His voice grows more serious, his face now stern. "I'll make it up to you. I promise."

__chapter three__

Sarah

Make it up to me? How?

These words constantly run through my head for the rest of the day. After Zander left the classroom, I didn't see him at all. Something about his devil-may-care attitude told me he had left school.

Making my way to my independent art class, I can't help but think about what he might have in mind. Maybe he'd make me cookies or something.

The smell of oil paints gets my mind off Zander for a minute. Art has been my second favorite pastime since I was in fifth grade. Ms. Wilson gave us a watercolor assignment, since that was basically all we could use. "This can be anything that inspires you. Paint something you love. Or even something you hate!" she said as she paced in front of the class. I painted a pizza, something I loved. I got an A+ on it.

I also had a rival, Samantha Willow. She has had it out for me ever since my pizza painting got a higher grade than her flower. We had been friends since pre-K up until that point. I used to stay at her house all the time, spending hours playing in their large yard or cooking with her parents. Her parents loved me, treated me as their own daughter, even. It was then that my parents helped me realize that she wasn't my friend, but was simply using me to make herself look better. I was nothing more than a measuring stick that showed off all her superficial qualities like athletic skill, number of friends, fashion status, and sense of humor. Despite being just kids at the time, Samantha has never let my pizza painting success go, and has continued on her war path to one-up me any chance she gets.

When Gina and I met, she really helped me overcome a lot of day-to-day issues I was facing. She made me stop eating my lunch in the library every day and staying behind after class to avoid Samantha in the halls. Samantha plays nice just enough to save face, which has resulted in her being one of the most popular girls in school, like Regina George in *Mean Girls*. Some days, I wonder exactly what it was that made her hate me so much. I don't recall us ever having a fight as kids, and she was always more popular than I was.

Which makes me wonder, is Zander popular? He hasn't really been present the few days he's been here, but he still could be.

I find a seat in the back. Since I'm the only one here, I can finally read. Not even two minutes in, someone taps on my shoulder. I hold back an annoyed groan. Looking up, I see none other than Zander himself, as if my thoughts conjured him. "Can I sit here?" Zander points to the chair next to me.

Forcing a smile, I nod. He plops down in the chair. The other kids start to trickle in.

"So, about Home Ec earlier. I'm really sorry about that." He scratches the back of his neck, gives me a slight smile, and starts—*Oh my gosh, is he? BLUSHING?*

James, who often gives me grief, walks by and shoves my notebook off my desk, coughing out "fattie" under his breath. His friends snicker off to the side. This is nothing new. I glower down at my crumpled notebook, quickly glancing up when Zander frowns and leans down to grab it for me. When he hands it to me, his face is devoid of a reaction, giving me no indication whether he heard what the guy said. *Does he think the same?*

Before I can say anything, Mr. Hanks walks in and silences the class. I give Zander a nod before tucking my book and glasses away, then focus on the teacher. I take notes on what he's saying, but that doesn't stop me from stealing a few glances at Zander. He seems rather tense, his eyes glancing around the room. I brush it off, focusing on Mr. Hanks instead.

"Alright, class. For our next assignment, we will be doing a group project. I will explain the assignment, then you can choose your partners."

Great. I hate group projects. *I don't want to be partners with anyone!*

"Okay," says Mr. Hanks. "What I want you to do is to get to know your partner, find a common interest, then make a drawing of said interest. It can be anything you'd like. I just ask you to keep it as clean as possible." Mr. Hanks shoots a pointed look towards the jocks in the room. Grumbling, they nod while the rest of the class—including Mr. Hanks—laughs at their dismay. "With that said, go ahead and start getting to know your partners! You have the rest of the period to do so." Mr. Hanks goes to his desk and starts looking through a jumble of papers.

I refuse to talk to Zander. I know that's not the point of the assignment, and I need to secure a partner, but I'm still silently hoping he'll choose someone else. Bent over my notebook, I focus on a doodle of a lily growing under a shower of raindrops.

Zander leans over in his chair and stares intently at the page I'm doodling on. It's making me nervous to say the least. Yet, I find myself subtly shifting my hand away from my drawing so he can see it better. I don't often share my artwork with others, but something about him has me wanting to understand him better.

"Ah, so you like rain and lillies?" he says, ignoring me pretending to be ignoring him. "I do, too. There's nothing quite like the smell of rain on a field after a good spring storm." He drops his head as a small smile tilts his lips. "My mom also loved lilies."

Past tense? Curiosity gets the best of me. "Loved?" I peer at him.

His eyes shoot up to meet mine, quickly realizing his slip. "Uh, yeah." He frowns and looks away. "She passed away a few years ago. We moved here to get a new start."

My eyes widen, regret taking over me. "I'm so sorry, Zander. I shouldn't have pried." I can't imagine not having my parents. Granted, they're away most of the time, but they're still present.

He smiles sadly and shrugs. "It's okay." He gestures to the rain. "That reminds me of a small clearing I found a few weeks ago. It's really cool at sunset right after a light rain. The sunlight practically makes the trees glow." His voice lights up as he tells me this, his previous sadness easing away the more he tells me about this place. I shift in my seat to give him my full attention. "There's a small creek that runs through it. It's the perfect place to soak up some alone time."

A guy who respects his alone time? I can appreciate that.

"That place sounds really awesome. I'd love to see that for myself some day." We stare at each other with small smiles, neither of us ready to break the moment. I finally glance away and bite my lip, changing the subject. "So it's settled. We'll draw rain, then." I turn pointedly back to my raindrops, shoving the small moment in the back of my mind for later.

"Something like that," Zander trails off, not sounding so sure of himself now. My hand hovers over the shading of a particular droplet, confusion blossoming in my chest. Is he rethinking his partnership with me? Is he realizing he made a mistake? My self-doubt sours my mood, my body curling into itself. He leans forward, rubbing his hands together. "Can we meet outside before you leave today?" I jump slightly in my seat and finally look up at him. He gives me a small smile, even going as far as to hand me my backpack as I start gathering up my stuff, then sits patiently for my answer. I shove everything into my tiny backpack and struggle to close the zipper.

Warm hands meet mine on top of the bag, stopping my furious jerking. My eyes flicker up to his and we stare each other down, neither of us daring to look away before the other. He zips up my bag with ease, then smiles in a way that turns my insides to mush. *What is happening?*

"S-sure, that works for me," I stutter. I pick my bag up from the floor. The bell rings, breaking our trance.

He blinks and shakes his head, standing up to throw his bag over his shoulder. "Okay. I'll meet you at the steps after school, then?"

Nodding, I study my shoes. "Yeah, that'll be fine."

He smiles then glances around again, spotting Mr. Hanks staring in his direction. He quickly waves goodbye before rushing out the door. My eyes follow him out the door then dart back over to Mr. Hanks, who is now staring after him with a confused frown. A girl bumps into my shoulder, muttering a "Move, fattie," under her breath as she goes. I shake my head, letting the comment sink in. I seriously need to pay attention to my surroundings.

Spinning on my heels, I walk out the door, then start speed-walking to Gina's locker. I spot her almost immediately digging around in her bag and stuffing papers into her locker. As I sneak up behind her, I have to hold in a laugh when she starts checking herself out in her little locker mirror.

"BOO!" I lightly grab her shoulders and shake her. Screaming, Gina spins around, dropping her eye liner.

"Oh my gosh! That was so freaking rude!" Gina picks up her eye liner only to throw it at me.

I laugh, blocking my face from the tube. "You should have seen your face!" Gina hits me again, now also laughing. "Anyways, want to go to the mall this weekend?" I pick up her books for her while she grabs her bag.

"Yes! We can have a girly day! And a sleepover!" Gina grins at me and claps her hands. She stops by the administrator's office and points her thumb behind her, "I gotta sort something out. I'll meet you at the car in a sec."

"Okay," I heave a sigh as I turn to the big double doors leading out of the school.

Standing at the steps in front of the school, I wait for Zander to show up so we can leave and start our project. It's been at least ten minutes since school has ended. Pretty much everyone is gone. *Where is he?* Tapping my foot, I fight the urge to go to Gina's car.

After waiting another five minutes, I get up from my spot on the steps and make my way towards her car, intent on blasting the heat. *I don't have time for this.* Just as I reach the car door, I hear Zander calling out to me. I turn around and see him running over to me, Samantha and a few of her friends walking out of the building behind him. She meets my eyes, a wicked smirk forming on her lips as she gives me a mocking wave. Her friends laugh, obviously part of whatever joke they are sharing at my expense.

"Where are you going? I thought we agreed to meet here?" Stopping a few feet in front of me, Zander glances between me and the car. He follows my line of sight behind him, Samantha blowing him a kiss. I watch for his reaction, taking note of the way his nose ever so lightly scrunches up before he's turning his attention to me, moving to turn his back to her completely.

"You were taking too long, so I decided to just leave. But, now that you're here, we can go get started on our project." I cross my arms, my focus now on him rather than the snotty girls behind him.

"Well, actually." Zander smiles sheepishly, rubbing the back of his neck, "I'm not going to be able to help you with your project...well, not entirely..." He walks over to his motorcycle, which looks totally awesome but absolutely terrifying at the same time, and hops on. I stand there gaping after him. Is he seriously going to ditch me now?

After starting it up, he makes a motion as if to say, "What are you waiting for?" I roll my eyes and turn back around, stalking off in the direction of my house.

"Oh, now look who's ready to go all of a sudden!" I grumble under my breath. His bike rolls up beside me. I pretend I don't notice him there.

"Are you really going to walk home when I can give you a ride?" he asks. "Let me drive you home. I was late. I might as well help you try to get home sooner."

I stop mid-stride and turn towards him. He smiles at me and pats the seat behind him. I roll my eyes and cross my arms again, "So you're late, don't apologize, then ditch me for our– no, I'm sorry–*my* project? Then expect me to just let it go?"

His smirk drops immediately. "No, I–"

I throw my hand up to stop him. "And you didn't even try to explain why you are! You can't just change your mind now. I can't change my partner!" I huff, my cheeks bright red from anger and embarrassment. I leave out the hurt I feel after having seen him with Samantha. Was he with her, though? Why does the idea of that hurt me so much? I don't even know this guy!

He shuts off his bike with a wince, "Listen, I am sorry for being late, but I had a good reason," *Yeah, hanging out with Samantha doesn't exactly qualify.* I open my mouth to retort, but before I can, he says, "I can't help you with your project because I'm not actually a part of the class."

My jaw drops. "What?"

He stares up at the sky, a tinge of a blush coloring his cheeks. "I wanted to talk to you, so I followed you into the room. I didn't realize it was an actual class until it was too late."

Silence engulfs us as I process this new information. He endured that whole class...just to talk to me?

"Why?" The word of disbelief shoots out before I can stop it. He cocks his head to the side, as if he's trying to figure me out.

"Because, Sarah, you seem...real." He must have noticed the confusion on my face because he quickly waves off his sentence and continues, "I saw you in the administrator's office and you intrigued me. A girl hiding behind a mask." He shrugs like it's no big deal, but my heart is pounding wildly in my chest. He steps off his bike, shoving his hands in his pockets. I stare into his eyes, trying to understand. Understand his interest. Understand these feelings blooming in my heart. My head is cautious to let someone new in my life, but my lungs are breathless and my heart says *jump*.

He smiles softly. "I want to get to know you, Sarah. You interest me." A beat of silence passes again before he's reaching out his hand to me, "Let me drive you home, at least."

I slip my phone out of my pocket and text Gina.

I'm getting a ride with someone else. I'll explain later.

I take off my shoes when I enter the house. Zander follows closely behind. After having accepted his offer to drive me home, we made it here lickety-split. I invite him inside for a few minutes.

I set my bag on the kitchen table. "Do you want anything to eat or drink?" I get myself a glass of apple juice.

"Sure, I'll have what you're having." I hear him walk in behind me. I glance over my shoulder and see him by the china cabinet, observing my family's photos.

When I turn to give him his glass, he's leaning against the counter behind me, and I bump into him. I squeak, surprised, as the glass slips from my hand, shattering on the floor. Zander stops me from falling too by wrapping his arm around my waist and pulling me against his chest.

"Careful. I don't want you stepping in the glass." I look up at him, forgetting where I am for a split second. Zander stares down at me before clearing his throat and moving me aside. He bends over the glass.

"You don't have to do that. I can get it." I grab the broom.

He stops me before I can get too close. "Stay over there. You're still barefoot. You might get hurt." He grabs the broom from my hands. I sink back against the table edge, watching him intently. I'll admit, I can't help but find him attractive. His unruly hair no longer sticks in place like it was this morning, providing an air of freedom around him. And the way he holds himself has me questioning so many things. Who is he, really? Truth is, I am as intrigued by him as he is by me.

After five minutes of sweeping, he puts the glass in a plastic bag to throw away, setting the broom off to the side. He straightens up, his hand rubbing the back of his neck. He seems nervous. "I should probably get going," he says. "I feel that I've caused more trouble than it's worth."

I wrap my arms around myself. "It's okay, the glass wasn't that important anyways…" I trail off, purposely avoiding mentioning his earlier confession. I still don't know how I feel. It's all so… new.

"I'll see you tomorrow, Sarah." He smiles softly, hesitating for a second before lightly tapping the counter and making his way to the door. I watch him go, my body slowly relaxing as my bubble of safety expands out into the silence.

The door latches shut and his bike roars to life. My heart continues to race up until the moment he pulls away, then finally a small breath escapes me.

"Bye, Zander..."

__chapter four__

Sarah

". . . And when Abraham Lincoln became president. . ."

Mr. Clark drones on and on. *When will class end?* I fidget and stare at the clock, willing it to move faster.

". . . Civil war . . ."

I really need to pee.

". . . American history . . ."

The bell rings. *FREEDOM!*

I rush to clean up my books and papers, then run out to the bathroom. I make it there, do my thing, and go to leave the stall when I hear more people come in. *Great. I'll just wait here until they leave.*

The girls start talking—about what, I couldn't quite understand. I pull out my phone to check the time to find I only have five more minutes to get to my next class. *Alright,* I tell myself. *You've already wasted time hiding. You need to get to class, so just man up and walk out of the stall. They're not going to hurt you...I hope.* I take a deep breath, then reach to open my stall door. The girls start talking louder. I hear Samantha's voice and freeze.

"Did you see how that guy looked at her?" One girl says, whose voice I now recognize as Claire's, one of Samantha's groupies. "It was like he was hypnotized!" My breath catches in my throat, my hand dropping back down to my side.

I lean closer to the door as the other girl starts talking. "Yeah, I don't see what all the fuss is about. She's just an ugly nerd. Who in their right mind would like that? They're all so buried in their books." The girl scoffs.

Maybe she should read a book or two. The nerd always seems to get the guy...

Then it hits me like a ton of bricks. I hear Samantha say, "Sarah doesn't deserve Zander. He's perfect. She's just... a fat, ugly, prude. Nobody—she's a nobody. What does he even see in her? Zander and I, though...it just makes sense. He would have so much more fun with me. We'd be such a cute couple, don't you think?"

Tears form in my eyes and anger boils in my veins. She's been going around telling people I'm gross, weird, and horrible to be around. It's no wonder why people avoid me in the hallways.

I reach for the stall door, quickly yanking it open so I can get out of here. The other girls are giggling and adding insults about me. All of that stops when I step out. Samantha turns around quickly, gives me a once-over, then smirks when she sees my tear-streaked face. She stalks up to me, her friends laughing and leaning on the sinks. My body stiffens as she comes closer, my fists opening and closing. She stops a few feet in front of me, still smirking. She laughs, reaching up to tuck a piece of my hair behind my ear. I flinch back, my eyes shutting tightly. *Please go away, please go away, please go away.*

"What's wrong, fatty? Did I hurt your feelings?" I open my eyes. She fake pouts and laughs again, glancing back at her friends.

A tear slides down my cheek as my hands start shaking. The others snicker and walk over to join in. Samantha reaches up again to tuck another loose hair behind my ear. She smiles at me as she plays with the strand of hair still in her hands. Her face turns serious, her hand pulling more of my hair. I yelp in pain.

I reach up to pry her plastic nails off my scalp. Her expression turns into one of rage, one that has me shaking even more at what could come next. She gets in my face. "Stay away from Zander," she whispers. She lets go of my hair, only to grab my chin, holding me in place so I can't get away. "Got it?"

I quickly nod, or at least try to nod as her hand grips my chin. She tightens her iron grip, pulling me closer. Her breath smells like Juicy Fruit gum. She screams the words in my face, making me shake even more. My heart pounds in my chest as I whimper a quick yes.

She pushes me back. "Don't get any ideas. Zander is mine." She looks at me in disgust, muttering, "Pathetic" under her breath. I rub my sore chin, hoping to soothe the pain.

Samantha's friends laugh, taking my stuff and throwing it all around the bathroom. Tears run down my face, my cheeks burning. Samantha joins her friends' laughter.

The words play like a broken record in my head. Fat, ugly, pathetic. I use my sweater sleeves to wipe the tears off of my cheeks. The girls laugh at me one last time, then leave the bathroom. The warning bell rings long before I can pull myself off the floor. More tears fall, splotching my sleeves. I walk around the bathroom, picking up my items and stuffing them in my bag, one by one. I stand in front of the bathroom mirror. Years of memories begin to surface. Kids avoiding me in the hallways, James knocking my lunch trays out of my hands, tripping in the halls with laughter following behind, bystanders staring at me with pity. Like that helped.

Worthless. . . Another tear escapes. I watch it slide down my cheek, then drop onto the sink. I laugh pathetically and wipe my face off again, as I push through the bathroom door to run down the hall. *I just want to be at home.* I hear him behind me. "Hey, Sarah!"

I run even faster. Zander catches up to me and turns me around, concern written on his face.

The next thing I know, his warm, comforting hands cradle my face.

"Are you okay?" I look up to meet his eyes, his concern shining brightly. I start shaking again. *Worthless. . . pathetic. . .*

Zander gently pulls me into a hug. I hesitate, Samantha's words echoing in my mind. Tears burn my eyes as I finally cave, wrapping my arms around him and letting the sobs out. I grip the back of his shirt as he holds me close. After what feels like forever, he pulls away. His hands rest on the side of my face, softly wiping away my tears. He looks at me with concern, sorrow, *pity*. All the things I don't like seeing on anyone are written across his face.

It's all too much. I've shown him too much. I gotta get out. I quickly pull away, grab my bag, and high-tail it down the hall. Anger slowly seeps in, fueling my sprint. I don't need anyone's pity. I don't need yet another person viewing me as a loser. I especially don't need more grief from Samantha.

"Wait! Sarah!" He tries to catch me, but I make it out the first door before he can. I hear him running behind me. The tears blur my vision, but I'm almost to the last door. Zander's footsteps grow closer. I pick up the speed. I burst outside and run towards my house. My breaths come out ragged as sobs rack my body; tears clouding my vision cause me to stumble and slow my pace. The sound of my feet hitting the ground and the pitter-patter of raindrops echo around me. *How could I embarrass myself in front of him like that?* I keep running. *Yet another person will think I'm a freak now. And what if she had seen? Would she hold true to her threat?*

The rain falls faster and I slow down. *Worthless...* I finally reach my house. I'm soaked to the bone. I shiver so much I fumble my key into the lock. Throwing my school bag to the floor, I go to the kitchen to get some food.

I quickly make a peanut butter and jelly sandwich, stopping midway to grip the edge of the counter and close my eyes. *I'm going to get in so much trouble for skipping school.* I shake my head and walk to the living room, plopping down on the couch and polishing off my sandwich. How can Samantha get away with all of this? Am I really such a nobody that even the teachers don't notice me?

The house is so quiet with just me here, further grounding me in this spiral of loneliness. Another shiver racks through me, reminding me of the rain-soaked clothes still stuck to my skin. I wish my parents were here with me. I'd run into their arms and hear my daddy say it'll be okay. Another tear drips down my cheek and I peel the wet clothes off, throwing them into a pile on the floor. I grab my dad's Led Zeppelin shirt from the other day's laundry, which I still haven't folded. I throw it over me and shakily grab my phone. I dial my parents number, hoping to hear their voices. Voicemail. Tears well up in my eyes again as I place my empty plate on the coffee table then lie down, curling into a ball. I reach for the nearest blanket and throw it over myself, finally blocking out the world. Slowly, I close my eyes and drift off into a deep sleep.

__chapter five__

Zander

Late again. Oh well. It's only my first week. They won't notice my absence. I pass by the class I'm supposed to be attending and continue walking down the hallways, dodging students as they rush to get to their classes on time. *They still have five minutes left. I don't see what the big deal is.* Soon, the hallways are empty, and only a few students are left rushing to class. I scan the hallways and beeline to the water fountain. Just as I bend over to drink, the door to the girls' bathroom slams open, Samantha and her group walk out, still laughing. They don't notice me. A rush of relief floods me. Samantha Willow had made it clear that she wanted me to know who she was the first day I got here. After meeting me in the administrator's office, she has made it a point to say hi to me any chance she gets: walking down the hallway, leaving class, and even following me out of the building to my bike.

Granted, she's not an ugly girl. On the outside. I can tell by the way she acts around me what type of girl she is. Glancing around to ensure everyone is looking at her, sliding up to any guy nearby, casting side eyes to other students in the halls. From past experience, I know those types of girls are nothing but a waste of time. They only date you to boost their social status, only want sleep with you, spend all of your money, then leave you once they get bored. Shallow. Samantha, unfortunately, is seeking that with me. Personally, I'm only interested in something long-term, or nothing at all.

My mind drifts off to Sarah. Those big, caramel-brown eyes that pulled me in the minute we met in that office. That bright smile she has when she's around her friend. A red sweater that hugged her curvy frame and matched her Converse. Freckles dot her cheeks and nose, accompanied by beautiful red hair. The girl is a looker.

I smile as I remember her shy demeanor. The way she shifted from one foot to the other when she stood in the administrator's office. She reminds me of my mom, quiet and reserved. Yet once people got to know her, anyone could see she was smart, funny, and quite opinionated.

Something that was smothered by my father.

Their laughter breaks me out of my thoughts. That loud, obnoxious laughter. Then, for a long time, it's quiet. Suddenly, the bathroom door swings open again, and I see a blur of red hair race down the hallway. *Sarah? Why is she running?*

I call after her, "Hey, Sarah!" but she continues running. Dread has my legs pumping faster to catch up to her, finally catching hold of her elbow to spin her around. Her tear-stained face strikes me cold. My hands move on their own accord to cradle her face. *What did those girls say to her?*

"Are you okay?" She starts tearing up again. I pull her into a hug, letting her cry as I wrap my arms around her. She doesn't care that I'm the one holding her together.

Finally after what seems like forever, I wipe away her tears as I look at her beautiful face. *And boy, is she beautiful.* She stares back but then quickly pulls away, grabs her bag, and books it to the door.

"Wait! Sarah!" I reach out to grab her arm but she's too quick. She runs out the door, halfway down the hall by the time I make it out myself. I follow her, her little legs taking her farther away from me with each step.

Before I know it, we're outside in the pouring rain. I hurry to get on my motorcycle, revving it to life to race after her. I honestly don't even know why I'm following her; I just know that I have to.

The rain starts falling harder. She's only in a tee-shirt and jeans. She's bound to get a cold. Before I can speed up to give her a ride, she stops outside of her house. She's shivering, her clothes soaked, yet she stands there for a few more moments. Soon, she slips inside.

My heart lurches inside my chest. The way she looked at me in the hallway, so broken, so alone. I just wanted to hold her close until all her pain washed away. I know I just met her, but there's something about her that just seems different from all the other girls. *I can't let her get away.*

After she ran into her house, I sat in the rain wondering if she was okay—if I could do anything. *How could I just sit there? I should have run after her, to make sure she was actually okay.*

And how could such a lovely girl be hated so much?

The bell rings in the hallway, snapping me back to reality.

Why do I even care? She's just some girl, right?

Doubt flickers inside me as I head into my next class. I easily craft a half-lie to the teacher about where Sarah and I were. "She threw up in the bathroom, so I took her home after checking in with the school nurse." Ms. Hann accepts it and ushers me to a random seat, starting to go on about words I can't even focus on. As I sit in my seat, one word crosses my mind in a constant loop of doubt.

Right?

It echoes in my head until I get home from school. I park outside the trailer, turn off my bike, and put down the bike rest.

The car is still here, which means Dad is home. I shake my head and get off my bike, heading towards the door. Dread weighs me down as I make the trek to the run-down porch. The paint is chipped and faded, the roof leaning. The porch concrete is cracked and tilted, one earthquake away from completely falling apart.

I hear movement inside the house, probably Dad stumbling around. I roll my eyes and step away from the place I call home. Lately, he's always stumbling around like a brain-dead idiot.

I hear the door start to unlatch, so I move further away until I'm hidden behind the side of the house. Dad pokes his head out, his eyes straining to focus, but he's too hammered to even see properly. I hear him sigh and then he shrugs, closing the door and venturing back to whatever it was he was doing before. I walk around back, where my bedroom window is.

Dad bought the place when we moved here a few years back. After Mom died, most of our money went towards funeral costs and the move. Dad said he needed a fresh start, claiming it would be the best for both of us. He had sold our two-story home in the suburbs in favor of this dump in the woods without a thought.

Not that we were perfect before; Mom and Dad had their fights. He would go out and come home drunk. Mom would cry in their bedroom, and he would become angry. It usually never escalated more than yelling, but…

Grief changes people.

I move towards the large oak tree that stands right outside my window. The perfect way to escape—or come in without being noticed.

I jump up, grab one of the branches, and swing myself up to the base. I glance up at my window. I don't feel like going in right now. I lean back against the tree and take out my phone.

Most kids have iPhones or Androids by now, but all I have is a crappy flip phone. That said, my crappy phone works for me when I need to call someone. Besides that, it's all I can afford.

42

I hear a crash from inside the house and my father's string of curses, reality crashing back down on me like a tidal wave. A sigh escapes me as I rest my head back on the tree. I glance at the time. I have about an hour before I have to go into work at the grocery store. I close my eyes, pretending for a moment that things were okay. That Mom was still here. That Dad never changed.

But life is not so forgiving.

And reality always sets back in.

__chapter six__

Sarah

"Just some girl?! Sarah, if you were really 'just some girl,' as you say, why would he go to such lengths to help you?" Gina throws her hands up in the air as she paces, looking at me like I'm a madwoman. I had rushed here after church, begging Gina to stay the night with me before school tomorrow.

I shrug my shoulders. "Out of the kindness of his heart? I don't know. I just don't think he had any special reason." I fiddle with my nails and lay down on my bed. "I mean, what if he thinks it's a joke. 'Let's help the nerdy girl, only to turn around and slap her in the face'. I don't trust it, G."

She groans in frustration, dropping down on the bed beside me, "Honestly, Sarah, you always think the worst of things. Can't you just for this one time, I don't know, think that maybe he *wanted* to help you?" I shrug again, then look over at her. She's frowning.

She sighs once more, closing her eyes in defeat. "Okay, fine. But if he helps you like that again, I'm assuming he likes you! And all those other guys are a-holes. They're obviously missing out."

I roll my eyes, laughing softly. "Alright, if that's what you want to believe. Besides, we just met a few days ago. I highly doubt he would like me."

Worthless... I shake the thought from my mind, sitting up to lean against the wall. "G, what do you say we go watch some *Supernatural* while shoveling pizza and ice cream in our mouths?"

She leaps off the bed and rushes to the door. "Heck yeah!" she screams. Before I can even get to the door, she's turning on the TV downstairs.

Maybe he did do it because he wanted to. Maybe he only did it to make me owe him something in return. Either way, I don't think it'll turn into anything else.

It's Monday morning, and so far nobody has said anything about the bathroom incident. So I'm guessing nobody else knows. Which is good, considering how much they would laugh at me if they knew. *Laugh at the weak girl who couldn't even defend herself. She fell to the floor crying. Hilarious, isn't it?*

First period class is pretty boring. The math teacher drones on and on about something I forget to pay attention to. I am too busy worrying about a certain boy sitting behind me, whom I haven't seen since I ran away from him in the rain.

Tapping: that's all I hear. Almost like a song stuck on repeat. An annoying song that gets stuck in your head until you hear an even more annoying song to overlap it.

Tap

Tap

Tap

Until finally,

Tap

Ta –

You snap.

Whipping around in my chair, I catch the culprit, his pencil frozen in mid-air as he stares at me wide-eyed. I narrow my eyes at the pencil, then snatch it from his hand. Zander looks confused, then a little angry.

"Hey! Give that back!" He grabs at it, but I hold it behind me where he can't reach.

"No. Not unless you stop that annoying tapping. Otherwise, this pencil? Say your goodbyes!" I bring the pencil back around, ready to snap it in half.

"Okay, okay! Don't snap my pencil. It's the only one I have." His eyes look almost desperate but the anger is still there, slowly bringing me back into reality. My body instantly gets hot as the embarrassment rises through me. All the students in the classroom are staring at me either in annoyance or hiding their laughter.

"O-oh, s-sorry..." I set his pencil down on his desk and quickly spin back around in my seat. My hair shields my face from the piercing stares, but not from the teacher's frown.

Sarah, you idiot. Why would you make a scene? My fingers are wrapped tight around the sleeves of my shirt, trying to find some type of comfort there. My teeth are locked on my bottom lip, biting down enough to bring pain but not hard enough to draw blood.

The teacher continues her lesson and, what do you know, the tapping also continues. I don't know if he's doing it because he's bored or if he's doing it just to annoy me, but either way, it is getting on my nerves.

Zander will stop for a minute or two to write down something, then go right back to tapping again. There's only a few minutes left in class, and thankfully the teacher is basically done with the lesson. She had told us to write down the stuff from the whiteboard, then we could pack up our stuff and leave when the bell sounds.

The bell rings and everyone starts leaving. The tapping finally stops. Zander stands up the same time I do, grabs his bag, and follows me out the door. I feel him close behind me, and I grip the shoulder strap on my bag. I walk faster, weaving through students and dodging locker doors. *I'm not talking to him about it,* I tell myself. *I can't do that today.*

Second and third period are a breeze. I successfully dodge Zander in the hallways. The bells for lunch ring and everyone is off to get their fair share of food and gossip. Getting in line for my food, I grip my money in my hand as not to be a bother when it's my turn to pay. Someone bumps into me, causing me to drop my money to save myself from kissing the floor.

"I'm sor— Oh hey, Sarah!" Zander leans down and picks up my money for me as I regain my balance.

"Um, hi. Thanks for picking up my money." Slowly, my eyes trail up to his dark green ones. He gives me a small smile and hands it back, then stalks off through the crowd of students. My eyes trail after him, watching as his head disappears.

"Sarah! Snap out of it!" Gina waves her hand in front of my face. I mutter a quick "sorry" and hand my money to the lunch lady before Gina drags me off to our usual lunch table. We plunk ourselves down at the table and Gina digs into her salad. I sigh and start eating my bland pizza.

I glance up to find Gina worriedly staring down at her phone. I nudge her with my foot under the table. "Everything okay?"

Gina sighs and shakes her head, giving me a half-hearted smile. "It's just my mom. I asked how she was feeling today and she said she's really tired. I'm worried that she's getting worse."

Reaching across the table, I cover her hand with mine and give her a comforting smile. "I'm sure the doctors will figure out what's wrong soon enough, G." She nods appreciatively and takes a bite of her salad. Suddenly, water. Everywhere. I'm covered in water. I blink past the stream in my eyes, gasping. Gina coughs wildly, holding her hand over her chest as she gapes at whoever is behind me.

Samantha snickers behind me. "Oops, my bad." I turn in my seat to find her with an empty water bottle, an innocent smile on her face. She laughs and walks over to her table, sitting down with her friends. I look past her, straight into the eyes of Zander, who is sitting a few tables behind them. He frowns and glances between us, trying to decipher what's going on. My cheeks heat up, embarrassed that he saw it happen. I groan in frustration and angrily grab some napkins from my tray to dry off my face.

Gina throws her hands up in the air, almost knocking her salad over. "What an A-hole!" She picks up her fork again and starts stabbing the lettuce.

I shrug and rest my head on the table. "There's nothing I can do now. I'm already soaked." My words are slightly muffled by my arms as I rest my head on them.

She rests a hand on my shoulder, "S, anytime you want me to give that girl a taste of her own medicine, you just tell me."

I snort a little louder than I would have liked. "Thanks, G. But this is something I'll have to resolve on my own."

For the rest of the day, I fume about Samantha. I make multiple trips to the bathroom to dry off my shirt with the hand dryers. Gina had left school after lunch to go with her mom to a doctor's appointment, leaving me alone to my own thoughts.

At the end of the day, I finish putting my stuff into my locker. I glance at a picture of Gina and me. We were fifteen, and we were at Ocean City, having the time of our lives.

My parents had just gotten home from one of their longer events and declared that they were taking me on a vacation. They gave me an option to bring a friend, and despite only having met Gina that year, I invited her along. The trip really solidified my friendship with Gina. We went on our own adventures on the beach docks, spent hours bowling with my parents, and had countless late nights giggling under our makeshift fort.

The locker door slams shut, barely missing my face. I follow the arm up to the face Zander is leaning against the locker next to mine. And boy, he does not look happy.

"Uh, hello?" I glance around, wondering why he looks so angry. *Did I do something to him?* Jenny, who I know from gym class, stands across the hallway and gives us a curious stare. Her eyes bore into mine, girl code for 'all good?' Zander interrupts by dipping his head down into my line of sight.

"Home Ec is about to start any minute." He reaches out his hand, gesturing for me to take it. I stare at him bewildered. Why exactly does he want me holding his hand? He rolls his eyes at me, a small smile twitching at his lips, "C'mon, Sarah, I'm just escorting you to class."

"Oh, um, okay." The words barely leave my mouth before he grabs my hand and drags me down the hall. His grip is so tight that I can't feel my hand anymore. He dodges all the stares as he leads me into the classroom, taking me straight to our table in the back. He glances around the room before finally sitting down and motioning for me to do the same. Cautiously, I sit. "What was all that for?" I ask.

His frown instantly returns. "I wanted to make sure you made it here without any more...issues."

My cheeks are aflame. "Oh, uh, that..." I trail off with a wince, my hand running over the front of my still-wet shirt.

"Are you okay?" he asks me.

I shrug. "I guess." I lift my head and meet his eyes. Suddenly, the words are spilling out of me, "No, no, I'm really not okay." Tears well up in my eyes and I quickly look down again. Maybe it's the fact that he found me yesterday that has me telling him the truth. Or maybe it's because it's become too much. I'm not sure which.

He gently lays his hand on my shoulder. "That girl is just jealous, Sarah." His lips are in a tight line. I search his eyes. Jealous of what? She's already got everything she wants. *Well, short of the boy sitting in front of me.*

"Alright, students!" Mr. Barnes claps his hands at the front of the room, a large grin on his face. Zander gives my shoulder a soft squeeze before dropping away and facing forward. The place his hand was grows cold, and I begin to miss the comforting feeling of it there. *Where did these feelings come from?*

"We are going to do a group project as a celebration of bringing back our learning program. Each group will pick a classic book or movie to study. You will need to pick a dish described within the book to recreate and bring to class for everyone to sample." My heart erupts with excitement. *Finally! This is my chance!*

"Along with your dish," Mr. Barnes continues. "I would like you to prepare a presentation of sorts to explain the dish, the reference to it in the book or movie, and a play of the scene that took place in the book. Now, that part doesn't have to be accurate to when the dish appears within the storyline. It can even be an interpretation of the story to include the dish. So play around with it a little bit."

Zander and I look over at each other, small grins spreading across our lips. Although I hate group projects, I absolutely love this idea.

"This assignment will be due within the next two weeks," says Mr. Barnes. "I suggest that you all take the weekend to study up on your project's subject, then make a plan of action." He steps off to the side, revealing a table full of books and DVDs. "Pair up with your partner and come up here to pick out your project subject." Everyone begins forming a line, and Zander and I hurry to grab the best selection.

Zander whispers in my ear. "What classic are you hoping to get?"

His breath fans against my cheek, and goosebumps rise across my skin. I push my feelings away, determined to stay focused on the task ahead. "Definitely The *Princess Bride*. No questions asked." I glance up to find Zander smirking at me. I frown and cross my arms. "What?"

With a small laugh, he shakes his head and throws his hands up, "Nothing, nothing. I was just appreciating your determination there."

I lift my chin, relaxing my stance. "This is very serious to me."

He nods. "Well, here." He reaches into his pocket and pulls out a slip of paper. "Do you have a pen?" I pull out a pen from my bag and hand it to him. He motions for me to turn around, then uses my shoulder to write on his paper. Once I turn around again, he holds the paper out for me. "Since we'll be seeing each other more often."

I hesitantly take it from him. He's written his number and address on it. I give him a small smile, then tuck it into my pocket. "Thanks."

He nods. "Just text or call me whenever you're ready to make plans. We could do lunch tomorrow if you want."

"Zander and Sarah," Mr. Barnes calls us next, motioning us to the table. There are still lots of books and movies to choose from, but my eyes are instantly drawn to the perfect cover.

I grab the book and DVD and clutch them to my chest. I turn to Zander with a large grin. "It's here."

He smiles, amusement lighting up his eyes, "*The Princess Bride* it is, then."

__chapter seven__
Zander

I wave goodbye to Sarah as we leave Home Ec. She walks to her art class, dodging the stares of other students. I can't wrap my head around why everyone picks on her.

My phone buzzes in my pocket. With a frown, I look down at the small screen. It's an unknown number. A feeling of dread washes through me. "Hello?"

"Hello, this is the Melbourne Police Department. We're calling for a Zander Mills?"

I squeeze my eyes shut, holding back a groan. "That's me."

I hear tapping on the other line as the lady continues, "Hi, Zander. We're calling in regards to your father, Jeffrey Mills. He is currently in our holding cell for public intoxication. You are given the option to pick him up. If you choose not to, he will stay in the cell for twenty-four hours before release with a citation."

I can't keep doing this. Guilt eats away at me as I weigh my options. I should just leave him there. My mom's smiling face comes to the front of my mind. Her heart would break seeing us like this. Seeing him like this. She would come to the rescue, no matter how bad it was.

"I'll be there."

It takes me about ten minutes to get to the police department. The lady at the door greets me with a cheery smile, leading me to the jail cell. Unfortunately, I already know the way. Walking around the corner, my eyes meet my dad's. He sits up a little straighter now, ready to be released. I hesitate. Scenes from this morning flash before me.

"Zander!" Dad hollered from the kitchen. My body tensed. His footsteps stomped through the house, shaking the thin walls and rattling the few picture frames of my mother on my wall. Within seconds, my bedroom door swung open, my red-faced father on the other side.

I barely gave him a glance, "Yeah?"

He slammed his fist on the doorframe, "Why is there money missing from my stash drawer?!"

I scoffed loudly, finally looking at him. His body took up most of the doorway. Despite his beer belly, he is still a tall, red-faced man. Lethal. "I didn't take your money." I stated plainly, reaching down to scoop up my bag for school.

"Don't lie to me, boy," He growled, walking further into the room to block my path.

"I'm not," I retorted, a bite in my tone. "You probably spent it on more booze."

He scoffs, "You're just like your mother." He gets in my face, his hand shaking as he points accusingly. "Undermining my authority as if I don't provide you a roof over your head, food in your belly." He shakes his head, his lips twisting into a snarl. "You both are a disappointment."

My mind goes into a rage, "How dare you," I shove his shoulders, barely moving him an inch.

Before I could even blink his fist connected with my stomach, knocking the air out of me.

I stumble back a step, the feeling of the air struggling to reach my lungs still fresh. The officer glances behind her, noticing my discomfort. My dad's eyes fill with rage, his fists subtly clenching beside him. I know what that means.

I turn without thinking, booking it back out to my bike. I know there will be consequences later, but for just one night, I want to be free. I want him to pay for what he's done.

Revving the engine, I speed off downtown. I walk into the grocery store, heading to the back room, where my manager, Jim, is taking inventory. Jim has a bit of a pot belly, and graying hair pokes out from under his cap.

He turns around. "Hey, Zander! What're you doing here?"

I rub the back of my neck. "Hey, uh, I know this is weird, but do you have anything I could do?"

He raises his eyebrows. "It's not every day someone comes walking in hoping for a shift, Zander."

I wince under his gaze, shrugging again. "I know, I just really need something to do right now. Whatever you need."

Jim eyes me over. "Sure, kid. Let's get you clocked in, and then you can help me with some displays." He pats me on the shoulder as he walks by, leading me to the time clock. I breathe a sigh of relief, thankful for the distraction.

For one night, I'll be free.

chapter eight

Sarah

I ponder the note. Today is Friday, which means we won't be here tomorrow. Which must mean, either he didn't know what day it was or he actually wants to meet up for lunch. After I finally regain some brain cells, I make my way home. The first thing I do is call not Zander, but Gina.

"Hey, G. I, um, need to tell you something."

"Sure, S! What up?"

"Well, Zander gave me a note with his phone number, then was talking about lunch?"

I can still hear her screaming on the other line. She comes over right after she hangs up and grabs the note from my hands to inspect it. "Girl, you've *got* to text him."

"No, I…" My stomach rolls. What have I gotten myself into?

"Then I'll do it for you!" She grabs my phone off my desk and texts him. Before I know it, it's official: he's picking me up at 1 tomorrow.

The next day, Gina's still screaming, this time as she dances around my closet.

"You're going to make my ears bleed!" I groan loudly and lay face down on my bed, covering my ears with my pillow. I'm already nauseous with nerves about meeting up with him. I don't need an earache, too.

"Make your ears bleed? What about my eyes? You need to go shopping again." Even with my ears covered, I can hear her throwing clothes onto the floor, making a giant mess. "Eureka! This is it!" She bounces out of my closet holding a maroon long-sleeved shirt, black leggings, and a pair of heeled combat boots. *I didn't even know I had these clothes...*

"Go put those on and I'll do your hair for you." She pulls me up from my spot on the bed, pushing me towards the bathroom. I change, then exit the bathroom to sit at my desk, which Gina has transformed into a vanity. She has all kinds of eye liners, mascara, hair clips, and wands.

"Okay, S! Just sit tight and I'll make you look so amazing Zander won't be able to take his eyes off you! Not that he has that problem now, anyways." She giggles. Rolling my eyes with a smile, I grab a YA Romance book out from under all the makeup and start reading. The story quickly engulfs my attention when the protagonist begins explaining her past while Gina starts working on my hair, giving it a slight curl at the ends. After she's done, she turns me around to do my makeup, snatching my book and making me look up at her. She simply swipes my lashes with mascara and does some winged eye-liner.

After an eternity of her swiping and brushing, she finally turns me around to see the finishing results.

I look so...*different*. My lashes accent my eyes, making the brown pop. My cheeks are a cute shade of pink, giving me a rosy look without smothering my freckles. I look like I'm ready for a night on the town. *I love it!*

"Gina! What did you do to my face? I look like a completely different person!" Gawking at myself in the mirror, I slowly reach up to touch my cheek. A slightly furious, slightly scared Gina slaps my hand away.

"Don't touch it, you'll ruin it! O.M.G. You don't like it? You don't like it. Oh no. I'm so, so sorry, I'll take it off!" She starts rushing around, spraying a cotton pad with cleaners and reaching towards my face.

Screaming and ducking away from her hands, I not so gracefully fall off the chair and roll onto the floor. "No, no, no! G, it's fine! I look fine, thank you. Now get away!" She stops short and bursts out laughing at my crumpled figure on the floor.

I roll my eyes and get up, straightening my shirt when the doorbell rings. We both freeze, our eyes going wide. Gina rushes out the door and down the steps to answer it. I take a deep breath. *Well, here goes nothing right? It won't be so bad.*

It's just lunch, Sarah. It's not even a date. Calm down! Deep breaths, in and out!

None of that works. As soon as I make it to the bottom step, I'm ready to faint again. Zander and Gina stand at the door chatting away about who knows what, not even noticing me standing there, almost ready to die. This is my first hangout with someone other than Gina or my parents. What if he thinks I'm weird? *Just treat it like we're at school, then it'll be like the same thing...right?*

Zander looks up over Gina's head and spots me slowly backing up the stairs. His face lights up, showing his pearly whites. A small bruise colors his cheek. I wonder what happened?

"Where are you going? The mall is this way." He grins up at me innocently, breaking me from my thoughts.

Gina snickers at me. "Get down here already." She shoves me toward Zander. "Take care of her, and have her back here by no later than 10:00!" I roll my eyes and trudge toward Zander.

He raises his hand and salutes her jokingly. "Yes, Ma'am." Zander takes my arm in his.

"This way, mi'lady." He grins and hands me a helmet. Here I thought chivalry was dead. A small smile makes its way onto my face as I climb onto his motorcycle, my nerves slowly calming down the more I'm near him.

"Zander?"

He looks up from his helmet in his hands. "Yeah?"

I fiddle with the straps on my helmet. "This is just a school thing, right?"

His arms go slack beside him. "Is it to you?" His voice is soft, unassuming. I feel myself relax completely, finally at ease.

I think about his question for a second, "I think so…?"

He smiles softly, "Then yes, it is." He mounts the bike and starts it up.

We arrive at the mall in record time. The parking spaces are pretty much filled, other than a few empties here and there. *Hopefully I won't see anyone from school here.* Zander shuts off the bike and steps off. He reaches a hand out for me. Softly smiling to myself, I take his hand and step off the bike. Once we take our helmets off, we start walking towards the mall.

__chapter nine__

Sarah

"May I have a sip of that?"

"Touch my cup, you die."

Zander and I are in the mall food court, eating pizza and sipping Slurpees. According to him, his stomach was about to burst out at any moment and ravage the world.

"Geez, didn't know you had that in you. So violent." He smirks and slides his hand away from my cup and back to his cherry Slurpee. My pizza was long gone, my blueberry drink almost finished as well. *All good things must come to an end.* Sighing softly as I reach the end of my drink, I slowly poke at the olives on my plate left from Zander's pizza. "You all done?" I meet his eyes, nodding and pushing my plate towards him.

"Thanks." I smile up at him and gather the rest of the trash.

"Here, I got it." He shoos my hands away from the pile and gathers it up, "I'll be right back." He disappears around a corner. I sigh and pull out my notebook and pen, turning to a new page devoid of doodles so I can start our project.

Our time together has been enjoyable so far. I don't feel as awkward as I thought I would, although I can't help but scan the crowds around me to search for a familiar face—actually hoping for a lack thereof. *If Samantha knew I was hanging out with Zander she would freak out.* My eyes stare pointedly down at my pencil. My thoughts travel back to Zander, curiosity eating me away. *What happened to him? Did he get in a fight?*

Just as I am convincing myself to stop thinking about Zander's business, he comes back and plops down in his chair, adjusting it closer to my side of the table so we both can look at the notebook. My eyes roam over his face, catching on the now purple bruise on his cheek. My words tumble out before I can stop them. "Are you okay?"

His eyes dart up to mine, surprised. I frown at this. Did he not think I would notice? He shakes his head, brushing it off, "Oh, it's nothing to worry about." His voice wobbles, setting off my suspicions even more. Did someone from school cause problems, maybe?

I quickly reprimand myself. I barely know him, so I shouldn't pry. "Okay..." I trail off. I watch him closely, noting the way he shifts in his seat and wrings his hands together.

"Alright, what do you think we should do?" He changes the subject, almost desperate to get off the topic. I file this information away, focusing on the notepad instead as he gestures weakly to it.

I tap my pen anxiously against the table. "Mmm, it depends," I sift through the different recipes and scenes of the story in my mind. Glancing over at Zander, I notice he's staring expectantly at me. I blush and continue. "It depends on what scene we decide to do. There's the infamous grilled cheese and apple sandwich, which depicts a day in the life on the farm. Then there's Fezzik's soup, depicted from the scene with the giant who dunks his head in the hot water, then the cold, then back to–"

Zander barks out a laugh. "Whoa, okay. You're obviously very passionate about this movie."

I smile and look down at my hands, "Yeah, I used to watch it with my parents all the time."

He smiles back. "Are they around today? I'd love to meet them." He says it so nonchalantly, as if it'd be no big deal for me to introduce the first guy friend I've ever had to my parents. Mom would freak. Which reminds me, now that I think about it, I really should call to check in.

I shake my head, disappointment flooding through me. "No, I'm not sure when they'll be home again." At his confused expression, I add, "They travel a lot for their business, *Jonesing For It*. It's a–"

"Moving food truck that caters at Comic-Con?! Your parents own that?" His eyes light up.

A surprised smile reaches my lips. "Uh, yeah. How do you know about them?"

"Pfft, are you kidding?" He stares at me like I'm crazy, a large grin on his face. "Everyone knows them. I didn't realize I was sitting with royalty here." His comment makes me blush. He continues. "I used to wish I was old enough to go to some of the events they attended just so I could get something from their truck. I've only actually eaten from it once, about three years ago. My mom had brought home some leftover dessert from a wedding she had planned." His smile slightly fades when he mentions his mom, his eyes dropping to the table. He must have loved her very much. Almost immediately, he regains his previous gumption, shaking off his sadness. "It was Turkish Delights from *Narnia: The Lion, The Witch, and The Wardrobe*. The flavor was so amazing, I have yet to forget it."

Pride washes over me. My parents did that. And one day, I will do the same. I smile widely, "I'm really glad you liked it so much. I'll have to get you hooked up with another dish." Meeting his eyes, I quietly add, "Your mom sounds wonderful. You must miss her a lot."

The sadness returns, and he looks away, across the food court. It must be hard to talk about it, so I don't pry. Changing the subject, I focus back on the task at hand. "So I think we should pick a scene from the movie that's fundamental to the plot, then pick the dish to accompany it?"

Zander nods. "It would probably help if I actually knew what we were talking about." He gives me a sheepish grin.

I shake my head in disappointment. "Uncultured, I see." I tease him with a small smile. "Now we're definitely going to have to watch the movie for...research of course."

He laughs again and bumps his shoulder with mine. "Okay, you're the expert here." He nods down to my notebook, "Should we make a list, then? Things we'll need, scenes we could use, that kinda stuff?"

I nod along and start writing things down. Different recipes that I already know, scenes we could incorporate, when suddenly it hits me. "We should probably decide first which characters we'll focus on first." He gestures for me to continue. "Really, there are two that I'd like to choose from. The previously mentioned scene with the soup involving the giant and the guy who -"

Zander throws his hands up over his ears. "Whoa, spoilers!"

This gets a laugh out of me. "Or we could go the easy route of Westley and Princess Buttercup."

Zander leans back in his seat, "Well, I think we know the obvious answer here." He smiles widely, "Of course, we'll need to go do more research." He moves out of his seat, picking up my notebook, pen, and bag for me. I quirk an eyebrow at him as he stretches his hand out for me, giving a slight bow. He peeks up at me, "Come now, Princess...what's her name?"

I giggle. "Buttercup."

He nods as if he knew along. "Right—Princess Buttercup. We shan't keep the castle waiting!"

I take his hand and step down from my chair, another laugh bubbling out, "That is *so* not how they talked."

"Shh." He puffs his chest out and hooks my arm through his. He clears his throat and says, "Hear ye, hear ye!"

I punch his arm, my eyes wide as people turn to look at us. We both dissolve into laughter as he leads me out of the mall. I stare up at him. Where did this carefree, funny, and actually kind of dorky guy come from? I find myself being less intimidated by him, and it's actually quite refreshing. I like this side of Zander. *Maybe a little more than I'm willing to admit.*

__chapter ten__

Sarah

Sundays are always amazing to me. Although Monday is right around the corner, it's the perfect day to just relax and watch all your favorite shows and movies while snacking on ice cream and chips. Another great thing about Sundays is that my parents are actually home every other week. It's the one day of the week I get to see them all day and actually talk to them before they leave for another adventure...without me.

That's what I planned for this Sunday. All of that is put to a halt when I find the note on the dining room table.

Went away for a business trip. We should be back in 2-3 weeks. Here's some money to buy food and other necessities. Call us when you see this.

Love,

Mom and Dad

That's it? No warnings against boys, parties, or drugs? Sighing softly, I crumple the note, throw it in the trash, and stick the money in my pocket. Might as well go to the store now and get some pizzas.

I send a quick text to Gina asking if she wants to go, then head up to my room to change. After throwing on some black leggings, a sweater, and my favorite Converse, I sit down on my bed to wait for her reply. Now is as good a time as ever to call my mom and dad.

They answer within the first ring, the sound of the car on the ground muffling their voices. "Hey, sweetie!" Mom's cheerful voice greets me first. I smile sadly as I stare down at my hands.

"Hey, Mom." I open my mouth to say more, my dad cuts me off.

"Hey, sweetheart! We're so sorry we didn't get to see you this morning. There was an issue with our next event and we had to leave right away to keep our spot. I hope you understand." I can just picture the pleading way he would look at me through the rearview mirror any time they drove me home from school, dropping me off before they bolted out the door to another event. Even though I did understand and support their dreams, my disappointment would always be the same.

"Yeah, I get it."

My mom answers next. "Oh, sweetie, we're here now. We'll call you later, okay? We love you!"

I barely get to say, "Love you, too," before the phone goes dead. A loud sigh whooshes out of me, tears pricking my eyes. I really wish we could spend more time together, like we used to. Movie nights every weekend accompanied by board games before bed. When my parents first started traveling, they would always ensure that they were home for the weekends so we could spend time together. But now it seems that the older I get, the more they hit the road on the weekends. I just feel like I have so much to tell them, but not enough time to do so.

I had really hoped to tell my mom about my day with Zander, but I suppose that will have to wait. My phone pings loudly. Gina will be there in five minutes. Those five minutes stretch into ten. *Of course she's late. Wouldn't be Gina if she wasn't late.* The horn blasts outside, scaring me half to death. My phone beeps as a text from Gina comes through.

"I'm here!"

Yeah, you don't think I wouldn't have known from you blowing the horn? Grumbling, I slide off my bed and head downstairs. Gina waves frantically when she sees me and I can see her slightly bouncing in her seat. As soon as I open the car door, she bombards me with the never ending questions.

"How was it? Did you have fun? What time did you come home? What was he like? Did he kiss you? Did he *try* to kiss you?! Oh my gosh, if he pulled a fast one on you I'll beat him up. Omigosh, I'm so excited! Why aren't you talking? Are you sick? What took you so long? Why do we have to go to the store? Wha-"

"Oh my fudge, woman, let me speak!" I shout. Her eyes go wide with shock.

"Sorry," she whispers. She starts her car and heads to the store.

Shaking my head, I place a hand over my forehead. "It was fine. We had a lot of fun. No, he didn't try to kiss me. He didn't try anything. It was just a friendly get-together for school, not a date." The last words came out a little quieter than expected. *Had I been wanting it to be a date? We had both agreed that it wasn't, but...*

Gina smiles at me sheepishly. "Sorry for all the questions, I just got a little excited." I simply shrug and turn back towards the window, watching the buildings and trees pass by until we arrive at the supermarket.

I grab a cart and start pushing it towards the fruit section. "I honestly don't even know what I need. I just know I have a hundred dollars to spend."

Gina starts coughing wildly, stopping me in my tracks. "Gina, what the heck? What're you doing?"

She points toward the lettuce, where a tall boy has his back turned towards us. Dressed in a red shirt and black slacks, with a black hat covering his hair—he obviously works here.

I furrow my brows, about to ask who he is. But the words die on my tongue when he turns around. He gives me his signature smile. I smile softly back at Zander and before I know it, Gina is pushing the cart towards him with me in tow.

"Hi, Zander!" Gina greets him as she approaches, keeping her hand firmly wrapped around my arm. He turns and nods in acknowledgment then leans against the lettuce racks with a smirk.

"Hi there, you must be...?" He stops short. He's forgotten her name. I smile in victory. *Ha! Nice try being smooth there, buddy!* As I laugh internally, his smirk falters and he stands up straight.

"Gina? Sarah's best friend? Dude, we literally just met yesterday...?" As Gina goes on her tirade, I hope against hope that she won't be mean. I don't want Zander to start hating us. He nods along to Gina, a small smile on his lips, his eyes darting to the man further down the aisle. Oh no, he looks uncomfortable. I take Gina's arm and tug her away, waving to him over my shoulder. I should have talked to him, but it still feels kinda awkward with other people around.

"Geez. What's the rush?" she asks. "I was just trying to talk to him." I roll my eyes and swing around to meet her innocent smile.

"No, you were trying to get *me* to talk to him. Besides, he's working." My cheeks heat up and I cover them with my hands, groaning. *Stupid cheeks and stupid boys and stupid stupid stupid.*

She sings out teasingly. "Oh, stop it, you're just being dramatic. It's not like you spent the whole afternoon with him or something." Then she races the cart to the ice cream aisle, nearly hitting a small child. I think about her words. She's right, I need to stop being so weird about it. We did perfectly fine together yesterday. I should be able to talk to him today!

I have to run to catch up to her. I find her digging through the ice cream cones, looking for who knows what. An elderly woman watches her like she's a lunatic.

"Gina! C'mon, they don't have it. You're drawing attention to us!" I try to pull her out of the freezer, sending an apologetic look towards the elderly woman.

She holds onto the side of the freezer and keeps digging with her other hand. "No, Sarah, there's got to be some in here. I just know it!" She rests her leg on top of the ledge, shoving herself further in. My cheeks heat up in utter embarrassment as my idiot best friend climbs into the freezer and emerges with a box of chocolate eclair bars.

She turns around and gives me a smug look. "Got 'em." She skips over to the cart and delicately places them in it. I shake my head and push the cart towards the dairy section, way too eager to get out of here and just go home. *Sam and Dean and their supernatural adventures are waiting for me.* At that thought, another idea pops into mind. I should invite Zander over to watch The *Princess Bride* for our project.

After another twenty minutes or so, I have all the stuff I need, and Gina and I are headed back to her car. Unfortunately, I didn't see Zander again after the whole lettuce rack thing. We unload the groceries into the car, and I take the cart back. After I push the cart into the holding area, I whip out my phone and shoot Zander a text to invite him over.

"Sarah, are you coming or are you just going to stand there daydreaming?" Gina teases as she stands by her car door waiting for me to get in.

"Yeah, sorry." I get in. She starts up the engine and we head home.

She gets this evil smile on her face, and I know whatever she's about to say, I won't like it. "What were you daydreaming about?" she asks. "Or should I ask, who?" I cast a mocking glare at her before sighing in defeat.

"Okay, maybe I was thinking about him. But it's not like that." I shake my head and my cheeks start flushing pink. I hate that I blush so much. "I was actually going to suggest I invite Zander over...He needs to watch *The Princess Bride* as a part of our project."

"Oh my gosh, I knew it! You totally like him, don't you?" She squeals and dances around in her seat, making me concerned for our safety.

"No, no, no! I don't like him like that. I mean, sure, he's cute and all, but I don't have feelings for him. We're just friends, I think..." My mind starts going wild. *Are we really even friends? I mean like, neither one of us have said that we are...and we haven't said that we weren't. So, are we friends or...?*

Gina immediately stops dancing and frowns at me. "You think? Sarah, from what you've told me, he's a nice guy. And considering that you both have hung out multiple times— and yes, school counts!—I don't see why you wouldn't be considered friends." She shoots me a knowing look, "You know, we didn't really hang out outside of school until our trip to Ocean City. Would I have gone on a two-week vacation with someone just because we talked at school?" When she puts it like that, it makes sense.

I give her a small smile and jump out of the car when we pull into the driveway. I feel my phone buzz in my pocket, but don't bother with it until all the food has been unpacked. Once everything is put away, Gina leaves to practice, and I finally pull out my phone to see a message from Zander, confirming he's on his way.

__chapter eleven__
Sarah

While I wait for Zander to show up, I prepare a small vegetable pizza. With my cookbook propped open on the counter and dough in my hands, I hum softly while I begin kneading it out onto the pan. Popping it into the oven, I move on to the next step.

This recipe is a staple for my family's Christmas dinner. Every year, my dad would help me make this while my mom prepared the table. Because my parents cooked so often, we didn't have a traditional dinner. Instead, we snacked throughout the day until we exchanged presents and watched our favorite Christmas movies. My humming turns into singing as I sprinkle the vegetables into a bowl, then take the crust out of the oven to cool. I dance as I spread the cream cheese and ranch mixture onto the crust. I grab my bowl of veggies from off the counter and dance my way back over to the oven.

"May I join in on the fun?"

I scream, dropping the bowl of veggies to the floor. Zander stands in the door frame, holding his hands up innocently while chuckling. I clutch my chest and try to catch my breath. "What—How—?"

He smiles sheepishly. "The door was unlocked. I was knocking for almost ten minutes." His hand cups the back of his neck. "I poked my head in and heard you singing."

My cheeks burn bright. "You weren't supposed to hear that."

He walks further into the kitchen, stooping down to clean up the array of vegetables on the floor. I remain frozen in place, still reeling with embarrassment. He smiles and lifts the semi-full bowl up to me, "I'll pretend like it never happened," A sigh escapes me as I reach for the bowl, my brows jumping up when he pulls it away for a second as he says, "But only if you make me those Turkish Delights we talked about yesterday," his tune hopeful.

I fight back a smile as I finally take the bowl from him and say, "I think I can handle that." Eyeing up the veggies left in the bowl, I'm relieved to find that not many escaped. Zander stands up and dumps a handful of broccoli in the trash can nearby. Taking handfuls at a time, I begin sprinkling the veggies on top and clarify, "Although it won't be done today." He comes up beside me, taking a handful of veggies. My eyes widen and on reflex I reach out to stop his arm, "Wait!"

His eyes are wide. "What?" He glances between me and the pizza, his eye brows raised. His skin is warm against my palm, and I quickly realize I am still holding onto him. I drop my hand away, immediately blushing as I ask, "Did you wash your hands first?"

His lips purse and he promptly walks over to the sink. He glances over his shoulder as he rinses off the veggies in hand with a sheepish smile, "Sorry, Chef."

My heart skips a beat at the nickname. I quickly turn away, hiding my grin. He comes up beside me again, lightly bumping his shoulder with mine as he reaches over my hands to sprinkle the veggies on. I steal a glance at him, taking in the curve of his jaw and the small smile on his lips. Goosebumps raise where his shoulder brushes mine, and a wave of warmth washes through me. What would it be like if he were to hug me?

Whoa, where did that come from?!

I shake myself from my thoughts and take two steps back, beelining for the sink to wash the vegetable remains from between my fingers. *I should not be feeling like this. I barely know the guy!* My eyes betray me, glancing over to look at him again.

His eyes meet mine and he smiles, "This looks really good. Do we have to bake it or anything else?" He leans back on the counter, looking so at ease. Almost like he belongs in that spot.

I shake my head, "It just needs to refrigerate for a bit." *Man, I need him to not stand there looking so...himself!* I jerk my thumb behind me to the living room, "Would you mind setting up the movie real quick? I have the dvd laying on the coffee table…" I bite my lip, gripping onto the towel to dry my hands.

He pushes off the counter, "Yeah, absolutely." He brushes past me to get to the sink, quickly washing off his hands as well. A small wave of relief goes through me. *I just need a minute to*—My eyes jerk down to the towel as his fingers brush mine, then up to his face as he smiles widely, "I kinda need that if you don't mind."

"Yeah, sorry!" I release it and step back, ramming into the counter behind me, "Oh!" With a surprised squeak I sidestep away from him, hurrying to cover up my mistake. He chuckles but doesn't say anything, then leaves the room.

Oh my gosh, I'm so embarrassing. I cradle my head in my hands, taking a deep breath before I push my hair back from my face and drop my hands to my sides. Let's hope that the rest of the day isn't like this.

Once I regain my composure, I join Zander in the living room as the movie starts. With light commentary here and there, he quickly gets into the movie and points out scenes we could try. Having just walked back from throwing away our dinner plates, I settle back into the couch as the poison scene continues.

"This is hilarious." Zander sits cross-legged on the couch, practically on the edge of his seat, with a wide grin. A grin of my own forms at his eagerness. It's always a great feeling when someone loves what you've shared with them. He glances over at me, "It would be awesome to act out, but terrible as a 'meal'."

I nod as I settle back into my seat, "Yeah, I don't think Mr. Barnes would appreciate us putting some apples and grapes on a plate then calling it a day."

The movie progresses into one of my favorite scenes, which typically has me grinning and quoting every line—but now with Zander beside me, I hesitate. Is this weird? To watch a kissing scene with a really good looking boy who just so happens to be sitting *very* close? *When did he get so close?!*

I catch him glancing at me as Princess Buttercup kisses Westley, the scene proving to be a very heartfelt and romantic moment. A sigh of relief escapes, my shoulders easing now that the scene is over. Soon, the movie is coming to an end, and yet again Princess Buttercup and Westley share an intimate kiss. *When did this movie have so much kissing in it?!*

My hands are sweaty, my nerves out of whack having him so close. He shifts in his seat, his shoulder brushing mine as his eyes practically burn holes into me. I gulp back my nerves. "Well?"

He turns his head. "Well?" I turn to look at him, my breath catching at the proximity of our faces.

"What did you think?" My words are barely a whisper, my heart beating rapidly. He's so close. The green of his eyes is mesmerizing, flecks of gold swirling within them. I see now that his nose is slightly crooked, like it had been broken before.

The scar on his lip is even more prominent now. He has a hint of stubble on his cheeks, and his hair is kind of messy today.

I can't help but admit that I find him extremely attractive.

"Honestly?" He gets a little smile. "I really liked it. It was the perfect mix of funny and romantic."

My heart does somersaults as I smile back. "That's why I like it, too." I rest my head on my hand. "So what scene do you think would best suit our project?"

He looks up at the ceiling in deep thought, talking out loud. "Well, after viewing the scene involving the soup, I fear I won't be able to accurately portray that to the class." I laugh. His lips turn up at the sound before he glances back over at me. "I'm thinking when they're reunited would be best. We could incorporate the dish afterwards?"

My eyes widen as the scene comes to mind. "The kiss?" The idea of kissing Zander has my heart in my stomach. Butterflies swarm as the image comes to mind. Would I really want that?

Does he?

"Yeah." He smiles shyly. "It was the best scene of the movie, super heartfelt and romantic," *which is exactly why I thought he wouldn't choose it!* He continues, "We would have to practice, of course. Get used to the idea and all..."

I gulp back my fear. "Yeah..." I trail off, hoping he'll make the first move. "What do you have in mind?" My fingers grip my leg, anticipation clawing at me. I don't know what to expect here. I'm scared, but excited as well.

"Just one kiss, every day."

I bite my lip anxiously. "Just one kiss?"

He looks back up at me, something like hope shining in his eyes. Nodding, he takes my hand in his. "Just one."

I take a deep breath, then take the leap. "Okay, yeah. Let's do it."

__chapter twelve__
Sarah

Just call already!

No! No, don't call, it's a bad idea.

I groan and dial her number, then quickly hit the end call button.

This is the fifth time I've done this. *Okay, okay. Just call her. It's what a good friend would do. She can help you!*

I bite my lip and nod. I groan again and rub my face with my hand.

Finally, I hit the dial button for the last time and wait for Gina to pick up. After about three rings, she finally answers.

"Hey, S! What's up?"

I take a deep breath. "Well, um...I have *a lot* to tell you." I trail off, nerves and excitement bubbling up inside me. "I sold my soul to the devil."

"You what? Why?" Gina's voice rings through the phone and into my skull.

"I sold my soul to satan, Gina!" My words come out panicked and I place a hand on my forehead. Zander left about twenty minutes ago and I haven't been able to calm down since. I'm shaking and I can feel the sweat forming on my forehead. Oh gosh, I can't go through with this. "What do I do?" I pace around my room.

"Well, I guess you just wait till your ten years are up and try fighting off the hellhounds. Although, your chance of survival is very minim— "

"Gina, seriously! What do I do?" I stop pacing and sit down on the floor, bringing my knees up to my chest.

"Um, I don't know. What exactly did you say you would do?" I hear her pull out one of her chairs. *Good, she's got her thinking cap on.*

"Well, I uh, agreed to give him a kiss every day until..." My words fly out a mile a minute, coming to an abrupt halt. *Wait a minute.* My breath stops for a split second.

"Until what, Sarah? Until what?" Gina screeches into the phone, again making my ears ring.

"Oh my cheeseballs, Gina, he didn't even give me an 'until!'" I smack my forehead and fall back on the floor.

"Sarah, I'm having a really hard time understanding what's going on..." She sighs and I can hear her worry creeping in.

"Gina, I'm not cut out for this kind of stuff. What if he changes his mind halfway through and does something awful?" I groan and go limp on the floor. I put Gina on speaker and then lay my phone beside my face, letting my arms drop down beside me. "I actually think I kind of like him."

A stray tear slides down my cheek, crashing onto the carpet and dissolving into it. *I don't want to ruin my chances, no matter how slim.*

"Sarah, you've got this. There is absolutely no reason why you can't do this. You are a beautiful young woman who deserves a nice guy. And if it ends badly, oh well, 'cause he's the one who will be missing out. All you have to do is give him a small kiss on the cheek, every day until he gets bored and moves on. Or until he completely falls in love with you and you two get married and have fifteen babies and make me the godmother and—"

I laugh softly as she drones on and on about spoiling our potential babies. My tears finally dry up and before I know it I'm a laughing mess on the floor.

Sometimes you just need a little best friend therapy to get by.

I tap my chin in thought as I look back and forth between my comfy gray sweats and my ripped blue jeans. "Sweatpants or jeans, sweatpants or jeans, sweatpants . . . or jeans . . . ? Sweatpants, definitely." I nod in agreement with myself and grab them, holding them close to my chest as I walk to the bathroom. I throw on my sweats, sweater, and Converse. I rush out the door, tying my hair up into a messy bun as I walk to school. The leaves are changing colors as fall sets in. A cool breeze blows the fallen leaves across the road, making that scraping sound I love. Today is the first day of our agreement. I'm nervous, yes, but I'm keeping in mind what Gina told me. *I should not compare myself to other girls, and I am fully capable of doing this. Besides, he was the one to ask me. That has to mean something, right?*

The sound of kids screaming, teenagers talking, and feet shuffling reaches me as I finally make it to the school steps and head to my first class. The hallways are packed as usual, kids cramming their books into their lockers and bags, bumping into each other with no remorse. The typical morning scene. I make my way through the middle and pass by Gina's locker, pouting slightly to myself because she's not here.

I end up bumping into someone, knocking their books out of their hands.

"Oh my gosh, I'm so sorry!" I quickly lean down to pick up their books. Once I have them all I look back up to hand them back, when my eyes meet with the devil in disguise. *James.*

"Get your lard fingers off my stuff." He glares down at me, ripping his books from my hands. I flinch away from him, my eyes dropping to the floor.

"Maybe you should watch where you're going." Zander suddenly appears in front of me, shielding me from James' view. I peek around Zander's shoulder at his clenched jaw, his eyes shooting daggers at James.

James scoffs loudly. "Yeah, whatever. Keep a leash on your girlfriend."

My mouth drops open as I search for my words, "No, we're not..." James rolls his eyes at my pitiful attempt, finally shoving past me.

Zander turns around to face me. "You okay?" His hand lightly brushes my cheek, which is flaming red now. I blink back tears.

"Yeah, I think so?" He quirks an eyebrow. I quickly shake my head. "Yes, I'm fine. Thank you."

He nods in approval. "Anyways, as I was going to say before." He smiles widely, his stance finally relaxing. "Hello there, Princess Buttercup."

"H-Hello." I stutter, gripping the handle of my book-bag. My cheeks flush. Memories of our deal rushing back to me. He takes my free hand and starts walking down the hall.

"Where are we going?" I gulp. I try pulling my hand from his, but to no avail.

"To first period?" He gives me a confused look, then turns back to navigating us through the swarm of teenagers.

"Oh..." My shoulders finally slump.

He finally stops outside of the door and lets go of my hand. My eyes drop down to where his hand just was, a feeling of sadness washing over me. My palm grows cold, already craving his hand in mine again. I cringe at my own thoughts. *Geez, Sarah, it wasn't even that serious!* He walks in without saying another word, leaving me standing there looking like an idiot.

Oh, fun.

The day goes by fast, not another word exchanged between us. Even in Home Ec, he only speaks when he needs me to pass him the salt. He seems as if he had a lot on his mind, but isn't willing to share. I can't help but get lost in my own thoughts, the self-doubt starting to creep in.

Maybe he doesn't care about it anymore? Could he have gotten bored already? Is it for the best?

Conflicted with my own feelings, I rush down the school steps as I leave.

Then I run into a brick wall.

I fall back onto my butt and all my stuff spills out. Thankfully, nobody seems to have seen my embarrassing fall.

"Whoa there, that's the second time you've run into someone today. Sarah, are you...are you falling for me?" Zander bends down to help me, an amused smile on his lips.

I roll my eyes. "Haha, really funny. People just happen to get in my way a lot." I grumble and start picking up my stuff. He stretches his hand out to help me up and I begrudgingly take it. *I've had enough embarrassment for one day.*

He pulls me up so fast I feel like I got whiplash. I gasp softly as I crash into his chest, his arm around my waist to steady me. My hand rests over his heart beat. His heart pounds against his chest. A small sliver of satisfaction shoots through me. *Did I do that?* His lips part as he lets out a small breath, his hand lightly squeezing my hip before he gently releases me and hands me my books. I take them, finally breaking eye contact when I turn to put them in my bag.

I turn back around to face him, jumping in fright when I see his face merely inches from mine.

"I think you're forgetting something." He stares at me, waiting with a quizzical smile on his face. His voice teases me, daring me to make the first move.

"T-thank you." I stutter and blush, trying to move away, but he only draws closer.

He laughs softly and shakes his head. "No, that's not what I meant."

I stare at him. "Then what did you mean?" *I know exactly what he means.*

He moves his hand up and lightly taps on his cheek. "I think we need to start practicing."

"R-right." I gulp nervously, my body starting to shake with anticipation and nerves.

His smirk turns into a soft smile, his eyes going soft as he looks at me. "Don't be nervous. It's only a kiss."

Yeah, that's what The Killers *said and look how that turned out.*

"O-okay." I stare up at him and bite my lip. He turns his head slightly, looking at me from the corner of his eye. I take a deep breath and lean forward.

Then I do it.

My lips press against his smooth cheek, the stubble he had last night nowhere in sight. I quickly lean back down and look down at my feet, fiddling with my fingers. That was the closest contact I think I've ever had with a boy in my life.

My heart is racing and jumping hurdles, my hands sweating and clammy. Zander doesn't say anything at first, both of us seemingly stunned into silence. My legs feel like jelly, all of the adrenaline leaching from my veins. I can't believe I actually did it. Pride consumes me. For once, I stepped out of my safety bubble.

And my goodness, I liked how it felt.

__chapter thirteen__
Zander

It wasn't what I was expecting. No, not at all. Her lips are so soft. No hint of chapped lips. The smell of strawberries sticks to her skin, wafting up to my nose as her breath fans across my cheek.

It ended just as quickly as it started, and I am left wondering why it ended so soon. Sarah looks awkwardly down at her feet, her fingers twining together. We both stand in silence, nothing but the sound of our breathing filling the space between us. I can't quite tell if she enjoyed it, but I know I sure did.

I finally come back to my senses and lean back, taking a small breath in as I do so. "Bye, Buttercup." The nickname slips out. She sucks in a small breath, and her cheeks flush even darker. Doubt creeps in, and I force myself to walk away before anything else can happen. *Before I let anything else happen.*

I get on my bike and rev it up. Sarah continues to stand there, eyes wide with shock over. I don't blame her. I feel the exact same way.

I shake my head, revving the engine again then taking off in the opposite way. Through my side mirror, I see her look back at me before turning and speed-walking to the school steps. With my focus back on the road, my smile slowly dims the closer I get to the house. The house I refuse to call home.

I pull into the driveway alongside Dad's car and shut off my bike. Walking up to the door, I get the key out and unlock it. Before opening it, I listen for any noise inside but hear nothing. Relief eases my steps. I have been avoiding him since the day at the jail. I had left him there all night, and the next morning he had cornered me on my way to work. Words were said, and fists flew. I barely dodged his swing before I scrambled out the door, away from his enraged state. It's best to let him simmer for a few days before I see him again, but sometimes that doesn't always work out.

As I push the door open, beer bottles go rolling across the floor. I roll my eyes at the mess and bend down to pick them up. Tossing them in the trash can nearby, I then walk into the kitchen. Empty pizza boxes and take-out bags litter the table, dirty dishes piled high in the sink.

I sigh softly and shake my head. "Can't even clean up after himself." I glare down at the sink, gripping the edge as the rage starts boiling. I take a deep breath in, closing my eyes and thinking of something else, something that makes me smile. Before the rage can bubble over the edge.

My mom would have never allowed this. Our home life wasn't the greatest, but they both tried their best to keep up. Now, he has completely given up hope.

Shoving off the counter, I move towards the fridge. When I open it, the foul smell of rotting eggs punches me in the face. I choke back a cough and cover my nose with my arm, slamming the door shut and backing away. I could swear I saw flies in there.

I can't stay here. Not right now. I move towards the door, grabbing my keys and coat on the way out. I start up my bike, then head back down the street. Slowly, I pass by all the buildings until nothing but trees surround me. I continue until I see the little pull-off along the side of the road, leading to a small path into the woods.

I pull over and park my bike, shutting off the engine and putting down the kick stand. I swing my leg over and get off, taking foot on the dusty ground beneath me. I pull my phone out of my pocket. *No service. Just the way I like it.* I shove it back in my pocket.

The wind slightly picks up, sending a cold breeze through the trees. The branches sway back and forth, mesmerizing me. I look away from the branches and start up the path. I step over fallen logs, unturned rocks, and some blue flax flowers still standing tall in the cold weather.

I reach the end of the trail, where a small creek flows through the woods. Not many know about this place. As far as I know, I'm the only one who comes here. It's out of the way, a place you could go if you don't want to be found for a while. Or in my case, ever.

Taking a seat on the log closest to the water, I pick up little pebbles here and there to throw in. The little fish quickly swim away from the intrusion, then herd back together further down the bank. Down the stream, a frog croaks away.

I look up to the trees and smile, closing my eyes as I listen to everything at once. This is my safety net, my escape from everything that's happened. The place I go to be stress-free, even if it's only for a few minutes.

I frown again, then cast my eyes on the ground. I pick up a stick and poke at the dirt, digging little holes then covering them back up again. I can never truly get away from it all. *Away from him.*

It's all your fault.

I squeeze my eyes shut and I tighten my grip on the stick till the bark digs into my hands. His voice rings in my head, the words like a bite from a viper.

If it weren't for you, she'd still be here.

I push myself up from the log, yelling out in rage as I hurl the stick across the stream. It lands with a thud on the leafy floor on the other side. My head pounds, and I can't get enough air in my lungs.

That night disaster had struck. My mom had gotten into a fatal accident on her way to the store, crashing her car into a tree. The police couldn't explain what had happened, why she would have done it. But I knew. Deep down I knew. Her heart was broken. When she drove off that night, her mind wasn't in the right place.

It's all your fault. She would have stayed if it weren't for you.

His voice penetrates my head as tears stream down my cheeks. My fingers tangle in my hair, tugging at the strands. I rest my elbows on my knees, shutting my eyes as tightly as possible.

You'll drive that girl to do the same. Stay away.

"No, no," I cry out, opening my eyes and looking up at the sky. I shake my head furiously. "She's not like that." I look back down and sniffle, thoughts of the kiss earlier today flooding my brain. Sarah's beaming smile brings a bit of light back into my gloomy world.

She was so disgusted, you saw how fast she wanted to get away from you. You're nothing but a lowlife scum to her. You're nothing.

I shake my head again, the tears falling down my face and onto the ground. I think of the look on Sarah's face, how her cheeks flushed after she kissed mine, how her eyes wouldn't meet me. *That couldn't have been disgust, could it?*

What, you think you're so special now that a girl can't help but fall in love with you? Is that it? Stay away, Zander. Don't get too close.

I pound my fist against the ground, casting my gaze back up to the trees. The trees' swaying now seems to mock me with their freedom. "Why? Why can't I have one good thing?" I yell up at the trees, but nothing happens. They continue to sway without a care in the world.

Because you'll ruin her.

I drop my head down, my shoulders slumping in defeat.

You'll ruin her.

"No, I won't! She's too sweet. I wouldn't dare!" I tremble as sobs escape me. Pain echoes through the trees, only to be lost in the wind.

Yes, you will, because no matter what you do, you'll always be your father's son.

___chapter fourteen___
Sarah

"What are you doing?" Gina touches my shoulder, breaking me out of the spell of that one little kiss.

I turn around to face her. "Nothing. Are you ready to go?"

She raises her eyebrow, but lets the matter go and nods. "Yeah, I actually bumped into Kyle in the hallway!" She skips to her car and gets in, starting it up before I can touch the door handle. She stops midway and frowns. "Although I had a total word vomit moment."

Chuckling, I ask, "What did you say?" I get in and buckle my seat belt. We pass the stairs to the school, where I kissed Zander, and I find myself staring at the spot.

It was just one little kiss, yet it felt like the whole world just kinda stopped for a second. And the way he stood there afterwards makes me wonder, maybe he actually liked it? I was expecting him to immediately walk away, but he looked just as shocked as I was. Maybe—

"Sarah, are you even listening to me?" Gina snaps her fingers in front of my face then turns back to the road, glancing over at me.

I shake my head and take a deep breath. "Yeah, sorry. What did you say?" I look over in time to catch her rolling her eyes.

Maybe he'll ask me sooner tomorrow. Like in the morning before he goes in? Or some time around lunch?

"Sarah!" Gina looks at me, her eyes narrowed.

"W-what?" I snap back into reality and see that we're parked in my driveway. I sheepishly look over at Gina. "Sorry."

"What're you daydreaming about that is so important that you keep ignoring your best friend?" She narrows her eyes at me some more. "And it better be good, like, puppies or hot-guys-type good or so help me..."

I laugh and shake my head. "It's nothing really. It's just that Zander had me kiss his cheek..." I bite my lip and wait for her screams of joy, but they never come. Confused, I look over at her and almost lose my cool when I see her face.

With her mouth hanging open and her eyes wide as plates, she stares back at me with shock. "You alright over there?" I raise my eyebrow and reach over, shutting her mouth with my finger. "You were about to start dripping."

"You and Zander... you kissed his cheek..." She blinks at me and gulps, looking like she just got kicked or something.

I furrow my eyebrows and nod. "Yeah, I did. I thought you'd be happy."

She gasps and places a hand over her heart. "Be happy? Of course I'm happy! But I'm also upset!" She grabs my shoulders and pulls me over to her side of the car now, the console digging into my ribs.

"Good lord, woman! What are you—"

She shakes my shoulders. "I can't believe you kissed him and didn't tell me beforehand so I could watch!"

"What?" I push away from her. "You creeper! It wasn't like I knew it was going to happen anyways!"

She shakes her head and looks away with disappointment. "I can't believe you would do this to me. I was supposed to take pictures to show your future kids when their mommy and daddy had their almost-first kiss." She crosses her arms and turns to the window, pouting.

I stare at her in disbelief, then bust up laughing, clutching my stomach as I lean over in my seat and laugh. "Oh my gosh, Gina, you're so ridiculous." I make eye contact with her. It's silent for a minute before we both burst out laughing again, wiping away tears.

She punches my shoulder lightly. "I was being serious, you jerk!" She shakes her head and unlocks the car.

"Which makes it so much funnier!" I open the door and jump out, taking deep breaths between my laughs.

She pouts again. "Whatever. Bye, jerkface."

I wave sarcastically, blowing kisses as I walk away. "Bye, loser!" She rolls her eyes and pulls out of my driveway, leaving me there to laugh by myself. After I regain my composure, I feel my phone buzz. It's Zander. **Are you free to practice later?**

A butterfly flutters around in my stomach. I think about how soft his cheek felt, about how much I'd like to kiss him again. I text him back: **Sure. How's 5?**

"Can you even act?"

I sigh and glare over at Zander. "Yes, I can act. Can you?"

He smiles sheepishly. "Uh, no, I can't. Probably a good thing you can, then." He scratches the back of his neck. I roll my eyes and turn back to the slightly empty paper. He's jotted down an outline of our scene, but that's pretty much it.

"That's what I thought," I say smugly and grab the notebook, filling in the missing pieces of the scene with quotes. "It's a good thing I have these quotes already memorized."

Zander leans over my shoulder and examines my work. "It looks good." He steps back. "Okay." I spin around in my chair, raising a brow at him. He shakes his arms out, clearing his throat. *Oh, he's acting!* I quickly stand up, positioning myself too. He smiles sheepishly, "This is what I've got so far—" He points to me. "You yell at me to die."

A bubble of laughter escapes me, "That's one way to put it."

He struggles to hold back his smile as he waves off my comment. "Then push me." He reaches out to me, placing my hands on his chest. My breath catches, his hands still gently resting atop of mine. "I say, 'As you wish' then fall, and you follow suit." Our eyes lock as we both sink to the floor, our hands still joined. I struggle to breath, butterflies erupting in my stomach, knowing exactly where this is headed. His voice is barely above a whisper, his eyes dropping down to glance at my lips as he says, "And then…"

The silence is deafening, "And then…?" My eyes drop down to his lips, too. He leans forward, our lips only inches apart. My heart beats erratically, my palms sweating under his.

Suddenly, he leans back. "The scene would end." His voice is…disappointed? His hand hesitantly drops from mine. Just like that, the moment ends. What was that? He backs away and flings himself face-first onto my bed, cuddling into my pillow and blankets. "Except I'm terrible at remembering lines." His words are muffled by the pillows.

I shake myself from my thoughts. *Quit overthinking it.* Leaning back on my hands, I raise an eyebrow and laugh. "What are you doing?"

He grunts in response. I laugh softly and turn back to work on the scene outline. Since it's meant to incorporate a dish, I figured I would rearrange a few things in order to add it in. The dish itself—butter bread cupcakes, or buttercups, my own recipe—a nod to Princess Buttercup, will be introduced as a gift to Westley. *I just can't figure out where.* I hear him roll around a bit before he speaks.

"Hey, can I ask you a question?"

"Sure," I murmur. I skip to the end of the scene. *Where to put it, where to put it...*

"Do you hate me?"

My hand pauses mid-sentence. I turn to look at him as concern makes its way through my body. "Why would you ask that?"

He sits up and looks at his fingers while he bites his lip. "I just—I don't know. I don't want you to hate me, that's all."

I smile softly and walk over to sit beside him. "Don't give me a reason. Then you won't have that problem, okay?" It's obvious something else is weighing on his mind, but I can't figure out what. It warms my heart that he's concerned about my feelings. It gives me a sense of hope that maybe he's just as affected by this as I am. Does he get butterflies when we're together? Do I run through his mind constantly afterwards?

Am I the only one falling?

He looks up and stares at me, a small smile spreading across his face. "Okay."

"Good." I grin up at him, determined to distract him from his own thoughts, and reach behind me, slowly wrapping my hand around the pillow behind me. "What's that over there?"

I point towards the corner of my room, getting a good grip on my weapon of mass destruction.

"What?" He looks over to the corner and then frowns in confusion, "I don't see an—"

I cut him off with a pillow to the face. He falls backwards onto the bed, and I double over with laughter. I clutch my stomach and wipe the tears from my eyes.

Zander sits up and glares down at me before a few chuckles escape him. "Oh, you *so* should not have done that."

I stop laughing immediately and rush to get off the bed. I only make it about halfway across the room before he grabs me from behind and throws me back on the bed. I scream and laugh, curling up in a ball to protect myself as he pelts me with pillows.

"Surrender!" He laughs and wraps his arm around my hands.

"Never! Death before dishonor!" I scream out what I think is a warrior's cry, that probably sounds like a strangled shriek, then kick him off the bed.

"Oof." He tumbles onto the floor in a heap. I take the chance to hit him with pillows.

"Die, evil knight! This is my kingdom!" I shout. Before I know it, my leg slips out from under me and I tumble down to the floor. I scream and grab at the air, then land with a thud.

I groan and hold onto my side. *For a floor, it's awfully soft.* I hear a moan from under me and the floor shifts beneath me. *Oh my gosh, Zander!* I quickly roll to the side and off of him.

He lays clutching his stomach, his eyes shut tightly in pain, but laughs still slip out of his mouth. "Geez, Sarah. Did you fall for me *again*?" He opens his eyes and looks over and smirks at me.

"Shut up." I roll my eyes and punch his arm, small giggles escaping my lips. He laughs again and looks back up to the ceiling, sighing softly. I stare at him, noticing the bit of stubble on his sharp jawline.

He catches me, his smirk turning into a soft smile. I blush and look away, turning to lay on my back and stare up at the ceiling.

"Thank you, Sarah." His voice turns serious.

"For what?"

He sighs softly. "I haven't laughed like that in a long time. Not since my mom died." My breath catches at his small revelation, but I remain silent as he goes on. "Things haven't been the same since she passed." He trails off, his eyebrows drawing in.

My eyes roam the ceiling as I search for the right words to say. Finally, I find myself admitting, "My parents are hardly around anymore. And although I'm glad they're living their dreams, I feel like they forget about me sometimes." A small scoff escapes me. "Sometimes I wonder if the things Samantha says about me are true." He remains silent. We sit in the other's admission. It feels...good. Like a small burden has been lifted, not totally gone but just lighter.

I turn my head and find him staring at me. He smiles and closes his eyes. He's never looked so kissable in all the time I've known him. Perhaps it's this moment we shared that drives me to do it. That flutter comes back into my stomach. I bite my lip and take a deep breath. *I can do this.*

I quickly plant a kiss on his forehead, then lean back. His eyes snap open and he looks at me, eyes wide with shock.

"Did you just—"

"Yup!" I gulp and quickly sit up, a blush flooding my cheeks. *That really just happened.*

Zander laughs and sits up as well, leaning back on his hands. "Gee. I didn't see you as the daring type."

I huff and cross my arms in defiance. "I can be daring!"

His head falls back as he laughs, the deep, velvety sound rumbling up through his chest. *Good lord, have mercy.* Our laughter dies off into a comfortable silence.

He sighs and gets up, reaching his hand out to me, as well. "I should get going."

I take his hand and he pulls me up and into his chest. I rest my hands on his chest and look up at him, surprised by his warmth. "Okay." The words are a whisper as I stare into his green eyes.

He smiles down at me, then wraps his arms around me tightly and buries his head in my shoulder. My heart pounds in my chest as I wrap my arms around his neck, telling myself to relax against the hug. I don't think I'll ever get used to the excitement and nervousness that comes with being this close to him.

Zander gently pulls away and grins down at me. "I'll see you tomorrow, Buttercup."

I smile up at him and nod, "Okay, see you tomorrow."

__chapter fifteen__

Sarah

"So he hasn't texted you since?"

I shake my head and purse my lips. "Nope, nothing." I had just finished telling Gina about the moment I had with Zander yesterday. I haven't heard from him since and can't help but worry. *Did I say too much?*

Gina frowns as she pulls into the school parking lot. "Maybe he's just really busy?"

I shrug and get out of the car. "Oh well, who knows." Despite my nonchalant attitude, I can't stop the way my heart drops at the idea of him possibly avoiding me.

"Well, I've got to get to my early class. See you later!" She waves goodbye and rushes into the school. We're already ten minutes early, and she's still going to be late.

Kids stare at me as I walk by, making me question my outfit for the day. *Are jeans and a hoodie such a bad thing or something?* I wonder. I walk a little faster up the steps, nervously pulling at my sleeves as the staring continues.

"Hey." Someone behind me says in a deep voice. I stop dead in my tracks and turn around to meet the bright blue eyes of the person it belongs to.

I smile politely at the boy, who looks like he's popped right out of a movie set. He's of medium height, and his hair is dirty blond. His blue eyes pop against his tan skin, which makes me think he spent a lot of time at the beach. "Hello," I say. "Can I help you?"

He smiles down at me, his pearly white teeth threatening to blind me. "Yeah, actually. I'm new here and could really use some help finding my way around." He chuckles shyly and scratches the back of his neck.

I nod slightly. "Okay. I can lead you to the office to help you look for someone to help you." I nervously jerk my thumb towards the administrator's office, which is only a few feet away.

He grins at me and shakes his head, "No, I meant you." He chuckles again, then throws his bag over his shoulder. "You don't have to if you don't want to," he says, shoving his hands in his pockets.

I blush, feeling awkward and surprised. "Oh, okay. Yeah, I can help you. Do you have your schedule yet?"

"Uh no, actually. I need to get that." I nod in agreement and motion for him to follow. I open the door for him, smiling and gesturing for him to enter.

He grins and bows sarcastically, both of us laughing while we walk in.

Samantha scowls at me at first, but then she notices the boy. "Hi there, how may I help you?" She smiles flirtatiously as she adjusts her name tag, her eyes locked on the boy.

"I'm here to pick up my schedule," the boy says. I glance at the clock above the door. The warning bell should ring any second. I look back over at the two. The boy takes subtle steps toward the door, but Samantha keeps batting her eyelashes at him. I force down a laugh and wrap a hand around the boy's arm, pulling him away.

"If we don't go now, we're going to be late!" I avoid looking at Samantha, then rush the boy down the hall. On the way, we glance at his schedule and learn that his first two classes are right next to mine.

We stop in front of his classroom and smile at each other. "Thanks for the help." He pauses. I don't know his name and I haven't told him mine. My eyes widen in the silence as I hurriedly stick out my hand.

"Sarah. Sarah Jones." I chuckle lightly and take his hand, giving it a firm shake.

"Keagen. Keagen Richland." He grins down at me and shakes back. "Nice to meet you, Miss Sarah. See you after class?"

I keep pumping his hand up and down. He has a kind smile. I snap out of it and pull my hand away, an embarrassed blush rising across my cheeks. "Of course," I say. "See you then." I smile at him one last time. He chuckles and waves goodbye, then walks into his class. I sigh heavily and head into mine as well, a small smile stuck on my face the whole lesson. *I think I just made a new friend! Take that, Samantha!*

"And then—ha!—and then he slipped on the ice and fell, breaking it even more!" We laugh loudly, both of us barely able to breathe.

"I don't get what's so funny." Gina walks over to our table and sets her plate down, giving me a questioning look, before shooting a smile at Keagen. "Hi, I'm Gina Robertson, Sarah's best friend. You are?"

"Keagen Richland. Nice to meet you!" He grins up at her with a warm smile.

"Nice to meet you, too. How did you two meet?" Gina plops down across from us and digs into her hamburger. Even as she chomps on her hamburger, she still smiles and chats with Keagen in a way that only adds to her cuteness.

I sit and listen to them talk. Anytime Keagen would smile or let out a little laugh, a girl somewhere nearby would do a double take. *But his smile isn't nearly as heartwarming as Zander's...* I blush at my own thoughts.

"Hey, S. Are you okay?" I glance up and meet Gina's worried gaze. I flicker my eyes from her to the cafeteria doors. She immediately takes action.

She smiles widely at Keagen and gets up. "Excuse me, but I actually have to go use the restroom. Sarah, come with me?" I quickly nod and follow her.

"Okay, I'll wait here for you." He smiles widely and turns back towards his food.

We leave in a rush, Gina dragging us to the bathroom. We barge in and quickly check if we're alone, then she quickly starts drilling into me.

"What's up? Who is he? Friend, foe? Do I get to throw down today?" She jumps up and down in her spot, clapping her hands excitedly.

I shake my head, reaching out to grab her shoulders so she'd stop jumping. "I just met him this morning. He asked for my help around school and hasn't really left my side since." I shrug and release her shoulders.

"Ohhhh, interesting!" She starts giggling and jumping again, clapping her hands like a happy seal. My eyes widen slightly and I open my mouth to protest.

"O-M-G! So exciting! Not." We both jump in fright when the voice intrudes, both of us whipping around to face her. The blood drains from my face when we turn to see Samantha, hands on her hips.

Gina glares daggers at her and crosses her arms. She steps out in front of me. "What's it matter to you?" She sneers at Samantha.

"Oh, nothing really. Just reminding you that he's mine and neither one of you can have him." She rolls her eyes and inspects her nails.

Gina rolls her eyes and snorts. "You can't just claim every guy in the school, Samantha."

She looks back up at Gina, still disinterested. "Oh, I wasn't talking to you, honey." She moves her gaze to me, giving me a sickly sweet smile. "I was talking to Sarah here. Did you hear me, Sarah?"

I gulp and nod quickly, looking down at my feet. Her heels click against the floor as she walks closer to me. She gets up in my face, and her breath is hot against my forehead.

"Stay back, fatty," she whispers menacingly. She turns away laughing, flipping her hair off her shoulder. Her blond waves hit Gina in the face on her way out.

"Why, you fu—" Gina starts after her but I quickly grab her arm.

"Don't. It's not worth it." I whisper the words, already exhausted, not even believing them myself. I sigh and let go of her arm. "There's no use."

She turns back towards me, still fuming. "Of course there's a use! The use is to make that witch pay! Sarah, you don't deserve this. You deserve to like a guy without being bullied for it!" She stomps her foot and glares at the door. "Besides, she hasn't even talked to Keagen yet. How can she claim him like that?"

"She wasn't talking about Keagen. At least not for the most part," I whisper softly, afraid of hearing my own voice break.

Gina whips back around and frowns in confusion. "Then who was she talking about?"

"Zander." I avert my eyes and gaze down at the floor. "Ever since she first saw Zander and me talking, she has been reminding me that she 'claimed' him. I guess she must have seen we were still talking and decided to remind me again." I sigh and splash some water on my face. I blurt out, "I haven't even heard from him or seen him today."

"She is literally so selfish, it disgusts me to no end. Girl, you're allowed to like whoever you want—or even just be friends with whoever you want. I will back you up, okay?" She walks over and smiles at me in the mirror, gently rubbing my back. I smile back and nod, a feeling of relief washing over me.

"Okay." I give her a quick hug before we head back to the cafeteria. I spot Keagen staring down at his phone while eating his salad.

"Hey," he says. "You're back." He locks eyes with me and seems to give me an exceptionally bigger smile than Gina, making me confused. What's going on here?

"Hey." I smile and take my seat beside him again.

"Hey there, too!" Gina interrupts our smiling session, giving me a knowing smirk. I roll my eyes and turn towards my food, lightly poking at my fries with my fork. Once in a while, I join in the conversation, too, but I mostly just listen while my thoughts wander back to Zander. I want to text him, but I don't want to seem clingy. It's only been a day... Lunch quickly passes by, and the day is over before I know it. Keagen and I walk out to Gina's car.

"So I'll see you tomorrow?" He grins down at me and shoves his hands in his pockets.

I smile sarcastically. "Well, it's school so yeah, I'll see you tomorrow." He laughs, nods, and starts walking away, waving goodbye. I sigh softly and get into the car, patiently waiting for Gina to finish up in the library then take me home. I watch as Keagen gets in his car and pulls out of his parking spot, slowly driving away and out of sight.

I feel my phone buzz in my pocket and I immediately take it out to look at it.

Hey

A small glowing ripples through me. I quickly type back.

Hey! What have you been up to?

Having some issues at home. You, Gina, and I should have a movie night Friday. I could use some friends. What do you say?

Worry seeps in around my excitement. Is he okay? I reply again.

You got it. I'll let her know.

__chapter sixteen__
Sarah

"Ha! You really said that? Wow." I slowly applaud.

"I cannot believe you would say something like that, let alone to a teacher!" Gina leans her head against my shoulder, her shoulders shaking with laughter.

Keagen winks. "Can't help it. I'm a rebel." He joins in our laughter, pointing at Gina's beet-red face.

We're sprawled out on the bleachers, watching as the football team trains. Keagen dragged us out here after school, insisting we sit there with him until he got the guts to go over and ask the coach how to sign up. Twenty minutes later, and practice almost over, he still hasn't gotten up.

I reach up to wipe a stray tear from my eye. "So wait, all these great stories, yet you still moved here? Why?" I ask. Gina sits up and looks at him curiously.

"Well, my dad got a big promotion, but for said promotion we had to move. So here I am." He shrugs and turns his attention to me with a soft smile. "I'm glad we did. Otherwise, I wouldn't have gotten to meet you."

I blush immediately and look at the ground. Gina holds back a laugh and pokes my thigh. She wiggles her eyebrows at me knowingly. Keagen's already gotten up, stretching his arms up into the air. His shirt raises slightly, revealing the tanned skin of his stomach. I quickly look away again and towards the school building.

He doesn't look as toned as Zander does.

He turns slightly and salutes us, then jogs over to the coach. I watch him jog, then quickly turn back towards Gina. She's staring at me, a huge smile plastered across her face.

She smacks my knee and squeals. "He totally likes you."

I groan immediately and shake my head. "G, we just met. There's no way."

"Mhm, *sure.*" she says. I huff out a sigh and glance towards the field full of players. *I wish Zander were here.*

"Well, you're definitely starting to like him." She smirks and looks over at Keagen smugly, watching as he laughs along with the coach.

I shrug my shoulders. "Maybe." My mind drifts off to Zander again, "Hey, have you seen Zander around school today?" I frown and look down at my phone, checking for any messages from him. Nothing. *Ugh, where is he?*

She frowns. "I could have sworn I did. Didn't you see him in any of your classes? I seriously thought I saw him in the hallway today."

My heart drops to my stomach. "No, I didn't see him at all." *Maybe he didn't want to see me.*

"That's weird. Try texting him!" She bounces in her seat and points to my phone.

I give her a weird look but grab my phone anyway. "Okay?"

Hey. Where have you been? Do you still want to hang out with me and Gina today?

"That's good. Now send it!" she says, a huge smile plastered across her face.

"Why are you so excited about this?" I ask suspiciously.

She quickly leans back and looks at me with wide eyes, "Me, excited? No! Uh...I gotta go, see ya!" She gets up and sprints to the parking lot.

I stare after her, stunned into silence. My phone buzzing breaks me from my silence.

Hey. Come find me, lot 2.

I frown down at the text, even more confused than I was before. *So he* is *here? In the stadium parking lot?*

Okay, on my way now.

__chapter seventeen__
Zander

I see her smile first, her long red hair bouncing as she runs and glinting in the sun. Her movement colors her cheeks in a way that captures me.

She is so beautiful.

Stay away. You'll only hurt her.

Shut up.

"Hey. Have a nice run?" I chuckle past my intruding thoughts and hesitantly rub her back, trying to help her catch her breath.

"No. No, I did not." She stands up straight and fake glares at me, her lips forming into an adorable pout that threatens to make me weak at the knees.

"Aw, you're too cute." I tease as I pull her into a hug. She nestles her head against my chest, and my heart speeds up when she hugs me back, a soft sigh escaping her lips.

"Where have you been?" she asks, staring up at me with doe-like eyes.

My heart clenches when she asks. *Don't think about it.* "My dad..." I trail off, hesitant to tell her this piece of me. One glance down at her patient, worried expression has me spilling the details. "He had to do community service, and needed me to sign off as his witness or something. I don't always understand the details." I shrug it off, shifting the conversation, "Why, did you miss me?"

"Pfft, no!" She rolls her eyes, but smiles anyway. Her cheeks redden ever so slightly. "Okay, maybe a little." My heart flips in my chest.

I laugh. "Ah, you're too much." I softly pinch her tinted cheeks. Her nose scrunches up, giggles rising from her when she slaps my hands.

"Stop it!" she squeaks, pushing my hands away. She takes off running in the opposite direction.

I bite my lip and watch her run away giggling for a second, my heart racing in my chest. *The things this girl does to me.* I run after her. "Get back here!" I shout. I finally catch her and toss her onto my shoulder.

She laughs and starts hitting my back lightly. "Put me down, you jerk!" I tighten my hold on her.

"Alright." I sit her down on my bike and hop on before she has a chance to get off. I grab the only helmet I have and hand it back to her. "Here, put this on," I tell her.

I hear the soft click of the helmet latch, then start off. She clutches my waist the whole ride, and I feel her head pressed against my back, like she's counting on me to keep her safe.

The five-minute drive is all too short. I shut off the engine and gently tap her knee for her to release the death grip she has on me. *Even if I don't want her to let go...*

I get off the bike and offer my hand to her. "Are you just going to sit there? C'mon, we've got a mini party to prepare for!" She takes my hand, her fingers small and soft against mine. It takes everything in me to not wrap my fingers up with hers. I quickly put the helmet on and reach for the key.

"Where are you going?" she asks. "Aren't you coming in?" I shake my head no.

"Not yet," I say. "I'm going to go get snacks. Text Gina!" I rev the engine and pull out of the driveway.

I zip through the drugstore, tossing snacks in the basket. I stop in front of the candy section and eye up the different varieties, trying to find one she might like. *Chocolate? Skittles? Do I even know what she likes?*

"Need any help, Zander?"

I look over and see a girl my age, dressed in the drugstore uniform. I narrow my eyes immediately. It's Samantha. She has a wide, glossy smile, her blonde hair tied up in a ponytail so tight it looks like it's pulling at her temples. It looks painful, and kinda terrifying.

"No, I'm fine, thanks." I turn back to the candy, mentally battling over the two options.

She touches my arm, forcing my attention back to her. "Are you sure you don't want any help?" She beams at me again eagerly. "I'd be glad to help you."

I'm sure you would. I take a step back. "I said I was fine, thanks." I quickly grab some Skittles and M&M's, then rush down to the checkout line, excited to get back to Sarah. After waiting a good ten minutes to get through the line, I'm out of the store.

I run back out to my bike with the bags and shove them into the small compartment under the seat. Ten minutes later, I pull into the driveway and park beside what is, I'm assuming, Gina's car.

Hurriedly, I grab the bags and go inside. "I brought food!" I say.

Squeals come from the living room, then next thing I know, Sarah and Gina ambush me. They grab the bags from my hands and run off with them again. I chuckle and follow them back into the living room, where I find a mess of different movies sprawled across the floor.

"Zander, help us pick movies!" Sarah motions me over to her from her spot on the floor beside the huge mess.

"In other words, 'Zander, team up with me and choose a movie I'll like instead of one Gina will like!' Pfft, I see how it is." Gina fake glares over at Sarah, chomping down on a piece of licorice.

"How about we just all agree on one category?" I smile in amusement and make my way to Sarah. Her head bops in agreement. She's thrown up her hair in a messy bun that suits her well.

"Okay, on the count of three we'll all say the one we want." I sit down beside Sarah and put my hand into the air, counting down from three.

"Horror!" I shout.

"Comedy!" Sarah chimes in.

"Romance!"

"Why?" I look over at Gina incredulously, my nose scrunching up. Sarah busts up laughing, lightly clapping her hands like a seal.

"What? They're good movies!" Gina crosses her arms. "Fine, then I pick horror. That makes two against one!" She sticks her tongue out at Sarah.

Sarah shakes her head and giggles. She picks up *Zombieland*. "Here, we can watch this one. Zander, would you start the popcorn?" She smiles sweetly at me. I'm putty in her hands.

"Sure." I smile and get up, heading into the kitchen to start the popcorn. After a while, I head back into the living room with a bowl full of buttery goodness. *I know exactly where I'm going to sit—*

I nearly drop the popcorn bowl when I see him. His arm draped across the back of the couch like he owns the place. A pulse of anger runs through me. *I should go over to him and pummel him into a pulp.*

"Zander?" Sarah asks. "Are you going to sit down?" I quickly shake my head, coming out of the daydream. Sarah stands in front of me, her hand gently resting on my shoulder.

"Y-yeah. Sorry." Sarah moves past me and plops down beside him, but then turns sideways to say something to Gina.

The guy nods over at me, a smile on his face. Despite his friendliness, I'd still love to punch his pearly white teeth in.

"Oh! Zander, this is Keagen," Sarah says. "I hope you don't mind that I invited him, too..." She trails off, a look of innocence on her face. My heart melts and the rage fades away slightly. Begrudgingly, I shrug and head over to the other couch. I sprawl across it.

"Let's start the movie." I glare at the TV and try not to analyze my daydream too much. *Am I turning into my father?*

"Okay, let's get this party started!" Gina claps excitedly and hits the play button, starting the longest ninety minutes of my life. I glance over at them every so often, how they're softly laughing together. I take note of the way she unknowingly leans towards him during a scary part. Hot rage and jealousy surge through me, along with a tinge of sadness. *Would she be happy with him?*

The buzz of my cell phone interrupts my musing. I flip it open to find a text from Gina. **If looks could kill, Keagen would be a pile of ash right now!**

I roll my eyes, my mood darkening even more.

Why is he even here? I've never seen this guy before. I text back.

I hear Gina snort softly from across the room. "Sorry," she says. Her response comes in seconds.

She met him at school today, and invited him so he could make new friends.

I huff in annoyance and flip my phone off. Gina motions to the kitchen, then gets up without a word. Sarah is so focused on the movie that she doesn't notice. Curiosity gets the best of me and I find myself wandering into the kitchen. Gina fixes herself a glass of water, motioning me to join her beside the sink. As soon as I'm beside her, she lightly punches my shoulder.

"What the heck?" I gape at her, "What was that for?"

She points a finger at me and whispers, "You need to step up your game." My mouth opens and closes. She waves off my confusion and continues, "She likes you. Or is starting to. This guy has charm, and she's a hopeless romantic."

"What do I do?" Although we haven't known each other long, what I do know is that I haven't felt this way for anyone else before. *I don't want to lose it so soon.*

Her eyes dart out to the living room. "Here's the plan." She whispers her instructions to me.

After a while, the movie finally ends and the credits roll across the screen. I stretch as I sit up, watching him out of the corner of my eye. Keagen sits up as well and yawns loudly, checking the time on his phone.

"Geez, it's late. I gotta get home." He turns towards Sarah and smiles widely. I glare at him and roll my eyes.

I look over and see Gina hiding her laughter behind her hand. I roll my eyes again and lean back on the couch, moping.

"Okay, thanks for coming over." Sarah smiles up at him as he gets up.

Gina springs out of her seat as well, quickly sending me a wink before turning towards Keagen. "Actually, I need to head home, too." She walks over and pulls Sarah into a hug, blocking Keagen from her. She pulls away from Sarah for a second. "Hey, Keagen," she says. "Do you need a ride?" A smug smile makes its way onto my face.

"Yeah, thanks!" Keagen says. Gina gives him a thumbs-up and hugs Sarah one more time.

"See you all later. Bye, Sarah," says Keagen. He waves to her and smiles, then quickly slips out the door. Sarah doesn't seem to notice his departure.

"Bye, S," says Gina. "Don't want to keep Keagan waiting. Love you! Bye, Z!" She lets go of Sarah, then rushes out. Soon enough, she's gone and it's just us.

"So, have you decided what recipe we'll be using?" I ask. She spins around and smiles widely at me, and I can't help but smile, as well.

"Yes!" She bounces in place, launching into a description of the buttercups she wants to make. "And then, instead of saying 'powdered with confectioner's sugar on top', we can say 'be careful of the iocane powder!'"

It takes me a second to understand the reference. A second too late. Sarah gasps. "Zander! Have you read our script? We only have a week left to get this right!"

I wince and rub my neck. "Yes….no?"

"That's it." She throws her hands up and stomps over to the TV Once the movie is playing, she hands me our script and motions for me to start. "We're going to get this right. Tonight."

An hour and a half, three breaks, and twenty-some mess-ups later we're both exhausted. We've barely worked out the kinks of the first few lines, and my Westley needs to be more suave than stiff. Sarah shuts the TV off of the rolling credits, glancing at the time with surprise. "Oh man, it's already ten!"

I chuckle. "Yeah, and I'm expected to be awake early." She laughs and walks toward me. I gently pull her into a hug. She wraps her arms around me, snuggling her head against my chest. I nuzzle my nose into the crook of her neck, basking in the sweet strawberry smell of her perfume.

"I've got to go. It's getting darker." I smile against her neck and her arms tighten around me as if she doesn't want to let go. I chuckle again and gently pull away, the happiness returns full force.

"Okay," she says. "Promise I'll see you again tomorrow? I need you to do a taste test for me." She grins while she walks me to the door. She opens it for me and leans against it.

I nod and move outside. "Promise." I grin back at her, then slowly walk over to my bike. I mount the bike and start the engine. I pull the helmet over my head, my grin never faltering.

"Wait!" Sarah yells out to me. I lift my visor as she rushes down the steps. She jogs over to me and whispers, "You forgot something."

"What—" I barely get the words out when she leans forward and plants a sweet kiss on my cheek, completely catching me off guard. My skin heats up.

"See ya." She leans away, giggling, then runs back inside before I can even say anything.

And I swear, my heart melts into nothing right then and there.

__chapter eighteen__
Sarah

"Hey, Sarah." I look up from my paper and smile up at Keagen.

"Hey, what's up?" He pulls out a chair from beside me and plops down, sliding his tray out in front of him.

"Just finished a chemistry test. That stuff sucks." He turns to his food, eyeing up his sandwich hungrily.

I open my mouth to respond but another tray slams down on the table beside me, cutting me off. I jump and look over at a moody Zander plopping down beside me. He's thrown the hood of his jacket over his head. Something isn't right, though I can't put my finger on what it is.

Soon after, Gina sits down across from me too. Her eyes scan Zander cautiously. She looks over at me, and we exchange questioning looks. She looks back over at him then turns back to me, clearing her throat and giving me a pointed look.

I quickly shake my head, shoving fries into my mouth. *No way am I poking the angry bear!*

She rolls her eyes and straightens her back, turning to him with a plastered-on smile. "Hey, Zander. How's your food?"

He doesn't even look up at her, just glares down at his food. "It's okay." He stabs his fork into his noodles. Gina and I jump in surprise.

"Dude, what crawled up your ass and died?" Keagen laughs, raising an eyebrow at Zander. I kick him under the table, effectively silencing his laughter. He shoots me an incredulous look, his grin only slightly faltering, but my eyes stay trained on Zander. *Something must have happened...perhaps with his father?*

Zander becomes completely motionless in his seat. Keagen still has a huge grin spread across his face and doesn't seem to notice the tension in the air. Zander slowly looks up, glaring straight forward, then slowly turns to Keagen.

Keagen raises his eyebrows in surprise, but his grin doesn't falter. "What? PMS'ing today?" Keagen holds back a laugh.

Zander goes to open his mouth, his shoulders stiff in rage. I gently touch the small of his back. *Please,* I plead with him. *Don't do it.* His eyes switch over to me and soften slightly. He turns back to Keagen, then shakes his head and goes back to stabbing his food.

"Ah, not one for talking?" Keagen laughs and leans back in his seat, carelessly shoving more fries into his mouth. My own anger starts to boil. *I wish Keagen would just shut up right now.*

Zander balls his hands into fists, squeezing his fork so hard the thin plastic snaps in half. He grabs his bag and storms out of the cafeteria.

"Whoa, he needs to chill. I was only joking." Keagen stares at the cafeteria doors and laughs.

I look over at Gina and she's staring over at Keagen incredulously. I glare at him.

His eyes widen and he immediately stops laughing. "What?"

"You shouldn't have egged him on like that," I say through gritted teeth.

He throws his arms up in surrender, muttering an apology under his breath. *Yeah, right.* I roll my eyes and grab my stuff, moving to go after Zander. I feel a hand on my arm, stopping me from slinging my bag over my shoulder.

"C'mon, Sarah, just stay here," Keagen says. "He'll be fine, he just needs to cool off or something."

I yank my arm away, standing up quickly and glaring down at him. "As if you'd know what he does and doesn't need." I turn away from him, catching a glance at Gina's amused smile as I stomp away. I push open the doors and step out, the hallway clear of students.

"Okay, if I was Zander, where would I go?" I mutter to myself, making my way down the hallway and checking the classrooms.

I check the library, the Home Ec classroom, even the art room, but nothing. I huff in defeat and lean against the wall to catch my breath. I check the clock. Only ten minutes left for lunch. I huff out a sigh and look outside, my heart jumping in my chest when I spot him leaning against his bike. *Bingo!* I push off the wall and walk outside, going slowly so I don't upset him more.

I hesitantly stop a few feet away from him, afraid to intrude. He stares at the ground, kicking small pebbles.

"You can come closer, you know," he says. He doesn't look up, but instead keeps his gaze on the stones. Slowly, I approach him. The cold bites into my skin, and I shiver a little. He finally looks at me when I'm only a few inches away. Then, he reaches for me and pulls me into his chest. I gasp softly when he wraps his hands firmly around my waist, and he buries his face in the crook of my neck.

"Are you alright?" I softly whisper, worry setting back in. I gently cradle the back of his head, softly rubbing circles across his back with my other hand.

"No." He mumbles the words into my neck. I start running my fingers through his hair, and he tightens his hold on me.

"Want to talk about it?" I ask quietly. His warm, soft breaths tickle my neck.

"Not really," he says. "This is good." He sighs softly, moving his head back to look into my eyes. I smile up at him and move my hand from his hair to his cheek, frowning when I finally notice the dark circles under his eyes. My gaze drifts down to the blackened bruise along his jawline.

I eye it up and slowly brush my fingers across it. He winces, drawing my hand away from the bruise.

"What happened, Zander?" I ask. He sighs and slides down to take my hand in his. I stare up at him, searching his eyes for the answers to calm myself. He hesitates, still nervous. What is he hiding from me? In that moment, I make a decision. "Come home with me."

His eyes dart up to mine with shock. I take his hand. "I will make dinner and the buttercups for our project and you can tell me what's really going on. If you want to." He turns away, battling with himself. I drop my head to meet his gaze and give his hand a reassuring squeeze. "Okay?"

He smiles weakly. "Okay." I shiver again. He lets go of my hand and unzips his jacket. I blush and step back, looking down to fiddle with my fingers. Something warm drapes over my shoulders, instantly heating me up. I look up and meet his eyes.

"Thank you, but won't you be cold?" I smile up at him, tightly wrapping my fingers around the warm fabric.

"Nah, I'll be alright." He helps me put my arms through it, then zips it up in the front. It's entirely too large for me, making me feel smaller than I am. I giggle and flap the extra arm sleeves, pushing my hands through.

"Thank you," I say. He nods, motioning me onto his bike. I whip out my phone, shooting Gina a text to let her know where I am. A rush of adrenaline hits me as I mount his bike. I've never skipped school like this before. Sure, in moments of panic, yes. But to run off with a boy? Never.

Zander revs the engine, and within minutes we're at my house. He steps off the bike and offers me his hand, something I've now come to love. I grab his hand, hopping off the seat and taking off the helmet.

Zander snorts loudly, his hand flying up to cover his mouth. I raise an eyebrow at him, "What?"

He tries to hold back his laughter as he points at me, "Your hair is *very* staticky." He finally lets out a small laugh, despite my now flaming cheeks. I reach up and try to smooth out the frizz, shooting him a tiny glare. A smile struggles to form as I lightly punch his shoulder, a small laugh escaping me.

"C'mon, let's get inside." We both make our way to the front door, Zander patting down my hair from behind me as I work to unlock it. I swat at his hands, both of us laughing as we step inside. Moving to the kitchen, I shrug off his jacket and lay it on the back of one of the kitchen chairs as I begin digging through the kitchen cabinets.

A chair scrapes along the hardwood as he takes a seat, his laughter finally subsiding as reality sets in. He doesn't have to tell me. I won't force him. But as I gather the ingredients to make my infamous Crack Chicken Casserole, I can feel the tension in the room thicken as he gears up to tell me.

"My dad is an alcoholic."

I freeze in place, my back turned to him. I hear him take a deep breath, the words a weight on his shoulders. How long has he been keeping this to himself?

"Even before my mom died, he had a drinking problem. Back then, it was only here and there. A few nights a week. He would come home from work, drink a few beers, then plop himself in front of the TV. My mom would try to say something about it, and he would lash out at her. At first, it wasn't bad. They would yell and he would storm off to either a bar or to bed, leaving my mom and me to ourselves." His voice shakes. I finally dare to turn around and find him staring down at his hands on the table. He continues, "I was young at the time, so I never realized what was going on. It wasn't until I was older, around twelve, that he started becoming...violent."

A small gasp escapes me. The bruises...his father did that to him?

He laughs bitterly, "I would try to stand up for my mom, shield her from his wrath, but I was still so young. I hadn't realized that my getting involved had only made things worse. My mom would get beaten worse, told that she should have never told me what was going on. Even if I came to the conclusion on my own." He shakes his head, his brows furrowing down at his clenched hands. I quietly continue my meal, shifting my dish so I can look at him as he goes on.

"My mom died when I was fourteen." Tears well up in his eyes, silently falling down his cheeks as he continues, "I had gotten the flu. It wasn't anything out of the norm, but my mom was really worried about me. She had kept me home from school, restricted me to my bed, and checked on me throughout the day. When my dad got home from work and found out what had happened, he was annoyed. He claimed that I was faking it for attention, which he always claimed I would do to 'take her away from him,' and wanted her to leave me alone. When she told me she would go to the store for some medicine, he flipped out. I watched as he dragged her out of the room." My hand flies up to my mouth, my eyes wide with shock. He chokes out the next sentence. "She left in a hurry and sped off down the street. Because of her panicked state, she swerved off the road and wrapped her car around a tree. The police never found out what really happened, but my dad reminds me every day that it was my fault she left. It was my fault that she died."

A sob breaks free from his chest, and I drop my spoon to wrap him up in a hug. He clings to me, his hands gripping the fabric of my shirt. I whisper sweet nothings in his ear, gently petting his hair as tears of my own fall down my face.

"Sarah," he whispers. He pulls away to stare up at me, "Is it really my fault? Am I the reason she's dead?"

I cradle his face. "No, Zander." I take a deep breath, staring into his eyes with as much sincerity as I can muster. "You are in no way responsible for what happened. How your father has treated you and your mother is wrong, and she was simply doing what any mother would do." I search his tear-stained face for any sign that he believes me. "It was a tragedy, Zander. It was not your fault."

He continues to stare up at me, speechless. Using my thumb, I gently wipe off the drying tears. My heart aches for the boy in front of me, for how much he has carried by himself. His eyes shine with an emotion I can't put my finger on as they roam my face. I gently bring his attention back up to me, my voice firm. "You are not alone, Zander. Not anymore."

His lips press into a thin line and he looks away. "Sarah, I can't drag you into all of this. I won't." He glares down at the table, anger now replacing his sadness.

My hands drop to my sides. "Zander, you're not 'dragging me' into anything. I'm here for you." I gently touch his shoulder, trying to bring his attention back to me, "Let me be here for you." The words are but a whisper, afraid I'm crossing a line.

"No!" He stands up abruptly, shoving the chair back as his hands tangle in his hair, "I won't let you get hurt. Not like she did." He grabs his coat off of the chair, shrugging it on as he avoids my pleading stare. I can't let him go like this. I just can't.

"Zander." I follow after him, gently grabbing his arm. He finally hesitates, just long enough for me to wrap my arms around him from behind, giving him a backwards hug. Shutting my eyes, I whisper, "I understand." His breathing is ragged, his hands twitching at his sides. I give him one last squeeze. "I'm here. Whenever you need me. I'm here." I release him, taking a few steps back and trying to regain my breath. I add in, "Our project is due Monday...promise you'll be there? " He hovers for a minute, his head turning ever so slightly, just enough for me to catch his pained expression before he nods. Then he opens the door and walks away.

My body collapses on the door frame behind me, the air whooshing from my lungs. His engine revs and then speeds off down the road.

__chapter nineteen__
Zander

That moment shared with Sarah was…too much. The sadness in her eyes broke me. I can't deny how good it felt to be held in her arms, the sound of her soft heartbeat soothing me. But letting her in so much—it'll only hurt her, just like it did my mom. I close my eyes, pushing back the tears as another memory replays.

The bottle connected with the beer-stained wall behind me and shattered, barely missing my face. I cowered against the wall, beer dripping onto my shoulders. My father shouted at me. This was the worst I had ever seen him.

My mom scooped me up in her arms, cuddling me close to her. "Zander, honey," she murmured. "Just look at me, baby. It'll be alright." She tilted my tear-stained face up to hers, her eyes boring into mine and reflecting brokenness back at me.

"Mommy, I'm scared," I whispered, flinching into her as another bottle shattered by her head.

She cried into my hair. "I know, Sweetie, I know." She repeated sweet nothings into my ear, but I couldn't calm down. Not now.

He screamed with rage. He ripped open drawers and threw them at us. One slammed into Mom's back. We fell together, and she cried out in pain. Her blood trickled down her back and onto my hands.

"Where the hell is it, Maria? Where'd you hide the money?" Another bottle crashed against the wall.

Mom ushered me up the steps, hunched over in pain. "Mom," I pleaded. "Don't go back down there." She did not answer, but I heard her yelling back after shutting my bedroom door.

"Jeffrey, please calm down!" she cried. "You're scaring us." I jumped into my bed and pulled the covers up over my head. Whatever came next would not be pretty. I sniffled as the yelling continued.

"You were going to leave me. How dare you! I do so much for this damn family. You're so ungrateful." I flinched as I heard his palm connecting with her cheek. Her loud sobs echoed throughout the house. I clenched my blankets tighter, violently shaking.

"You can't keep doing this, Jeffrey. Not to him, not to me. How could you treat us like this?" More glass broke. I silently pleaded that someone was home next door, that anyone would intervene. We have plenty of neighbors, but they never called the police or checked on us.

"What the hell do you want me to do, Maria? Huh? I put food on our table, and pay for the clothes on your back. What more do you want from me?"

The fights were always like this, only ending when the sun came up and Dad slept off his hangover. Then he'd apologize, promise to get better, last for two days—maybe three—then we'd go right back to where we started.

"Stop this nonsense. Please, Jeffrey." Her voice was broken, hoarse from screaming. "You were so kind. What happened?"

I sobbed into my pillow, desperately trying to tune out their voices. The fighting continued until daybreak. I tossed and turned all night, falling asleep for a short while, only to be awakened again by something else being thrown or another loud shout.

She asked him to change. *But that's the thing, Mom. He never did.*

I speed out onto the paved road, the memory blurring along with the trees and buildings that pass by, the wind matching the stony cold feeling in my chest.

Pulling into the familiar dirt path, I park my bike and head into the woods. The leaves crunch beneath my feet, the tree branches dancing overhead as they always do. Calmness and peace wash over me, draining the worries from my mind. I need to decide what I want to do. Face my fears and take the leap? Or leave her alone completely?

The rocky path leads me down to the river. The waters are slow today, and the fish are easily visible as they dart beneath the surface. I sit down on a nearby rock and watch them, listening to the birds and the bugs. I close my eyes and imagine myself as a bee buzzing to collect from a flower, as a grasshopper playing its song. My father's voice threatens to resurface, but I squeeze my eyes shut harder, willing the pain to hide once more. I focus on the various sounds around me, and the calm returns to me.

I've made up my mind.

__chapter twenty__
Sarah

Last night was intense. I can't help but mull over every detail Zander told me about his family. How can his father get away with treating him like that? My mind struggles to wrap around the idea of Zander being hit by another male—his father, at that. The idea is almost too much to fathom, yet he's living it every day. How can I help him?

My night had progressed into watching The *Princess Bride* (again) and going over our lines for our project. I had forced myself to finish preparing the buttercups after he left. Then I called Gina to come stay with me, not mentioning any of what had happened. Currently, I'm in the library studying chemistry, distracted by thoughts of Zander, when I hear someone approaching my table. "Hey, Sarah?" I look up from my textbook to see Keagen.

"Yeah?" I shut my book and turn my full attention to him.

He blushes, his smile hesitant. *Why is he so nervous?* "I was, uh, wondering..." His voice trails off.

"Wondering..?" I smile up at him, confused. *Wondering what?*

He pulls out a chair beside me and sits down. He reaches forward and gently grabs my hand, awkwardly playing with my fingers. My eyes dart down to our hands. Something feels off about this. My thoughts drift off to Zander, how soft and warm his hands feel in mine. Keagen seems very nervous. I wonder if he has done something wrong? Did someone say something to him? He closes his eyes and takes a deep breath then opens his mouth to speak. "I was wondering..."

"Hey, guys! What...Did I interrupt something?" Gina plops down beside me, glancing between us curiously.

"N-no, you didn't," Keagen stutters. "It's okay. I'll find you later." He smiles at me and leaves in a dash. I stare after him bewildered.

Gina raises her eyebrow at me. "What was that all about?"

I shrug and page through my textbook to find my place. "No idea," I say. "Guess I'll find out later."

Gina only hums in response, shrugging it off as well. She launches into telling me about her interaction with Kyle Cunningham, a football player she has a crush on.

"Then he smiled at me, Sarah! He smiled at me!" She squeals in glee, lightly hitting my arm in excitement.

I laugh and pat her shoulder, shutting my textbook. "That's great! Now you just need to talk to him." I smile over at her knowingly. "Coherently."

"Pfft, yeah, okay, you're funny." She snorts, but then starts giggling again. Her laughter subsides and she nudges my shoulder. "How are things with Zander?"

I immediately blush as thoughts of our night resurface. "Good…" I trail off, meeting her eyes with a wide smile. "Great, actually. We're almost finished with our project, and I feel like we've become really close in this short amount of time."

Her eyes shine as she smiles back at me. "Do you think it'll become anything more?"

I think about it for a second. Do I want it to be more? I feel as if we've developed a really great friendship, and it's been a while since I've had any other friends. Sighing, I shrug. "I don't want to ruin it by assuming, but it is nice to hope."

I'm walking home from my study session with Gina when Keagen finds me again. "Sarah!" he yells. I jump and turn around as he runs up to me.

"Yeah?" I haul the strap of my heavy book bag up onto my shoulder more, the thick material rubbing against my skin.

"Mind if I walk you home?" he asks hopefully.

I shrug. "Sure, if you want."

He grins, then points to my bag. "May I help you with that?" My heart warms and I nod, handing it over to him. He slings it over his shoulder. *Such a gentleman.*

"Thanks," I say, rolling the tension from my shoulders. I focus on the walk ahead, my mind wandering to what I'll make myself for dinner tonight. Perhaps I'll call my parents to see when they'll be home again?

Keagan falls into step beside me. "You're welcome. So, um, about earlier..." He trails off.

I peer at him. "Yeah, you said you had a question?" I smile at his nervous state. His blonde hair dips down across his eyes as he walks, the freckles across his cheeks prominent in the afternoon light.

He bites his lip softly. I look away, focusing on the cracked cement beneath my feet as to give him some space to think.

"Yes, I was wondering if, uh..." He stumbles over his words, kicking at the stray gravel on the ground.

"Keagen, just spit it out already." I huff, looking over at him as the curiosity slowly kills me. My driveway is only a few steps away.

Keagen shocks me by grabbing my hand, his breathing heavy and uneven. He shuts his eyes tightly, then opens them and looks right into mine.

"I was wondering if you would hang out with me on Friday. O-or whenever you're free to, it doesn't have to be on Friday. It can be whenever it doesn't really matter when, I just— "

"I would love to." My heart stops in my chest. What am I saying?

He takes in my words, then grins down at me. "Really?" he asks, hope glittering in his eyes.

It has been a while since I hung out with someone other than Gina. Or Zander. That's probably all Keagen wants. "Yeah." I chuckle. "Why not? I mean, you probably won't murder me."

He laughs with relief and gently pulls me closer, his hand cradling mine. I glance down at our hands, subtly taking a step back while still smiling at him.

"Will tomorrow at six work for you?" He bites his lip again. My eyes dart down to it for a second before flickering back up to his clear blue eyes.

"Tomorrow will be perfect." I lightly squeeze his hand, hoping he'll let it go now.

"Okay, I, uh, guess I'll be over then. Wear something casual." He slowly lets go of my hand, taking a step back and clearing his throat.

"Okay, see you then." I wave goodbye, watching as he turns and walks away. I sigh softly, then turn towards my own house. Did I just agree to something else? It seemed a little more important to him than just a friendly hangout.

"Wait!" he cries. I whip around to face him again. He runs back over to me, lightly panting as he reaches behind him. He slings my bag off his shoulder and holds it out for me. "I forgot to give your bag back." He smiles sheepishly, running his hand on the back of his neck.

I blush and take it from him, throwing it back over my shoulder. "Thanks."

"Of course, see you tomorrow." He walks off again, a slight bounce to his step. I shake my head and smile, finally turning to walk up my driveway. I shouldn't overthink it. I'll just go and see how it turns out.

The house is silent as always when I walk in, nothing but the sound of my own footsteps across the wooden floors. I pull out my phone and dial up Gina's number, gently biting my lip nervously.

"Hello?" She shuffles around on her end, then closes a door behind her.

"Are you busy?" I get out the peanut butter and jelly to make a sandwich, my excitement from earlier now drained. I'll just make dinner later, a snack won't hurt for now.

"Nah. What's up, Chica?" She shuffles some more, then I hear her jump onto her bed. Through the phone, I hear her opening up and digging into a plastic package.

"Well, Keagen walked me home today..." I trail off, taking a bite of my sandwich.

"And? So?" She crunches on her snack. Sounds like chips.

"And he asked me to hang out. I don't think it's a date, though." I close my eyes and pull my phone away from my ear, bracing myself for the screams of joy from her end.

They never come. I look over at my phone confused, checking to make sure she's still on the line. I bring it back up to my ear, "Gina? You still there?"

"W-what? He did wh-what?!" She sputters, coughing when she finally responds.

"Yeah...You're not mad, are you? You seem upset. Did you . . . did you have a crush on him or something?" Oh gosh, what if she secretly liked him too?

She coughs again. "No! No, it's not like that! I just...don't you think it's a little soon? Is it a date?" I ponder her words. I mean, yes I just met him. But I don't mind hanging out with him.

"Well, no...He didn't say it was...But he also didn't say it wasn't." Doubt returns as I rethink this whole thing. "It doesn't hurt to go, right?" I ask softly, my heart clenching uncomfortably in my chest. *Would Zander think it's a date?*

"No, it doesn't," she says finally. "I'm happy for you. When is it? I'll come over and help you get ready!"

With a rush of relief, I say, "It's tomorrow at six. He said to dress casual."

She starts closing up the bag of chips. "Alright, I'll be over right after school!"

We both hang up. I hesitate putting my phone away, then quickly type out a text to Zander.

I hope you're okay…

My thumb hovers over the send button before I finally huff out a sigh and press it, shoving it back into my pocket. It's so weird to not have heard back from him yet, especially considering our deal.

I spend the rest of my evening in the kitchen, trying to hone one of my sauce recipes. This one, a marinated bourbon glaze, is meant for a smoked chicken sandwich. Every time I've tried this recipe so far, I have either overcooked or undercooked the sauce, throwing off the flavor.

As I work to add in my seasoning, my eyes keep darting back over to my phone that is now resting on the counter. Zander never texts me back.

__chapter twenty-one__
Sarah

"What about this?" Gina holds up a sweater, washed-out jeans, and a pair of black combat boots.

I look up from my spot on the bed, throwing up my thumb in approval. "Are you done yet?" I yawn, stretching my arms above my head.

She shuts the closet door and throws the clothes at me. "Yup. Now go change and then come back out here so I can do your hair!" She claps and rushes me into the bathroom. "Hurry up!" She grins then shuts the door, leaving me to get ready.

I look down at the outfit, a small smile growing across my face. The washed out jeans accent the pastel pink sweater, the fabric tight enough to hug my curves. *I wonder if he'll think it's too much, or too little...* I softly bite my lip, worry bubbling up inside of me. *But why -*

"Sarah! Stop it and put the clothes on before I put them on for you and go on the date myself!" Gina lightly bangs on the door, shouting at me over the noise in my head. I grin and shake my head, then quickly get dressed. I look up and glance at myself in the mirror, my cheeks flushed slightly, my skin paler than usual. *It's just the nerves, calm down.* Closing my eyes, I take a deep breath then release it, opening my eyes once more to smile at myself in the mirror. *You've got this.*

I wonder what Zander would think?

The thought seemingly comes out of nowhere, especially since I haven't heard from him since he bolted yesterday. Pulling my phone out of my pocket, I bite my lip as I type out yet another message to him.

Hey...

The text is like all the others. Am I being too needy? No, I'm just worried about my friend, that's all. And, our project is on Monday—it's logical to be worried about that, right? I shake my head at myself. Opening the door, I spot Gina working on a dance routine near my dresser, a slight frown prominent on her face. "Hey, are you alright?" I ask. "Is something wrong?"

She quickly glances up mid-dance, the frown disappearing immediately. "Nope, everything is peachy! Let's get your hair done." She leads me over to the chair, plops me down, and then grabs the curling iron with a grin that makes me a little nervous. *Maybe I shouldn't let her do my hair...*

A good half hour later and a lot of fussing, mainly from me, she puts the finishing touches to my hair.

She turns me to the mirror, beaming at her work. "You look great!"

I smile softly and lightly touch a curl, loving the way it bounces back once I let go. My phone buzzes on the table. I reach over and grab it, Gina leaning over my shoulder to read it.

Was leaving and realized I forgot where you live. Address? :)

I quickly send my address, butterflies floating around in my stomach. Or is it just nerves?

"He's on his way! Are you ready?" Gina claps, squealing in glee.

I nod, blood draining from my cheeks. "I feel like I'm going to throw up." I place a hand on my forehead, "I don't even know where we're going."

"You'll just have to go to find out. No backing out now! And remember, don't be nervous. You know him. It's practically like going out with me or Zander!" My smile falters slightly when Zander's name comes up, dread seeping into my very core. I hope he's alright. Should I be checking on him? Is he stuck at home with his father?

I look up at her, panic in my eyes. "I should cancel. I can't do this." I look around the room in a frenzy as I think of all the possibilities.

Gina spins me around in the chair and slaps me hard across the face, my head whipping to the side. I gasp as the pain spreads like a fire. She glares down at me, grabbing my chin with her fingers. "Listen here, and listen good. You are a strong, beautiful woman. You are perfectly capable of hanging out with someone new, and you will have loads of fun. Stop doubting!" She glares down at me with passion and fury. I nod as best as I can with my head in her grip.

We stare up at each other for a few seconds. Then the doorbell rings. "What're we gonna do now? My whole cheek is probably red!" I panic, rubbing my cheek.

Gina looks around the room, trying to figure out what to do. She looks back at me, then moves my hands away from my face. "Brace yourself."

I frown in confusion. "Wha—?" She brings her hand back and slaps my other cheek. "What the fudge, Gina?!" I cup my cheek, blinking back tears.

She grins down at me proudly. "We needed to make both sides red. Now c'mon, he's waiting!" She drags me down the steps. I try to keep up, occasionally tripping on a step or two until we're finally at the door, eyeing up the figure standing behind the stained-glass window. Gina glances back to me, her hand hovering over the knob. I nod, taking a deep breath, then letting it out again. *Here goes nothing, right?*

She nods back and opens the door. Keagen smiles at me, nearly blinding me with his bright white teeth.

"Hey," he says breathlessly, his eyes flickering up and down my body then to my face. "You look stunning."

I smile, a blush rising across my already bright-red cheeks. "Thank you. You do, too."

Gina rolls her eyes, then grabs my arm and shoves me out the door. "Go! Have fun! Have her home before ten, mister!" She points a finger at Keagen, then turns to me. "Love you, see you later!" Gina giddily shuts the door, leaving us together in silence.

Keagen gently wraps his arm around my shoulders as he leads me to his car. "You look really beautiful, Sarah." He opens the door for me, a shy smile on his lips, his cheeks tinting a light shade of pink. His compliment should send a wave of butterflies through me, but all I can think of is the way Zander looks at me. *Is he safe?*

I shrug out of his hold. "Thank you." I get in, clicking my seat belt into place before he gets in himself. He starts the car, pulling out of the driveway and driving off towards town.

"So, where are we going?" I watch as little corner stores and buildings fly by.

I feel his eyes on me while I stare. "It's a surprise," he says. "You like surprises, right?"

"Yeah, I like surprises!" I shoot him a wide smile, focusing out the window again. My palms begin to sweat, and I desperately try to push my worry away so I can enjoy my night.

"Good, that's good."

"Keep your eyes closed and take my hand!" He laughs at me as I stumble out of the car, stretching my arms out to find him.

"I'm trying, where are you?" I stumble some more, then slam into his chest, hitting my nose a little too hard. "Ouch." I reach up and cover my nose.

I hear him laugh softly, then grab my other hand in his. "I'm right here, and sorry about your nose. Is it okay?" He gently pulls me along, the sound of music getting louder the closer we get. The smell of hotdogs drifts through the air, instantly making my mouth water.

"Yeah, it's fine. Where are we? Can I open my eyes yet?" I grip his hand with mine, hoping I don't trip over something and make a fool of myself.

"Just a little further. Take one step up." We stop, Keagen lightly gripping my shoulders as I take the step. "Now, open your eyes."

Slowly I open my eyes and am greeted with vivid neon lights, beautiful blues, pinks, and greens twined together to spell out Roger's Bowling Alley. *We're going bowling?*

He wrings his hands together. "Do you like it? I-If not I can take us somewhere else." I quickly turn my gaze back to him, a huge grin spreading across my face.

"It's perfect. I love bowling!" I jump in glee and grab his hand, dragging him into the alley. We go to the register to rent our shoes. I nudge his shoulder, giving him a smirk, "I hope you're ready to lose."

He raises his eyebrows in surprise. "Is that so?" He thanks the boy at the counter and grabs our shoes, leading me over to our lane. As we're lacing up, he looks over at me with a grin. "I'll have you know that my parents are in a professional bowling league."

Now it's my turn to be surprised. "You're kidding."

He sits up and rolls his shoulders. "Not in the slightest." He laughs at my expression, knocking my arm with his. "Nervous now?"

I quickly pick my head up high. "Not in the slightest." We laugh. I nod over to the food court. "We better fuel up first."

Once we've got our hotdogs and nachos, we settle into our lane and begin taking turns knocking down pins. I'll admit, I've got my work cut out for me here. Keagen gets another strike and whoops in glee, spinning around to pump his fists in the air. He strides past me to his seat, a confident smirk in place, "Beat that, Jones."

I huff, shooting him a mocking glare. "You're about to eat your words, Richland."

I grab my ball, then swing it back and forth one last time, determined to win. *You've only got two more pins to hit, then you win. You can do this, Sarah. Win it for mama!*

Keagen slowly comes up behind me, leaning over my shoulder to look at the odds. He chuckles softly, his breath feathering against my face. "Don't mess up," he whispers. I gasp when his lips lightly connect with my cheek, sending my heart into a frenzy. He quickly walks back to the chairs, leaving me in a blushing mess with only a few more minutes until our game is up. *What was that?!*

I turn back to the alley, then roll the ball. I take a deep breath, holding it in until the ball makes contact with the first pin, sending it flying over and into the second, knocking both over in one go. I spin around and shout in victory, doing a mini happy dance. I laugh at Keagen's slouched figure. He rolls his eyes, but smiles anyway.

"That was just a lucky shot." He leads me over to the chairs to change shoes. We take the shoes off and put on our street shoes, quickly drop off our rentals at the counter, then walk out the doors to the car.

I lightly punch his shoulder. "Admit it," I say. "I've got mad bowling skills."

He shakes his head, laughing. "No way, that was all luck!"

I giggle and lightly punch his arm again. "Say it: I, Sarah Jones, have mad bowling skills."

He opens the door for me, allowing me to hop in and buckle my seat belt. He leans against the door, poking his head in at me. He rolls his eyes and feigns defeat. "Ugh, fine. You, Sarah Jones, have mad bowling skills. You happy now?"

I frown and tap my chin, a small devilish grin spreading across my face. "I couldn't quite hear you. What was that?"

He laughs again, shaking his head. He looks back up at me, eyes shining. "I said that you, Sarah Jones, have mad bowling skills. And that's the last time I will repeat it." He shuts my door and jogs around to get in his side.

At precisely 9:59, we're back in my driveway. He turns off the engine and runs to open my door for me. I blush as we walk to the front door. To hide it, I grab my keys from my bag, keeping my face down. We stop in front of the door, the porch light illuminating our faces.

I dangle my keys from my fingers. "I had a lot of fun tonight," I say. I'm surprised by how much I mean it. What is happening?

He grins down at me, a small blush spreading across his cheeks. "Me, too."

I smile and unlock the door, moving inside before he can say a word. I poke my head out one last time. "Goodnight, Keagen."

"Goodnight, Sarah." We wave goodbye, then he slowly walks back to his car and drives off into the night. I lean against the door, replaying the night in my head.

"Well, don't just stand there, tell me everything!" My eyes shoot open, and I scream in terror. Behind me, I find Gina sitting at the end of the stairs, a mischievous grin plastered across her face.

"Goodness, how long have you been here?" I place a hand over my heart and try to calm it down with some deep breaths.

"I've been here since you left." She grabs my shoulders, her eyes full of curiosity. "Tell me everything!"

Here we go.

<h1 style="text-align:center">__chapter twenty-two__</h1>

<h1 style="text-align:center">Sarah</h1>

"Gina, have you seen Zander lately?" I twirl my finger around a strand of hair, a frown stuck on my face. I shuffle through my dresser for my dad's Led Zeppelin shirt to wear to school.

"Hmmm. Now that you mention it, no. Granted, it was the weekend."

I move as close to the couch as possible, stretching the cord to its limit. "Yeah...I just worry that he's avoiding me."

"Why would you think that?"

I sigh softly. "Well, he shared a lot of personal stuff the other night, and then bolted. I haven't heard from him since, and what about our deal?" I bite my lip nervously, eyeing up my cell phone from across the room. *Maybe I should text him?* "After what he told me I just want to make sure he's okay. Cheer him up, even."

"Ask him to hang out with us after school, then see what's wrong," she says. I hear crunching in the background. She snorts back a laugh, "And it sounds to me like you actually *miss* that little deal."

"Shut up, Gina," My cheeks heat up instantly, "It's a legitimate problem. We have to present our project today but we haven't practiced *that*." The sound of loud ruffling of a bag cuts me off. I huff an annoyed sigh, " Are you seriously eating chips right now?" I ask.

The crunching comes to a slow stop. "No..." she says guiltily.

I grab my cell phone, and type out a message, and read it back to Gina. "Should I send this text?"

"Sure," She says. "But what are you going to do about Keagen?"

I frown. "Keagen?"

"Uh, the kiss your cheek in the bowling alley, Keagen. Ring a bell?" She laughs loudly. "Sarah, the dude is seriously into you. You really haven't noticed?"

A vicious blush rises across my cheeks as I stutter. "I—I don't..."

"You don't like him?" Her question is pure curiosity, without judgment.

"I really don't know him..." I admit, groaning in frustration. "I mean, yes, he's cute. But I didn't have this...this..." I clench my fist, grasping for the words to say.

Gina fills in. "Spark?"

"Yes!" I exclaim, slouching against my desk. "I think I could start to like him, but it's too soon to tell."

She sighs softly. "Follow your heart, Hun. It's the only one that knows for sure. If it doesn't feel right, then it's not."

"You're right." I nod, my heart lightening. *If it doesn't feel right, then it's not.* "I'm gonna send the message. Do you want to come over now?"

"Yes, and I'll bring the popcorn and chips later tonight!" She squeals as bags crinkle in the background. "See you in a few!"

My thumb hovers over the text icon. Before I can hit the button, my phone buzzes in my hand. I check who texted me.

Hey...

My heart skips a beat. I immediately want to ask a million questions, but I restrain myself to a simple message.

Hey...how are you?

I anxiously wait for his reply, grabbing the stash of Nerf weapons to set on the coffee table. Plopping down on the couch, I stare at our messages until finally a new one appears.

I'm alright. Thinking about different things.

I bite my lip and stare at the text for a minute, finally deciding on a direct approach.

Need a distraction? Want to hang out after school?

I hit the send button before I can chicken out.

Yes.

I huff a sigh of relief and shove my phone in my pocket. Gina honks her car horn outside. Walking to the kitchen, I grab the tray of buttercups I made last night, then head out the door. Gina waves from the front seat, reaching across the seat to push open the door for me.

"You ready for your big project?" She asks once I'm settled in my seat.

I sigh heavily, my nerves making my palms sweat. "I don't know…" The idea of having to kiss Zander, for real, has me out of my mind with mixed emotions. Will he even want to kiss me right now? Or ever? Is he in the right frame of mind to perform the scene?

Gina shoots me a smile, lightly patting my shoulder, "It'll be okay, S. Don't stress yourself out!"

I hope she's right...

I sit in Home Ec anxiously waiting for Zander to show up. He had sat further away from me in English, then wasn't around in the cafeteria. I'm starting to believe my doubts are coming to life, that he truly doesn't want to be around me anymore. Mr. Barnes walks back to my table, giving me an encouraging smile.

"Are you ready to present your project today, Sarah?" He rests his hand near the buttercups, looking at them appreciatively.

"Kind of…" I force out a smile.

He glances around the room with a frown, "Where is Mr. Mills?"

"Right here."

Mr. Barnes turns around to find Zander standing behind him. He smiles at him and steps out of the way, "Ah, here you are then." He gestures to Zander's seat beside me, giving us another smile, "I look forward to your presentation." Zander nods, moving past him to lay his stuff beside me. Mr. Barnes leaves us to talk to the table across from us. Zander plops down in his seat, choosing to flip through the notebook that contains our lines. I bite my lip and stare at him, worry clouding my thoughts.

He glances over and catches me staring, his lips twitching into a small smile. "I'm okay, Sarah, I promise."

My worry finally eases. I smile at him, "Okay." I say. I settle into my seat and point at the notebook, "Are you ready for this?"

He gives me a nervous smile, "I think so? Did you make the buttercups?"

Reaching up, I nudge the container of buttercups towards him, "I sure did, have a look for yourself."

He opens the container, eyeing up the dessert. He grins, "Sarah, these look awesome. What recipe did you use?" His smile drops, and he glances over at me, "I should know that, I'm so sorry." He wipes a hand over his face while shaking his head.

I laugh and nudge his shoulder, "Hey, don't stress about it. As long as you carry the scene, we'll be good." He laughs and nods. I pull out my phone, showing him the recipe from my mom. "My mom helped me solidify the recipe, but other than that, I made it myself."

He looks over the recipe, "Wow, this is really awesome, Sarah."

I blush under his praise. "Thank you."

"Alright, class!" Mr. Barnes grabs everyone's attention at the front of the room. "It's time to present your recipes! I will say, I am quite excited to see what you all came up with. Susan and James, you'll go first."

Susan and James came up with a laughable rendition of *Moby Dick*, where they spoke of one of the monologs within the book, then ate a salmon soup to indicate The Whale. Which tells me neither of them actually read the book, seeing as the whale eats the people, not the other way around. I glance at Zander, desperately trying to hold back my laughter. He casts a curious smile, leaning over to whisper in my ear, "What's so funny?"

His warm breath sends a shiver down my spine. I grin and lean over, returning the favor, "They definitely did *not* read the book." His breath catches, then a small laugh escapes as we share a smile and he nudges my arm with his.

We sit through multiple presentations like that. The next is a rendition of Shakespeare's *Romeo and Juliet*, where instead of dying by drinking poisoned wine, he dies by eating poisoned cherry Jello cake.

Mr. Barnes laughs at the end of the last presentation. "Very interesting take!" He ushers the two boys off to their seats, the class clapping as they walk back. He points to Zander and me. "Next is Sarah and Zander. Please come on up." I glance over at Zander and give him a nervous smile.

I set the plate of buttercups on Mr. Barnes's desk to examine. Zander and I face each other. He mouths "Good luck" to me before I close my eyes, taking a deep breath. Opening them again, we begin reciting the scene of Princess Buttercup and Westley reunited.

"What can I do for you?" Zander asks, feigning a bow.

I narrow my eyes at him. "You can die slowly, cut into a thousand pieces." The room gasps, a few students chuckling.

Zander smirks. "Hardly complimentary, your Highness." He crosses his arms. "Why loose your venom on me?"

I glare at him. "You killed my love." We skip through the scene, glancing behind us as if horses are truly there. I shout, "And you can die too, for all I care!" With that, I give him a shove.

He stumbles back, like he's falling down a cliff, "As...you... wish..." he says, finally tumbling to the floor.

I gasp. "Oh, my sweet Westley; what have I done?" I tumble after him, falling to the floor in a heap beside him.

He turns his head to look at me. "Can you move?"

My heart races in my chest. I have been building up to this moment for weeks now. I swallow past the lump in my throat as I reach over for him. "Move?" I pull myself to hover over him, "You're alive. If you want, I can fly." And with that, Zander hooks his hand behind my head, pulling me down to kiss him. I'm surprised by the force of his lips, the passion that seems to spark from them. It's nothing I've ever felt before. His lips are so soft, his hand buried in my hair. My heart does somersaults in my chest.

Right after my lips touch his, I pull away from him, my face red with embarrassment. It was only a few seconds, but it felt like an eternity. *One that I wish I could remain in.* The class cheers as we pull ourselves up. Mr. Barnes laughs in his chair.

"That was brilliant!" he exclaims, then motions us over to his table, "Now, what have you made to accompany this scene?"

Zander nudges me forward, a large grin on his face. I blush deeper, clearing my throat. "It's Princess Buttercup Buttercups, a butter bread and cupcake combo featuring the warm flavors of vanilla, butter, and almonds." I take one of the cakes out of the container and hold it out so the class can see. "Topped with my secret ingredient powdered sugar—or is it iocane powder?"

Mr. Barnes laughs gleefully, "Great nod to the movie, Sarah and Zander. Well done!" The class claps for us as we walk back to our seats.

Zander pulls out my chair, leaning over to whisper in my ear. "Well done, Princess Buttercup."

I blush and elbow his side. "Couldn't have done it without you, Westley." He chuckles and settles back into his seat, both of us focusing back on the lesson. Even still, I can't help but think of how his lips felt against mine.

After class, Zander runs home as I walk home myself. I replay the kiss the whole way, my mind spinning. It felt so... real. Like it could have happened outside of the classroom. Does he wish it was real just as much as I do? I huff out a sigh and plop down on the couch. *I'm tired of overthinking.* Just as I relax onto the couch, the front door slams open and a crazy woman runs in, screaming a war cry.

"I'm here! Stop screaming, it's just me. I brought snacks!" Gina runs over to me and jumps onto the couch. I grip the back of the couch so I don't fly off, then look at her with wide, wild eyes. She stops bouncing immediately, staring back at me innocently. "What?"

"Are you on crack today? You almost sent us flying!" She opens her mouth to say something.

"What...is going on in here?" Zander hesitantly steps into the room, scaring both of us. We scream and grab our weapons and pelt him with Nerf bullets.

"Trespasser!" We scream in unison. We jump up on the couch and use it as cover.

He shields himself with his bag. "What the heck, guys?" He quickly drops it, runs behind the corner, then darts down the hall towards the kitchen.

Gina and I exchange looks, then sneak around the couch to peak into the kitchen. I motion for her to move to the other side of the doorway, then both of us position ourselves against the wall while reloading our weapons. In sync, we both turn with our guns up, scanning the area for him. Gina motions to me. *All clear.* I signal back, then both of us slowly move towards the hallway.

We quickly clear the corner, then slowly make our way back down the hall. Stopping at the living room entrance, we give each other confused glances before clearing the corner. *I wonder where he could be hiding.*

We turn in time to see two pillows flying our way. I duck down. The pillow flies over my head and crashes into the couch. Gina, on the other hand, takes a pillow to the face and collapses on the floor in a heap.

She reaches her hand out to me. "Go. Survive without me. Don-don't let him defeat you." Slowly, she closes her eyes and lets her head drop to the side, *a dramatist to the end.*

I mourn her death, then gently take her gun from her hand. "I will honor you, my dearest friend." I turn to Zander, a hard glare set in stone across my face. "Prepare to die." I raise my guns up and fire. He shouts and runs the other way.

Gina leans up from her spot on the floor and pats my back. "I'll get the popcorn and movie ready. Go whoop his butt!"

I make my way down the hallway, finding the kitchen empty. He must have run upstairs then.

I run up the steps, turning my stealth mode on. Slowly, I clear each room until I'm left with my own. The door is cracked open. Cautiously, I push it with one hand and scan the room with my gun up. Before I can look behind the door, he wraps his arms around my waist and lifts me off the ground.

I squeal and wiggle in his grip. "Let me go, you crazy man!" My guns fall out of my hands, leaving me with nothing to defend myself. *Crap.* He notices and smirks evilly. *Double crap.*

He laughs as he squeezes me tighter. There's nowhere for me to go. I'm pressed against his chest, our faces inches apart. His eyes scan my face, hesitating when they pass over my lips. I push against his chest, my heart racing within my own.

"Let me go," I whine, giving up on trying to free myself.

He brushes his nose against mine, then pulls away again. "Not until you give me the passcode," he teases.

I blush even darker, butterflies bouncing in my stomach. Actually, no. Forget butterflies, it feels like dragons in there. "Wh-what's the passcode?" I stutter, mentally smacking myself across the head for it.

He smirks. "You should know it, Buttercup."

I immediately look away shyly. I squeeze my eyes shut for a second then open them up again. *You've got this, just go for it!* Leaning up on my tippy toes, I gently connect my lips to his cheek in a soft kiss. The dragons in my stomach spit fire, my skin feeling like it's burning off. Quickly, I pull away blushing, then shyly scan his reaction.

He stares down at me with shock for a second, then a huge smile breaks out across his face. "I gotta say, I wasn't expecting that. Especially since the passcode was 'Princess Bride', but that'll work, too." He winks playfully, then lets me go.

I smack his shoulder. "You jerk! You could have stopped me!"

He grabs my hand, pulling me close to him again. "Why would I want to do that and waste a perfectly good opportunity to steal one of your kisses?" he asks.

I roll my eyes and glare at him. "Shut up, you butt."

He grins down at me slyly. "Make me." I gasp back a laugh and shake my head no. He picks me up and throws me over his shoulder. "C'mon, little sack of potatoes. I can smell the popcorn already!"

In that moment, Gina's words to me earlier rang through my head again. *If it doesn't feel right, then it's not.* And somehow, this felt perfect.

__chapter twenty-three__
Sarah

"This movie sucks," Gina whines from beside me. I push a piece of popcorn into her mouth. She sits up quickly and coughs, beating on her chest.

"Stop whining," I whisper, winking over at her. I pop another piece into my mouth.

"Why I oughta— "

"Shh, this is my favorite part!" Zander leans forward, eyes glued on Tony Stark's first suit. Gina and I stare at him blankly, then roll our eyes at each other. Plopping back against the couch, I lazily shove popcorn in my mouth while Gina rests her head on my shoulder.

"Why is this one your favorite?" I whisper, my eyes trained on the side of his face, taking in his expressions as the movie progresses.

Zander barely glances over at me as he says, "Stark is the coolest one out of all of them." Finally, he glances over and notices the appalled stares Gina and I are casting his way. He laughs, finally focusing on us, "What?"

I scoff loudly and throw a piece of popcorn at his head. "How dare you say that when Captain America exists."

He scoffs back. "Pfft, please. Stark built practically all of the Avengers' tech, and is still a hero without it. He's a mere man as well as a hero, and that's why I like him."

"But...Steve..." Gina sighs dreamily. "Stark is mean." Zander shakes his head at her, brushing off her comment.

I giggle softly and pat Gina's head while she pouts. "You're like a sad dog," I say, my hand still in her hair.

She snorts loudly and sits up, glowering at me. "If you're not careful, this doggy will bite."

I giggle and pat her head again, pulling her back to lay down beside me. "Yeah yeah. Go to sleep, doggy." I turn back to the movie. She falls asleep quickly, snoring low enough not to disturb Zander, but loud enough to annoy me.

Finally, the credits roll. As the names scroll up the list, Gina lets out a huge snore. Her mouth hangs wide open, drool dribbling down her cheek. Zander and I exchange looks and try to smother our laughter.

"Why don't we let the Sleeping Beauty sleep in peace?" he asks.

I nod and grab a blanket. After I toss it over her, I ask, "Now what do we do?"

A mischievous grin spreads across his face. "Why don't we see what's up?"

"What's up? Up where?"

He takes my hand and leads me onto the roof. While gazing up at the stars, one hand in the popcorn bowl, I point to one star. "That one looks like a potato!"

Zander snorts loudly. "They all look like potatoes if you bunch them together."

I pout and drop my hand. "But that one looks like a special potato."

"You're a special potato," he retorts. He bops my nose, pulling away quickly to dodge my attacks.

"Did you seriously just call me a potato?" I pout at him.

He scoots closer. "A *special* potato." He bops my nose again. I roll my eyes and slap his shoulder.

We both laugh, then sigh contentedly. "I like the idea that no matter where we are in the world, we're all looking up at the same stars and moon," I say. I think of my parents. It helps the loneliness at times to think that wherever they are, we're still connected. Some nights, my dad and I would sit on the phone together and stargaze. He would describe the constellations he could see for me to guess, and I him. My heart pangs at the thought of them. I really miss them. "Do you ever wonder what it would be like to be a star?" I ask, distracting myself from my thoughts. "To just sit in the sky for all to see?"

"Hmmm...no. I haven't really thought of it until now."

"What *do* you think about?" I ask, teasingly poking his ribs. He glares at me. I roll onto my side, propping myself onto my elbow.

He mimics my position and quirks his eyebrows slightly raised. "Are you sure you want to know the answer to that question?"

I gasp and punch his shoulder. "Ew!" He busts up laughing, his eyes sparkling in the dim light. My breathing slows, my heart stuttering in my chest. His laugh sounds like a melody in the night, his smile brighter than the moon.

What's happening to me?

His chuckles slow to a stop, his tone turning serious, "In reality, I don't think I would want to be on display for the world to see." He glances over at me, waiting for my reaction. I mull over his words, my eyes glancing back up to the stars.

"I can understand why." My thoughts drift back to my years with Samantha. I find myself missing those days. The simple friendship we had. I quietly admit my heartache. "I struggle to do the same. Between what happened to Samantha and me, and my constant desire to share my recipes with the world, I can't seem to find a balance between letting myself feel...free without compromising my fear of it all crashing in my face." I glance over at him. He stares at the sky, his brows furrowed.

I chuckle and look back up. "I know what you're thinking. Samantha and I used to be best friends, but after a while she began to resent me. She's been taking it out on me ever since." I frown and release a breath. "There are days I ask myself what I did to deserve any of it. If there is anything I can do to fix it."

"Hey." Zander gently takes my hand in his, pulling my focus over to look at him. He shakes his head, "You shouldn't hold that over your head. Sometimes people let their jealousy get in the way of something great." His eyes meet mine, sincerity sharp in his gaze. "Some things we cannot fix. At least not on our own."

My eyes roam his face, and I see layers of pain weighing him down, disguised behind a smile. The bruises on his skin are less prominent now than when he first told me about his dad. I wish he would let me inside his mind. To just allow me to understand him completely. Gently, I squeeze his hand back. "Do you want to talk about it?"

He smiles, tired. "Some things we cannot fix," he repeats. "At least not on our own." His eyes search mine, and an understanding passes between us.

My heart palpitates, my breath hitching. "You're not on your own," I whisper.

His eyes flicker down to my lips for a second, then back up to my eyes. My heart stops in my chest. My thoughts race at a mile a minute. *Does he want to kiss me again?* He moves my hand in his, intertwining our fingers together like pieces of a puzzle, tight but gentle.

Do I want him to kiss me again?

We both look down at our hands. I gulp and drag my eyes away from them to see Zander already looking back at me. I gasp softly, my lips parting. His eyes immediately dart down to them again.

Yes, I do.

"Sarah," he asks in a whisper that I almost didn't hear.

I shakily take in a small breath. "Yeah?"

His arm gently wraps around my waist, pulling me up closer to him. He stares into my eyes, curiosity and wonder shining brightly in his. "May I kiss you now, properly?"

The question sends my heart into a frenzy, the butterflies in my stomach bouncing around. I panic when I realize I haven't responded yet, and the words get stuck in my throat. I take a deep breath and close my eyes, opening them again with enough confidence to reply.

"Yes."

He doesn't hesitate, and he cups the back of my neck. I fidget nervously, my hands sitting idly in my lap. "It'll be alright," he says. "Place your hands on my shoulders and just close your eyes."

"O-Okay." I stutter stupidly, bringing my hands up to rest on his shoulders. I take another deep breath and let it out, closing my eyes tightly.

"Relax, Sarah, you'll be fine." He softly nudges my nose with his, reminding me of how close he is.

His lips softly press against mine, gently urging me to respond to him. It's nothing like yesterday, jerky and awkward as the feeling of eyes pressed on us. No, this is patient, perfectly slow. His lips are so soft and cold, tasting of sweets and popcorn. Slowly, I kiss him back, my mind turning into a puddle as his kiss takes over. It's shy, at first, then quickly becomes fervent. Like we're both trying to make up for lost time. I grip his shoulders, keeping me anchored to the spot.

Slowly, he pulls away and rests his forehead against mine. We're both out of breath. I open my eyes reluctantly, scared to see his expression. A goofy grin spreads across his face and a small blush covers his cheeks.

"Did I do okay?" I grin up at him, my hands sliding up to rest behind his neck.

He opens and closes his mouth like a fish. "That was—I want to kiss you again." He throws his head back and laughs happily. He stares down at me with the same mysterious expression as before. "I *really* want to kiss you again, Sarah."

My eyes widen and my blush burns across my cheeks. I smile shyly, then press a quick kiss to his lips. His eyes close, a happy smile on his face. His hand drops from my neck and falls into my lap. I giggle and stand up, gently tugging on his arm for him to follow. He follows me to the window, both of us safely climbing back inside my bedroom.

I shut the window and lock it, then turn to Zander. I squeal when he wraps his arms around my waist and pulls me flush against his chest, my hands resting over his fast-beating heart. He buries his head in the crook of my neck, a small sigh escaping his lips.

"Good night, Buttercup," he whispers into my skin.

"Good night, Zander," I whisper back, my heart beating wildly against my chest.

He plants a soft kiss on my nose before letting me go and heading out the door. I sigh softly, smiling goofily to myself as I watch him ride down the street from my window. I lay down on my bed and lightly touch my lips with my hand. *I can't believe that happened.* I giggle to myself and close my eyes, pulling the blankets tightly around my body.

This definitely feels right.

__chapter twenty-four__
Sarah

"Sarah." Gina whispers from beside me, slowly pulling me out of my deep sleep. She shakes my shoulder, and none too gently.

I groan in response, rolling onto my side and peeking one eye open. Sleepily, I yawn and stretch, then flop back into the pillows. "What is it, Gina?" I mumble quietly, slowly drifting back into a dream world of hunters and vampires. *Hehe, eat it,* Twilight.

"Sarah, wake up. This is serious." Her shakes become more violent, her voice trembling and cracking. I open my eyes immediately, my muscles tightening.

"What is it? What's wrong?" I whisper back, groggily rolling to sit up, wiping a hand across my face.

"There's someone in the house."

My eyes fly open, meeting with her nervous stare. "Wh-What?" I stutter nervously, my eyes darting towards the door.

She gulps and shakily motions towards the floor, indicating to the living room beneath us. "I was on my way up to see you when I heard the front door open. I didn't see who it was."

I nod slowly. "O-Okay where's my phone?" I scan the room, spotting my phone on the windowsill.

Gina shakes her head, "What if they hear you?"

I tip-toe over to my phone. Dialing his number, I look back over to a trembling Gina and give her a shaky nod of encouragement.

"Hello?" His groggy morning voice echoes through the phone, comforting my heart.

"Zander?" I whisper. My voice trembles.

"Sarah?" His voice clears. "Is everything alright?"

"Someone's in the house." My body suddenly starts to shake. I make my way back to Gina. She curls into me.

"Don't move. I'm on my way. Lock your door." He hangs up. My fingers tremble as I begin to dial 9-1-1, freezing at the sound of a voice.

"Hello?" Someone shouts from down the hall. My eyes dart to the lamp by the door. *Weapon.*

My heart jumps into my throat. "Get behind the bed, Gina," I whisper. I grab the lamp just before the door swings open. Gina screams and flings herself to the floor. I blindly swing the lamp, fear and adrenaline pumping through me. The person yelps in pain and falls backwards into the hallway, emitting a slight, yet oddly familiar, odor of bacon grease.

"Sarah Michelle Jones, what in the heavens are you doing?" Arms wrap around me, hands pulling the lamp away from my grip. The smell of bacon grease wraps around me.

"Sweetheart, it's me, Dad. Calm down!"

"Daddy?" I open my eyes, my body relaxing in his hold. Finally, the scent makes sense, and my heart skips a beat. I've missed him so much. "What are you doing here?"

He smiles down at me. "We finished business early, so we decided to come home and stay with you."

"Really?" I smile so wide, my cheeks hurt. I quickly turn and see Mom sitting up on the floor, massaging her shoulder with an amused smile on her face.

"You hit pretty hard," she says. "What'd you think we were? Robbers?" She takes the hand dad offers her and stands up.

"Yes. That's exactly what we thought you were." My parents turn to face Gina, whose hands still tremble as they rest clenched at her side. "We were even about to call the cops when you burst through the door."

Dad chuckles from beside me. "Gina! What a surprise. C'mere, sweetie." He opens his arms for her. Anytime they did stay home with me, they'd treat Gina as if she was their own. They really did try to be there for me, even though they're halfway across the country, they still made an effort.

She grins and jumps into his embrace. I softly smile as I hug my mom. She gently pulls away from me, grinning widely. "Let's go downstairs and catch up." She takes my hand and leads me down the steps with Dad and Gina following closely behind.

"I can make us dinner. I've been trying this new recipe that– "

I'm cut off by the door bursting open and Zander barreling into the room, gripping a baseball bat. I take in his appearance, biting my tongue as I hold back my laughter. His hair is in a mess, and he looks like he slept in his clothes. He stares at us for a second, red-faced.

My parents shove Gina and me behind them, my mom holding onto us as my dad squares his shoulders, his fists clenched at his sides. "Who the hell are you and why are you breaking into my home?" he bellows. Zander stumbles back. I reach out to my dad and place a hand on his shoulder.

"Daddy, it's okay. This is Zander. He's a friend of ours, and, uh, we called him to help protect us from what we thought were robbers..." I smile at Zander as he releases his death grip on the bat.

"Uh...Hi?" He smiles sheepishly, awkwardly waving at my parents.

Mom and Dad stare at him in shock, then Dad's face lights up with a huge grin. "Nice to meet you, Son! I surely hope you're treating our Sar-Bear well!" He moves forward and claps his hand onto Zander's shoulder, pulling him into a hug. Zander hugs him back, his eyes meeting mine with shock. I giggle softly, my heart warming. They're already getting along just fine.

"Uh, yes, I am." Zander clears his throat and smiles at my dad. His eyes roam over to my Mom, widening in surprise. I turn to look at Mom, as well. She glares at Zander with ice in her eyes.

Oh no.

"So, Zander, is it?" Mom settles down in her chair, a cup of hot tea cradled in her hands. Zander nods silently, a small hesitant smile on his face. He sits next to me at the kitchen table, while Mom and Dad sit across from us. Gina had already gone home, claiming she wanted to give us time to "bond." But really, she just wanted me to suffer on my own.

"How long have you known our Sarah?" she quizzes. Dad and I share a look, neither of us knowing what is about to come next.

His eyes flicker down to his hands, then back up to her. "A little under a month or so now."

Mom nods, her eyes narrowed. "Interesting. What are your feelings towards my daughter?"

I choke on my water. "Mom!"

She turns towards me innocently, her eyebrow raised. "What? It's a good question. I would like to know."

My mouth gaps as I struggle to come up with an answer. Why would she ask that? I groan inwardly. I mean, "friends" don't exactly kiss each other on the roof. Does he consider us just friends? Do we consider ourselves as more? I glance over at Zander, his eyes already fixed on me. I can't read his expression. My mom raises an expectant eyebrow at me. "We're just friends," I mumble.

"Yeah . . . just friends," Zander mutters bitterly, surprising me. My eyes narrow in his direction, focusing on the way his jaw clenches. My heart skips a beat and hope rises. Does he want to be more, too?

Mom brushes it off easily, jumping into her next question. "What are your intentions with our daughter?" Zander's eyes widen in shock. I cough loudly. *Oh my gosh, she can't just ask that, can she?*

Zander chuckles softly, his eyes catching mine. "Nothing but good intentions, Mrs. Jones." He turns back towards Mom, his eyes shining with honesty. My heart melts into a puddle.

Mom's tough facade slips, a small smile threatening to show. "Alright, I suppose that's enough for tonight. Johnny, why don't you show this nice boy to the door?" She turns back to Zander. "It was nice meeting you, Hun. I hope to see you around some more." She smiles sweetly at him, and I sigh with relief.

"C'mon now, Son. Show me what kind of ride you got!" Dad herds Zander towards the front door. I catch Zander's eyes before Dad gets him out of the kitchen. He smiles back softly then follows my dad outside. I sigh softly and lean against the chair, my body tired all over again.

"He seems like a sweet boy, Honey." Mom smiles over at me then sips her tea.

I groan in embarrassment. "Did you really have to ask those last two?"

She nods. "Yes, I did. It's best to give you as much parental guidance as we can to ensure you don't date a loser." She smiles widely, then winks. "Which brings me to ask you, what's his work life like? I know you're young, but would he be able to support your family on his career path?"

"Goodness, Mom! I haven't even started thinking that far ahead yet!" I groan and bury my head in my hands, my cheeks on fire now. She laughs as she gets up and gently pats my back. I watch her leave the room, a small smile pulling on my lips.

__chapter twenty-five__
Sarah

"Was it as awkward as you thought it would be?"

"No. It was worse." I groan, banging my head on the lunch table.

Gina giggles beside me and pats my back. "C'mon, now! It couldn't have been that bad!" The pats move into small circles, but do nothing to ease my embarrassment.

I groan again and turn my head towards her. "It was so embarrassing, though."

"It wasn't too bad," Zander says as he approaches our table. "It's normal for parents to ask those questions to the guy their daughter has been hanging out with, Buttercup." He chuckles and sits down beside me. I turn towards him, my cheeks heating up. "Besides," he says. "I wouldn't mind knowing the answers to a few of them myself."

My eyes widen in shock. His eyes hold my gaze until I awkwardly look away. Gina looks at me curiously, oblivious to what he could mean. *Oh my goodness, I haven't told her yet! She's going to kill me!*

I glance at Zander. "Okay," I whisper, fixing my stare on the sandwich in front of me. My thoughts drift off. I could have sworn yesterday I saw some sort of disappointment in his answer that we were just friends. My eyes meet Samantha's across the room. She sneers at me as she mouths the word "ugly" before turning back to her friends without a second thought. Tears well up in my eyes. Am I not worth a second thought?

He shifts around beside me. "Okay, great," he says. "Meet me by my bike after school, then." He leaves, his steps fading into the many voices around us. My eyes drop to my lap, feelings of hate swirling through me as I gaze at my stomach poking out.

"What was that all about?" Gina inquires, shoving a few chips in her mouth. "What're you thinking about?"

I smile weakly. "I'll tell you after school, okay?"

"Okay." She holds out her pinky finger. "Promise?"

I link our pinkies together. "Promise."

I groan softly, banging my head against my locker. "Man up, Sarah. Just go already."

I'm hiding in the girls' locker room. *C'mon, just go,* I tell myself. *It won't be that bad. Who am I kidding? It's dodgeball. Of course it's going to be bad.*

I sigh and shakily make my way to the door. I take a deep breath, then push the door open. Dodgeball has always been my least favorite game. I am terrible at throwing and dodging things. Gina, who is currently stretching out her legs, has the advantage of coordination due to her dance training. A bunch of girls look at me, and I scurry over to Gina, hiding behind her small frame. Thankfully, our gym classes aren't combined with the boys' class. Which leaves us with half the female high school population and a loud coach. *But it's still better.*

"Alright, ladies! Today is dodgeball. You know the rules!" Coach Mathers blows her whistle, bursting all the eardrums in a ten mile radius.

Gina and I wince. "I wish someone would take that from her and throw it away," Gina mumbles under her breath. I nod, grimacing as my ears ring.

Everyone else groans, and we line up without being prompted. We're so used to playing this that we already know which sides we want to be on. Coach Mathers points at each team, "Jenny and Samantha are your captains. Game starts in five!"

Our team captain Jenny, a really nice girl, smiles at us. "Alright, girls," she says. "Let's kick their butts!" I smile back at her. I've barely interacted with Jenny, but from what I've observed she's very passionate about sports. Gina and I have heard she's in line to play on Stanford's soccer team. I scan her tall, muscular frame. She's unapologetic about her appearance, and that's one of the things I admire most about her. It can be intimidating being one of the largest girls in the school, but she doesn't let that dampen her mood. I would love to have confidence like that. The other thing I like about her is our combined hatred for the opposing team's captain.

Samantha faces us now, a sly smirk on her face. "You ready to lose again, Kenny?" Samantha's little group snickers. The rest of her team stand by nonchalantly. My mouth drops open, glancing back to see Jenny's reaction. What does Samantha have against Jenny?

Jenny stares her down with a cool smile. "Sure thing, *Samuel.*"

Samantha glares at Jenny while the rest of us hold back our laughter. Samantha continues to glare daggers at us, then roughly throws the ball at Jenny's chest. Jenny catches it right in time. "Whatever," says Samantha.

The coach claps her hands, drawing our focus back to her. "On the count of three, we'll start." We all take our stances, getting ready to race towards the balls laid out on the floor.

"One."

I ready myself, Gina bending lower beside me.

"Two."

Jenny shifts her feet, giving us the signal to stay back. I connect eyes with Gina and nod, game faces on. *C'mon, c'mon!*

"Three!"

Everyone leaps forward, shoes squeaking on the floor. Gina shuffles backwards, taking on the defense. Jenny grabs a ball and throws it at a girl on the other team, getting her out. Balls fly around the room. Girls get knocked out of the game and brought back in. Soon, it's down to the three of us. Jenny, Gina, and me on our side, then Samantha and Claire on the other.

Samantha tightens her grip on the last ball. "Say, Kenny, who should I get out first? Fatty or wannabe Miss Popular?" She laughs maliciously.

Jenny rolls her shoulders. "Or you could just give me the ball and surrender."

Samantha laughs again, shaking her head. She sighs and studies her feet. Suddenly, her eyes snap back up at us. "Wrong answer." Her icy glare swings over to Gina and before she can block, the ball comes barreling at her chest. She falls down, the wind leaving her lungs.

"Oh my goodness, Gina!" I drop down beside her. Samantha's evil laughs ring in my ears. The other girls sit on the edge of their seats, worried but not daring to get up.

Jenny leans over to check on Gina. "Are you alright?" Gina takes in some deep breaths and nods weakly. Jenny turns to Samantha with a vengeful glint in her eye.

"You shouldn't have done that," she spits out. I pull Gina up to rest her head on my lap as we all watch the exchange intently.

Samantha rolls her eyes and turns towards her two friends. Jenny grabs the ball off the ground, swiftly throwing the ball at Claire. The ball bumps her arm, knocking her out of the game.

Our team cheers Jenny on, everyone at the edge of their seat as Samantha grabs the ball from the floor, throwing it back at Jenny so fast she can't dodge it. The ball collides with Jenny's shoulder, knocking her on her butt.

Samantha's team screams triumphantly. At the sight of her gloating, all of my pent-up anger propels me forward. Who says I have to keep bending over to her every word? If Jenny can let her insults roll off her back, so can I.

I huff and get up. Gina frowns and sits up on her elbows. "Where are you going?" she whispers, glancing over at the other team.

I look back with a sly smile. "I'm going to win." I stride forward, scoop up the ball, then throw it to the best of my ability. It smacks Samantha in the shoulder. She whips around.

"What was that for?" she shrieks, her arm turning red. Everyone around us goes quiet.

I plant my hand on my hip. "You seem to have forgotten that I was still in the game. So *we* just won. Not you." The quiet hangs over us, then our team hollers in victory. I run over to envelop Gina in a giant hug.

"S, that was so awesome, I'm super proud of you!" I giggle into her neck, my arms gripping her tightly. She laughs and pulls away. The other girls on our team run over to celebrate.

Samantha stomps off in a huff. Claire follows close behind, throwing glares at us over her shoulder.

Jenny bounds over to us. "That was awesome!" She pulls us into a hug, jumping up and down. "Did you see Samantha's face? Oh my gosh, she was pissed!" We all laugh, giving high fives to our teammates.

Tina, one of Samantha's friends, shyly approaches us. "Well done, Sarah," she says. I brace myself for her harsh words, but am surprised by the genuine smile she gives me. "Truth be told, we're all glad you guys won instead of us." Gina and I stare at her in shock. Tina blushes, ducks her head, and hurries out of the gym.

Coach Mathers blows her whistle from the sidelines, effectively shutting us all up. She walks into the little crowd and stops in front of me, eyeing me up with a frown. Slowly, her eyes light up and a smile spreads across her lips. "Well done, Sarah." She nods in approval, roughly patting my back. I smile past the pain and wiggle out of her hold as the girls cheer again and begin heading back to the locker rooms.

Gina smiles at them all, then links arms with me. "Well," she sighs, smiling. "That was dramatic!"

"Yeah, it was." We start walking back towards the locker room. Jenny runs up beside us, then falls in step with us.

"Thanks for your encouragement, Jenny," I say. "We couldn't have done it without you."

She blushes lightly. "Thank you, but I was actually here to congratulate you. And to make sure Gina is okay!" She bumps her shoulder with mine, "Samantha can be really awful when she's jealous. Don't let it get to you."

I link my arm with Jenny's. Gina shoots her a smile. "I'm okay, thanks." I give Jenny a smile of my own before we all head into the bustling locker room.

"There you are." Zander beams at me.

My stomach twists itself in knots. "Here I am." I shyly fiddle with my bag strap, stopping a few feet in front of him.

He leans back against his bike seat, his eyes cast down to his shoes. I watch him curiously. Why is he not talking?

I clear my throat. "So, uh, what did you want to talk about?" His eyes flicker back to me, his smile dimming slightly. Worry grips my heart.

He bites his lip then takes a deep breath. I take one as well, my heart hammering against my chest. Slowly, he looks back up at me and gets up, stopping when our shoes just barely touch. He gently takes my hands in his, his eyes locked on mine.

"Sarah, I..." His eyes drop down to our hands. My heart stops and tears well up in the back of my eyes. *No! Don't cry!*

He looks back up at me, confidence radiating from his face now.

"Sarah, I would like to take you somewhere. On a date."

W-What?

__chapter twenty-six__
Sarah

W-What?

I stare up at him, the tears drying up quickly. He stares back down at me anxiously. My mouth opens and closes as I try to respond. *What are words again?*

He looks away and bites his lip, sending my poor heart into a frenzy. *Oh gosh, is this real life? Did he really just ask me out?* His eyes lock onto his shoes, his brows creasing into a small frown.

"On a date . . . *A date*?" The words tumble out of my mouth. My heart feels like a bird that's just been released from its cage. *On a date.* I quickly nod. "When?" *He kissed me, and now he actually wants to take me on a date? This is like a fairy tale!*

A huge grin spreads across his face at my words. His smile is contagious. He gently wraps me up in his arms and spins me around, laughing loudly in delight. I can't help but laugh, too. He sets me down but doesn't let go, keeping our bodies pressed together in a way that has my cheeks flushing bright red.

He brushes away a few of my stray hairs, then cups my cheek in his palm. "Tomorrow night, I'll pick you up around seven. You'll want to wear something cute, even though you'll look adorable no matter what you wear."

"Okay." My arms are still wrapped around his neck. "I'll see you then?"

"See you then." He pulls me up again into a bone-crushing hug, taking my breath away. I squeeze back and shut my eyes happily, savoring the hard yet gentle embrace. I sigh softly and open my eyes again but almost gasp in shock. Out of the corner of my eye, I notice someone staring. I quickly look away and pull away from the hug, glancing around Zander's arm only to be met with a few bushes.

I'm losing my marbles.

"Everything alright?" Zander turns to look at the bushes, then turns back to me with a confused smile. I quickly smile back reassuringly and pat his cheek.

"Yup, everything's fine. Just thought I saw something."

He nods in understanding then pulls away, keeping a firm hold on my hand, and mounts his bike. He smiles up at me. "See you tomorrow, Buttercup."

I blush again and nod, gently squeezing his hand in mine. Slowly, he lets go of my hand to put on his helmet and start his engine. It roars to life, the loud sound vibrating right through me. He flips the visor of his helmet up to smile at me again, then moves to flip it back down. I grab his wrist and land a quick kiss on his nose. "Bye, Zander." His cheeks flush brightly before he flips his visor back down. He revs his engine then takes off, leaving me and a trail of dust behind.

I slowly make my way towards home, kicking little pebbles along the way. Gina's words ring through my head on repeat: *If it doesn't feel right, it's not.* A small smile forms on my lips when I think about all the little moments spent with Zander, all the sweet nicknames and kisses, all of it.

Then I think of the date with Keagen. I hadn't thought about him at all since the day we went bowling. Suddenly, I realize what I need to tell him.

I whip out my phone and send him a text, telling him to meet me at the park. He agrees. I hurriedly change my direction and walk to the little park only a few minutes away from the school. Kids run around screaming and covered in dirt. "Tommy, you put that bug down!" a mom yells from the park bench. A dad darts over to comfort a little girl crying under the monkey bars.

I spot a bench under a bunch of pine trees and take a seat, my legs anxiously bouncing up and down while I wait. *It'll be alright, he'll understand.*

"Hey, Sarah." His voice startles me, and chills run down my spine. He chuckles and takes a seat beside me. "Did I scare you?"

I let out a breathy laugh, brushing off the feeling. "Just a little bit, yeah."

He smiles sheepishly. "Sorry about that."

We both look away from each other, the silence growing thick between us. I take a small deep breath and prepare myself.

"I would like to hang out with you more," he says.

"I think we should just be friends." My words overlap with his.

We both stare at each other wide-eyed. He looks away, hanging his head. "Alright, then. This just got even more awkward, but okay. May I ask what happened? I thought we had a good thing going?"

My heart breaks a little bit the more he talks. "No, no, I had a really great time. It's just...I like someone else right now." I look away. His sadness hurts me. He nods, laughing almost bitterly to himself.

"You like *him*," he says.

"I—I'm sorry, Keagen, but I really, *really* do like him. I didn't want to lead you on."

"That's okay, Sarah," he says eventually. "I'm happy for you." He gives me a shaky grin. Again, tears well up in my eyes.

Gosh, Sarah, get a grip!

"Thank you." I smile and pull him into a small hug. "Friends?"

He chuckles softly and hugs me back, pulling away to give me a small smile of his own. "Yeah, friends."

My small smile turns into a grin and I hug him tighter, my heart finally happy again. *This has been a great day!*

__chapter twenty-seven__
Zander

I smooth out my coat, run my fingers through my hair, then give myself one more once-over in the mirror. I let out a small nervous breath. "Zander, you will not screw this up," I say to my reflection. I shake my shoulders, loosening up my tense muscles.

"Where are you going, boy?"

I make eye contact with him in the mirror. "Nowhere you'd be able to remember."

He scoffs and points at me, a bottle in his hand. "Don't speak to me like that, boy." He stumbles forward and grips the wall. I fix a stray hair before facing him.

"Don't call me a boy when you can't even be a man yourself."

He glares at me. "Don't speak to me like that. You know your mother wouldn't allow it."

I glare daggers at him, my eyes flickering over to the picture I have of her on my bedroom wall. Her beautiful smile stares back at me. Even then, I could see the bruises darkening her arms, the bags under her eyes from countless nights spent worrying about him. I clench my fists, desperate to control my anger. "Don't you dare bring her up." I take a menacing step forward. "Especially when you knew what she wanted."

"I—I don't..." His eyes dart around the room for an escape. I bump against his shoulder as I walk by. He stumbles backwards, gripping the wall to keep him steady.

"I'm going on a date. I'll be back later," I mutter under my breath, making it to the top of the steps.

"Zander..." I stop in my tracks. "You really like this girl?" I look at him over my shoulder. He stands there gripping the wall, his body slightly slumped and his face tired and desperate.

"Yeah, I like her a lot. She reminds me of Mom." Sarah's smile flashes in my memories, the way her cheeks flush brightly when she's embarrassed, the way her eyes would look so determined and would let me know that she was about to give me a kiss. She's a lot like my mom. Beautiful, goofy, caring, and let's not forget *she's a great cook.*

"I...Um...Good luck, Son." He stumbles over to the other wall, making his way back to his room. I sigh and continue down the steps, my nervousness returning full force.

Gosh, get a grip, Zander. It's not like she's the girl of your dreams and this date could make or break your relationship.

Okay, it's exactly like that.

I grab my keys off the table and head into the garage.

A smile spreads across my lips as I rev the engine, the door of the garage opening in the meantime. I quickly send a text to Sarah, letting her know I'm on my way. I can't wait to see her. Spending time with Sarah has become my new favorite thing. She's been the best thing to happen to me in a long time. From my mom's passing, to my dad's drunken outrages, to moving here with no plan for the future, I feel like meeting Sarah has really helped ground me back into normality. Sure, I still have to deal with my Dad, but having someone to go to, to talk to even, has helped so much.

After parking in the driveway, I hop out and run up to her door. It's in this moment that I wonder what my mom would think of her. I take a few deep breaths, then knock. Sarah opens it quickly, a shy smile on her face. She wears a maroon sweater and a gray skirt with tights and black flats. The skirt perfectly accents her hips, showcasing her curvy waist. Her beautiful red hair is done up in a bun.

Holy mother of all that was created, I struck gold.

__chapter twenty-eight__

Sarah

"H-Hi," I say, my fingers tightly clenched together as I anxiously await his response. My outfit is one that Gina helped me pick out from her closet, with her claiming I looked spectacular while I fretted in the mirror about the way my sweater and skirt hugged my hips. How I got in said skirt still shocks me, considering Gina's dancer frame is much smaller than mine. She was right, though. The ensemble looks casual, yet just dressy enough. And it's surprisingly really comfortable, that is, minus all the anxiety and self-doubt.

He stares at me with wide eyes, his mouth slightly parted as he gives me a once-over.

"Hi...You look beautiful." He stares at me with awe.

"You too, er, I mean, not beautiful—ah, not that you don't look beautiful. I mean handsome. You look handsome." I tumble over my words, embarrassing myself even more.

He struggles to hold back his grin. I smack his shoulder. "It's not funny!"

He nods, his grin finally breaking through. "It kinda is, Buttercup."

My heart flutters at the sound of the nickname. I cross my arms, jutting my lip out in a pout. "It's not. Are you just going to make fun of me all night? 'Cause if so, imma just go right back inside." I glare at him playfully, a smile tugging at the corner of my lips. *Do not smile. Do not break!*

He grins mischievously and leans forward, his face only a few inches from my own. My thoughts immediately go back to the night on the roof. His lips were so soft, and his kiss so gentle. My breath catches in my throat. *I really want to kiss him again.* "I might," he said softly, "but you like it."

I scoff, pushing him back out of the doorway. I can't control the smile breaking out across my face as I hook my arm with his to drag him towards his bike. He grins back down at me and grabs the helmet off the bike, holding my hand the entire time. I smooth my hands over the skirt, even more self conscious than before. Was a skirt the best idea for this? Zander nudges me with his shoulder, bringing my eyes back up to his. He smiles and glances down at my outfit again, "You look amazing, Sarah." I give him a shaky smile before mounting the bike, carefully fixing the helmet over my hair.

The engine comes to life, scaring me a bit. Zander laughs at my sudden jumpiness, flashing a smile my way before pulling his own helmet on. "Nervous?" he yells over the sound of the roaring engine.

I flip the visor of my helmet to hide my blush as I shout back. "Maybe."

He smiles again, but not as brightly. "Don't worry. I am, too." His words send a small pang to my heart, sending it skipping around with the butterflies in my stomach.

I study the side of his face as he stares ahead. His jaw is clenched tightly, his eyes locked onto the driveway. I glance down at his hands, which grip the handlebars.

"Done checking me out?"

I look up at him wildly. "I wasn't-"

He turns around and winks at me. "It's alright if you were. I don't mind. Besides, I can't say I haven't checked you out a few times myself."

I lightly punch his shoulder. "Jerk!"

He grabs my hands, pulling me flush against his back. "I can't help it, Buttercup, you're just too cute."

His leather jacket is cold as I rest against him, my fingers reaching to fiddle with the zippers on the front pockets. He revs the engine and then pulls out of the driveway. Sitting here with him, trees and houses blurring by, I can't help but think of Gina's words.

If it doesn't feel right, then it's not. I look at my hands, then at Zander.

And again, this feels perfect.

He notices me and flashes me a smile, his hand reaching to lightly squeeze mine. "Everything alright?" he asks as we stop by a red light.

I squeeze back. "Yeah, it's perfect." I sigh happily, gently rubbing my thumb across his. I still can't believe this isn't a dream.

He laughs softly. "Glad to know that, Buttercup."

I poke his shoulder. "I need to come up with a nickname for you!"

He scrunches his nose up and sends me a strange look. He shudders theatrically. "No, that's quite alright. Zander works for me."

I shake my head and poke him again. "No, you have one for me, and now I need to make one for you."

He laughs and shakes his head, "Alright, if you insist. What're you going to call me?"

I open my mouth to respond, but then I realize I don't have any. *What would fit him?* He looks over at me with his eyebrow raised, a smirk spreading across his lips.

"You can't even think of one, can you?"

I huff, annoyed. "It's not as easy as you think," I mumble.

"Sure it is. I can think of a lot for you. Cupcake, angel, kitten, sweetheart, flower..."

I turn to him incredulously. "Flower?"

He thinks about it, then scrunches his nose. "Yeah, you're right. That doesn't sound very cute."

"Yeah, no. It sounds like the skunk from *Bambi*."

"From what?"

I gasp loudly, my mouth falling open. "You've never watched *Bambi*?"

"No, is that a bad thing?"

"Yes, that's a bad thing!" I lean back in my seat in awe. "I can't believe you've never watched *Bambi* before."

He squeezes my hand again. "Don't worry, we can watch it together some time, yeah?" He smiles and looks over at me questioningly, a glimmer of hope in his eyes that sparks hope in me.

A car beeps behind us, scaring both of us to look up and find the light is green. I adjust my grip around his waist again as he speeds off. I shout back, "Yeah, we can do that." The road turns from pavement to dirt the further we go. Houses fade into trees until finally, we slow to a stop.

Zander squeezes my hand once more before turning off the engine. He gives me a huge grin, my forgotten nervousness returning again. "We're here."

I gaze in awe at the fairy lights illuminating the night. *Where are we?* I see the lake not far from us. A small circle table is set up on the dock, covered with a sweeping white tablecloth that gently floats in the breeze. It's set for two, with wine glasses and a beautiful rose centerpiece. Candles and lanterns light up the table. A tree stands a few feet away, its branches draped with fairy lights. The branches reach over the table, casting a soft glow on everything.

"Do you like it?" Zander's eyes flicker back and forth from my face to the set-up. I look over at him with awe, my heart exploding in my chest.

"No, I don't like it," I say.

His eyes widen and he looks down at his hands. "Oh, uh, we can–"

I place a hand on his shoulder. "Zander, I love it."

He gives me a flat look. "That was mean."

"I know." I grab his hand. "C'mon, let's go!" I revel in the beauty of the lights and candles. It's like the stars were draped over the table, *like he brought the stars down just for me.* My eyes well up with tears. I can't believe he cared enough to do all of this.

"Sarah? Are you okay? Why are you crying?" He cups his hands around my shoulders. I look at him through blurry eyes and I brush my hands over his elbows.

I sniffle. "Yeah, yeah, I'm okay." A small laugh bubbles out of my chest, growing into a fit of giggles. He looks at me as if I'm insane, his hands keeping me grounded. "I'm more than okay," I say. "I'm ecstatic!"

He pulls me closer, his arms wrapping around my waist. I rest my hands on his chest. He gazes into my eyes, "Let's go eat before the food gets cold." My stomach growls loudly at the mention of food. *Curse you, stomach, you traitor!*

His chest rumbles as a deep laugh escapes his lips. He comes to my side and leads me to the table, his arm still around my waist. A little path of flowers leads up to the table, each one placed perfectly to create a little walkway. My heart swells in my chest. A white bag is leaning against the leg of the table, but I barely notice it as I catch sight of the table top.

I can't help but eye up all the food hungrily. At each place setting is a white plate bearing a sirloin steak. There's a basket of steak fries drizzled with ranch dressing and some fried asparagus. A cooler full of glass bottles of soda sits by the railing. He pulls out my chair for me, then pushes me in once I sit down. He rounds the table to his seat, awkwardly fumbling with his jacket. "I hope you like what I chose," He pushes the plates of food and glasses on the table around, his motions jerky and frantic. "But if you don't like it, we can get something else." He shifts the salt and pepper shakers on the table, almost knocking the salt completely over in his haste.

I grab his shaking hands. "Zander."

"Yeah?"

I squeeze his hands in mine. *He's adorable. I never thought I'd be the one to make a guy nervous!* "It's alright. I love it, all of it."

His eyes search mine and he visibly relaxes. "I'm glad you like it," he says. "Can't take all the credit, though. Gina helped me with most of it." He points to the lights above us. "That required team work."

A surprised laugh escapes me. "I can just see her now," I say. "Climbing up the tree and hanging off the branches!" I look back at him only to be met with his shy gaze and bright red cheeks.

"Actually," he says. "That was me..."

I place a hand over my mouth to hold back my laughter. *C'mon, Sarah, don't be rude!* I sober up. "They look very nice. You did well!"

He grins over at me and then gets up to serve us. The steaks are cooked perfectly, not too raw and not too well done. The fries are delicious, just as I knew they'd be. I had thought that the fried asparagus would be gross, but I'm surprised to discover that I love it.

"So," I say in between bites, pointing my fork at him, "Did you make all of this?"

A sly smile spreads across his face as he leans back in his seat. "Are you impressed?"

My eyes roam over my plate with a small hum of approval. I glance back up at him with a smile. "I suppose I am." I shrug nonchalantly. "Although, you could have given me a bowl of Cap'n Crunch and I would have been happy all the same."

He chuckles, taking another bite of his own. "Come on now, only Froot Loops would be acceptable in that situation."

I scoff loudly. "Are you serious?"

"Uh, yeah?" He shoots me an incredulous look. "Froot Loops are the superior cereal."

I toss my hands up in surrender, a smile tugging at my lips, "Okay, Froot Loop fanatic, I'll drop it." We both laugh before falling into a comfortable silence. I allow him a moment before asking, "Where did you learn to cook so well?" He pauses, swallowing his food harshly. Did I ask the wrong thing? I set my fork down, leaning forward. "Zander, I'm sorry. You don't have to tell me anything you don't want to."

He winces and sets his fork down too, shaking his head. His eyes seem so distant, lost in whatever thoughts plague his mind. He sighs softly, "No, I–" He pauses and glances up at me, his face stern, "I want to be able to tell you these things." He scoffs and looks away, "I want to be able to say these things without feeling ashamed or embarrassed."

I reach across the table and take his hand that is gripping his fork, "You can tell me anything, Zander." I gently squeeze his hand. "It's hard to open yourself up to others like this, and trust that they won't judge you or throw your words back in your face."

Zander stares at me, his expression unreadable, then finally opens his mouth. "My mom taught me to cook some when I was younger, but I took to it more after she passed. It was a learning curve, and I never had help other than staring at recipes and trial and error." His fingers twirl his knife around, his eyes dropping down to focus on his plate. "Most days I had to create a meal out of the little items we had left, since my dad would spend most of his money on booze. When I turned sixteen, I was old enough to get a job to pay the bills. We had our water and electricity shut off quite a few times, one of the worst being in the dead of winter. It wasn't until he put the house up for sale that I was able to slightly catch my breath. I used some of the money we got to pay for my bike, which I got off some guy selling it along the road." A small smile forms. "I fixed it up in time for my new job across town."

I smile and squeeze his hand to get his attention again. "Is mechanical work something you want to do?"

His eyes roam my face for a moment, his lips finally pressing into a straight line as he shakes his head. "I'm not sure." He drops his gaze shamefully. "I know that doesn't say much about me, to not have my future planned out."

Shaking my head, I quickly pull his attention back to me. "Zander, nobody would expect you to have your life fully planned out when you've been fighting to live day by day." Tears sting my eyes as I gaze at his broken expression, so much guilt and remorse weighing him down. Listening to his story, and thinking back to my own of having to grow up too fast, I desperately want him to see himself through my eyes. A strong man, having lost his mother at a young age, still trying to stay strong enough to take care of his father and maintain a normal life. Most would have succumbed to something worse. I try to reassure him again. "What is important is that you find what you love to do, and chase it. What matters is that you're still trying in the meantime."

His eyes shine with unshed tears as he whispers, "I have been trying so hard not to crumble." He looks away again, a single tear falling off his cheek onto the white tablecloth. "I hate myself for not doing more to save her, to save us."

My heart lurches at his words. I stumble out of my chair, moving to kneel in front of him and gently grab his face in my hands, tears of my own dripping down my cheeks. He tries desperately to blink back his own tears as I use my thumbs to wipe them away myself.

"Zander, you are not your father," I say. He sharply inhales, his eyes searching mine wildly. "You were just a kid, and are not responsible for your father's actions." I barely manage my own smile. "I see you, Zander. I see all of you, your hopes and fears, and that's okay." I brush my thumb across his cheek again. "You will always have a home with me."

He exhales, his soft breath fanning across my cheeks. A smile fights across his lips as he lifts his hand up to cover mine. His face is so warm in my hands, and in this moment I decide to always try my best to keep a small smile tilting his lips. "Where have you been all my life, Sarah Jones?" he whispers, his eyes roaming my face.

My smile turns into a grin. "I've been right here, Zander Mills." Our eyes stay locked onto each other as he slowly leans forward. My fingers curl against his cheeks, pulling him down to meet my lips in a breathtaking kiss. His lips are salty with tears, and his kiss is gentle. It doesn't last long, both of us pulling away to rest our foreheads together, our breath mixing in the warm night air around us.

He chuckles, leaning back to look at me more fully. "Our food is probably cold by now."

I lean forward, planting another small kiss on his lips. "It was worth it," I whisper.

He glances back over our table of half-eaten food, then grabs my hands from his face, "C'mon, then," He pulls me back to my feet as he stands, crushing me to his chest as he wraps one arm around my waist. He reaches under the table and pulls out a large fleece blanket.

I gasp. "How did I not feel that under there?"

He laughs and starts leading us down to the edge of the lake. "You were distracted, maybe?" He spreads it out over the grass, gesturing for me to lay down. The moon illuminates the lake through the clearing of trees, giving us the perfect view of the starry sky above. I roll my eyes at him and laugh, lowering myself onto the flannel pattern. He stretches out beside me and turns to face me. I feel his eyes roaming across my face before settling on my eyes. I blush under his scrutinizing gaze and look back up at the stars, letting my imagination fly free.

I point up at a pattern in the sky. "That one looks like a cat!"

Zander snorts. "More like a dragon."

I roll my eyes and glare at him playfully. "It looks like a fluffy little cat."

"You do that a lot."

"Do what?"

He rolls over to lay on his side, propping his head on his hand. "Pretend you're mad at me when you're really holding back that gorgeous smile of yours." He reaches up and boops my nose. "You should smile more."

I swat his hand away. "I do smile. A lot. It's not my fault you're not around when it happens!"

He smirks at me. "Your sass levels are high today." His smile slips. Suddenly he grabs my hands and fidgets with my fingers, his face now anxious. "Sarah, I need to ask you something." I stare up at him skeptically, tilting my head. What is he thinking? He lightly squeezes my hands. "Would you be my girlfriend?"

My jaw drops. His eyes widen, the panic evident on his face. I let out a squeak before throwing myself into his arms, "Yes! Yes, of course, yes!" He scoops me up into his arms as he stands, spinning us around happily. He slows to a stop and places me back down, keeping his arms wrapped around me tightly. He buries his head in the crook of my neck and I gently run my fingers through his hair. I can't stop the grin from growing as I inhale his cologne.

"Tonight has been perfect." My gaze sweeps across the beautiful display, my grin widening. I finally glance up at him, finding him already staring down at me. My eyes drop to his lips, my breath catching. Leaning up, I smash my lips into his. His arms tighten around me, melting against my kiss. It only lasts for a minute, both of us pulling away breathless. He grins innocently and leads me to his bike, offering the helmet to me once again.

I furrow my eyebrows and glance back out to the dock where the table still stands. "Who's going to take care of all that?" I ask.

He starts the engine and pulls out of the parking spot. "I have someone to come by and clean up." I turn to look back at the lights one last time. Five minutes later, I find myself wanting to drift off into a light nap. I close my eyes and rest against his back, gripping onto his waist so I won't fall. The wind rushes past us, soothing me into a sleep-like state.

"You're home now, Buttercup." Zander's soft voice wakes me up. I blink a few times to register that we're back in my driveway. Disappointment fills me. I really wish this day would last forever. "Hold on, I'll carry you so you don't have to wake up too much." He takes the helmet off of me then gently lifts me up into his arms bridal style and carries me to the front door. I rest my head on his shoulder, my eyes fluttering closed. I could definitely get used to this. He walks up the steps to my room, gently lays me down on my bed, and covers me up. I look up at him through sleep-hazed eyes.

"Thank you for the wonderful date," I say, sleep slowly taking over me. "I can't wait to go on more."

He leans down to press a soft kiss on my forehead. "Of course," he murmurs. "Soon enough."

I pull the blankets up to my chin, cuddling into them. "Okay. Good night, Froot Loop."

He chokes back a laugh. "Good night, Buttercup." I smile and bury myself in my blankets. He softly shuts my door. The last thing that runs through my mind before I fall asleep is, *I could really eat some Froot Loops right now.*

__chapter twenty-nine__
Sarah

"Soooo, how did it go?" Gina shoves her tray to the side and leans closer to me.

I swallow my Froot Loops. "It was amazing. I loved it so much!"

She squeals and bounces in her seat. "I'm so happy that you're happy!" She wraps her arms around me tightly, almost knocking us both off the bench.

"Whoa! I can't tell if you two are overly excited or about to fight." Keagen blinks down at us, a ghost of a smile gracing his lips. I grin up at him and grip the edge of the table.

"Overly excited." Gina and I say in unison, surprising both of us.

Keagen takes his seat across from us, slowly picking at his sandwich. His eyes flicker back and forth between us. "What's the special occasion, then?"

I blush brightly and open my mouth to speak, only to be cut off by Gina's loud squeal. "She and Zander went on the big first date!" She claps her hands excitedly. A little *too* excitedly. People are starting to stare...

I reach over and wrap my hands around hers to stop her loud clapping, my eyes flickering around the room to the prying eyes. Gina looks at me questioningly, then notices everyone staring. "Oh," she whispers, tucking her hands in her lap. Keagen frowns down at his sandwich.

I gently rest my hand on his arm, causing him to jump and his muscles to tense. I take my hand back in surprise, my cheeks instantly flushing brightly again. "Sorry. Just wanted to make sure you're okay?" I look down at my forgotten Froot Loops, quickly taking a few bites before willing myself to look back up. *It's only awkward if you make it awkward . . . Or if he makes it awkward? Okay, now it's awkward.*

He clears his throat and shakes his head. *He seriously looks like he just heard that chocolate is no longer available. Well no; that'd be more tears than anger right? I mean, if it were me I'd be on the floor bawling my eyes out and wouldn't -*

Gina rams her elbow into my side, effectively cutting off my train of thought. I look over at her with wide eyes, oblivious to what I did wrong. She gestures to Keagen with her eyes. He had been talking to me the whole time, and I hadn't heard a thing he said.

I look back over to him with a sheepish smile, my hands fidgeting in my lap. He looks at me expectantly. I lick my suddenly dry lips, plastering on a wide smile. "Sorry, what?"

His frown turns into a huge grin, going all the way up to his eyes. "You're such a goof." He reaches out his finger, only centimeters away from bopping my nose when a hand comes out of nowhere and stops him midway.

"That's reserved for someone else." Zander pushes Keagen's hand away and takes a seat beside me. He puts his arm around my shoulders. I blush again, throwing Keagen a small apologetic smile.

"That wasn't very nice." I state seriously, earning a surprised look from Zander. His eyes dart to Gina, then back at me. I shake my head in mock disappointment, but can't help the grin from spreading across my face. "Now I definitely know Froot Loop suits you."

He raises an eyebrow, a smirk plastered across his face. "Oh yeah? And why is that, Buttercup?" He leans closer teasingly, trying to throw me off. I stand my ground as his face comes within inches of mine, my grin bigger than ever. Before I speak though, I catch Keagen in the corner of my eye making gagging motions, and I almost lose my cool. *Dang it, Keagen, I'm trying to focus here!*

Zander's eyes search mine, his lips parting in anticipation. I give him an evil grin. "Because your attitude is always different colors. Tell me, Zander, are you bipolar? Or is your mom just a box of Froot Loops?" Gina snorts back a laugh behind me and Keagen chokes on his sandwich. Zander gapes at me, his mouth opening and closing like a fish.

Keagen snorts again. His eyes linger on me for a second before sliding over to Zander, his grin turning into a half smile.

"No comeback from you?" Zander rolls his eyes at Keagen and turns to his food instead.

I catch Gina staring off dreamily at Kyle Cunningham at the football team's table. "Doesn't he just look so...handsome?" She sighs happily and leans her head against my shoulder.

I nudge her with my elbow. "You should talk to him!" Her cheeks heat up.

"No way!" she says. "He'd never talk to me."

"I bet he would if you were to go over there and talk to him." I give a brief nod towards his table. "He doesn't look busy. You could go now!"

She freezes up in her seat and furiously shakes her head. "Nope. I'm okay with just gazing from a distance." She sighs with disappointment, her shoulders slumping forward. "Besides, it's not like he's gonna profess his undying love to me, so what's the use?"

I gently rub her back. I want to see her as happy in love as she sees me. "Some day, G," I say. "You'll find someone to do just that, I promise."

She gives me a half-smile, her usual cheeriness coming back. "Yeah, you're right. Someday."

The bell rings loudly, cutting off everyone's conversations. Students hurry to the door, running each other over to get out first.

Keagen gets up first and slings his bag over his shoulder before grabbing his tray. "See you guys later!" He nods to Gina and Zander, then his eyes drop down to me. "There's a football game this weekend, see you—uh, see you all there?"

I nod. "Yeah sure, we'll be there."

He walks away grinning. Zander snorts and stands, slinging his bag over his shoulder and picking up mine. I link my arm with his as we walk out of the cafeteria.

"Ready for our next class?" I ask him.

His stone cold expression leaves Keagen's disappearing figure to look down at me, his eyes softening and a smile reappearing on his face. "Yup," he says. "I'm ready for my nap."

I elbow his side playfully, opening my mouth to chide him. Gina links her arm through mine.

"I'm ready for my nap, too," she says. "Let's go!" As ridiculous as they are, I can't help but laugh. *I really do have some great people in my life.*

__chapter thirty__
Zander

She glares at me intensely. "Zander, it's only fair." Her grip tightens on the remote, but I refuse to relinquish it. It's tug-of-war now. "Let go!" She fails to pull it out of my grip, losing her hold on the end of it. I slide my hand up to cover the spot hers just freed, giving more room to tug it in my direction.

"Do you guys think Kyle likes me?" Gina asks. We're too busy in our game to respond.

"Zander," Sarah says. "I swear to fudge."

An evil grin spreads across my lips as I yank the remote closer to my chest. Sarah huffs and keeps pulling, her body hovering halfway off the couch. If I were to just simply let go, she'd fall right to the floor.

"C'mon, Buttercup, you know it's my turn again. Just let go of the remote!" I give it one last yank, victorious. She goes down and yelps, reaching out for help. I wrap my arm around her waist and pull her into my chest. She stares right into my eyes, captivating me like comets in her gaze.

"You really should pay more attention," she says, smiling cheekily.

I look down at my hand, which is now remote free. *What the...?* Sarah springs off the couch and darts into the kitchen. I grumble and go after her.

"Give it back!" I say. I lunge at her, but she dodges my arms and runs down the hall.

"Never!" she cries. "Death before dishonor!"

I groan again. "You always say that!" Even still, I smile as I make my way back into the living room. I scan the area, then focus on Gina. "Where'd she go?"

She snorts loudly. "Like I would betray my best friend." I scowl at her and she throws her hands up in defense. "I don't know where she went, dude."

Something drops in the hallway. A coat lies on the floor. I look up and see Sarah hiding by the coat rack. Her eyes widen, and she darts off down the hall again. I catch up to her before she can get into the kitchen. I pick her up and drape her over my shoulder, laughing loudly when she squeaks in surprise.

She pounds on my back. "Unhand me, you Froot Loop dingus!" she shouts. She kicks, and I lose my balance. I carry her back into the living room and toss her on the couch.

"My goodness, you two are like an old married couple." Gina says, pointing her phone in our direction. I roll my eyes and sit beside Sarah, lifting her legs to rest on my lap.

Sarah sits up and pushes back her now wild hair, a silly grin spreading across her face. She looks over at Gina, her grin instantly dropping. "What, is there something on my face?" she asks. I frown in confusion and lean forward to see what's happening.

"Sarah," Gina says. "If I didn't know you and wasn't just here for the past ten minutes, I would've thought you guys just got outta the sack." She wiggles her eyebrows at us suggestively. I choke on air, my ears burning. Sarah's shirt is all rumpled, and her hair springs out all over the place. My shirt's all wrinkled, too. *What if her parents were to walk in and see us like this?*

Sarah throws a pillow at Gina. "Ow!" Gina yells. She cradles her cheek, playfully glaring at Sarah as laughter erupts from her. Sarah turns to me, giggling. Something in her eyes suggests to me that we should gang up on Gina.

I grab the pillow behind me and launch it at Gina, hitting her in the face. She immediately stops laughing and gapes at me.

Good job, Zander, you just signed your death wish.

Sarah looks at us with wide eyes, spluttering in her laughter. With a soft whisper, she gives me the confirmation I need.

"Uh . . . Run."

I jump off the couch like I'm on fire, bolting to the bathroom. I slam the door behind me and try to lock the door. There is no button to lock it. *How does this stupid door work?* Gina gives a war cry not far away.

Just as I figure out that the knob needs to be pushed in to lock, the door slams into my chest. I stumble back. "Ompf!"

Gina stares at me. "Oh my gosh, are you okay?" she asks. "I'm so sorry. I didn't mean to hit you with it."

I rub the middle of my chest, grimacing in pain. I'm definitely going to have a bruise there tomorrow. "Yeah, I'm fine."

Her shoulders relax a bit, "Okay, good. Anyways, where were we?" She aims a pillow right for my face. "Oh right, your demise!" She steps forward and lunges at me, the door lightly bouncing off the wall as she bumps it out of her way.

I back up slowly, my hands in the air. "Hey, man, let's talk this out, yeah? Look I'll give you, uh—wait, what *do* you want?"

She stops midway and cocks her hip to the side, tapping her chin. "Hmmm, how about a candy bar for Sarah and me the next time we go to the store?"

I start to nod in agreement, but halt and stand up straight again. "Wait, why am I—"

"Ah! No take-backs! You already nodded!" She skips back to the living room. "Did you hear that, Sarah? I just got us a free KitKat!"

I stand there, stunned. *What just happened?* Sarah giggles softly. "Yeah, I heard that. I'm pretty surprised, considering he's got nothing to be scared of!"

I walk out of the bathroom and plop down beside Sarah. "I still don't understand why I agreed." I gently wrap my arm around her shoulder, pulling her closer to my chest. She willingly leans against me.

"You must be a yellow Froot Loop today—scared of anything," Sarah says.

"Whatever," I grumble under my breath. Sarah rests her head on my shoulder. *She's so beautiful. How did I get so lucky?* Her hand lightly rests over my heart, and her body shakes in my arms as she laughs. My heart speeds up.

"Oh, crap," Gina says. She springs up off the couch and frantically rushes around the living room to gather her stuff.

"What's wrong?" Sarah asks.

Gina stops to brush the hair out of her face, a rigid smile on her face. She glances at the door desperately. "I almost forgot about Mom's appointment. Sarah, I gotta go."

Sarah nods. "Okay, yeah, hurry up. Text me as soon as you get back, okay?" She offers a comforting smile, getting up to give her a small hug. Gina nods solemnly. "Bye, guys," she whispers. Then she rushes out the door. *What just happened?*

Sarah gives me a tight smile. I flicker my eyes back and forth from the door and to her face. "Is she alright?" I ask. "Is her mom okay?"

"She's got some things going on, but yeah she'll be alright...I think." Her eyes drop down to the floor, then she lightly shakes her head, as if clearing her thoughts. "How about some music?" She spins around and skips over to the stereo above the TV, completely pushing away her worry.

If only I was that good with emotions.

She adjusts the volume as a song starts pumping from the speakers sounding something along the lines of a—*wait is this a Blink-182 song?* Sarah spins around, her grin making my heart stutter in my chest. She dances all around the living room, her hair flinging in different directions. The song hits a slow part and she dances my way, reaching her hands out to pull me off the couch.

"Dance with me!" She giggles loudly and spins, her hands still in mine, and I laugh with her, her hands still in mine as she spins. We face each other and twist our hips along to the chorus. She runs over to the couch, hopping onto the cushions and points at me while pretending to sing into a microphone. I jump along to the beat, shredding the air guitar. She flings her hair like a rock star, jumping off the couch to put her back against mine.

"Sing it!" I shout as she spins around again. She waves me over to her with a grin and I quickly follow her around the room. I head-bang to the last guitar riff, and Sarah leans against me while rocking back and forth. I play the last note with a flare, even doing a little spin. The song stops and we look at each other with giant grins. She jumps into my arms for a hug. I laugh, my heart full, and hold her tightly. I can't really remember the last time I felt this happy.

She smiles up at me sweetly, her eyes shining with something unrecognizable. Her arms tighten around my neck as she pulls me down to her level. She keeps her eyes locked on mine, then places a soft kiss against my lips. My eyes close on their own accord, my arms tightening around her and pulling her closer against my chest. All too soon, she breaks the kiss and giggles softly. I open my eyes and meet her brown eyes shining like comets.

"We should play that song again," she says.

"We should," I say. "But this time, I think I should try my hand at the drums."

"Okay," she says brightly. I grin down at her, then quickly peck her lips.

"Hey! You just stole that," she says glaring, but she's not mad, not by the way her lips struggle to hold back her grin.

I shrug. "I guess you could say I'm stealing kisses from the good girl."

She rolls her eyes before walking over to the stereo. She sets the song on repeat, then turns back to me with a wide grin.

"Alright, bad boy, let's see how good you are at drums."

__chapter thirty-one__
Zander

Sarah opens the front door with a giant grin. I meet her smile half-heartedly, wringing my hands together. I've never done an official "meet the parents" before, so this has my nerves all sorts of out of whack. She gently pulls my hands apart, intertwining our fingers. She raises onto her tiptoes to kiss my nose, then drops back to her heels. Her soft kiss does wonders to help ease my worries. She pulls me into the hallway and nudges the door shut behind her.

"You'll do great," she tells me. "It's just dinner."

I blow out a shaky breath and nod. "I'm just really nervous. I mean, our first encounter wasn't exactly on dating terms."

"I know, but—"

Her dad walks in with a wide grin. "Zander! Welcome back, son." He slaps his hand down on my shoulder. My body stiffens under his touch. I quickly remind myself of where I am, then glance at Sarah. She nods at her Dad, who is still waiting for my response.

I gulp and close my eyes, taking in a shuddering breath. Then I face Mr. Jones. "Nice to see you again, Sir." I grip his hand tightly and shake it, my cheeks warming.

He glances at our hands with amusement. "You've got a good handshake," he says before speaking to Sarah past my shoulder. "I like him already." He gives her a playful wink before gripping my shoulder firmly, staring me down with a stern glare. "Let's get one thing clear," he says. "My wife isn't the only scary parent, so if you hurt my daughter, I'll rip you to shreds. Got it?"

I struggle not to grimace and keep a straight face.

"Yes, sir. Loud and clear."

Her dad grins widely again and pulls me into a tight hug. I awkwardly hug back, my heart threatening to jump right out of my chest. *What is happening? Should I be worried or something?*

He pats my back roughly then pulls away, giving me a once-over before kissing Sarah's forehead. He nods for us to follow him. "Gen is serving dinner now. We'd better get in there before she gets too impatient!" He disappears around the corner. I hurry to follow him, only to be stopped by a light tug on my shirt. I look back to see Sarah staring up at me, her hand hanging onto my shirt.

I turn to face her fully. "What is it, Buttercup?"

She wraps her arms around me tightly, pulling me into a warm hug. My heart calms down immediately, my tense muscles relaxing under her touch. She leans her head back to look up at me, a soft smile gracing her lips. *This girl knows just what to do, doesn't she?*

"Just wanted to make sure you're alright before we head into the lion's den," she says. "You seemed..." She searches for the right word, "Troubled for a second there."

I brush my fingers across her cheeks. "Yeah, I'm alright. It's just not what I'm used to."

She quickly nods. "Right, of course."

"Okay." I take a deep breath then grin down at her. "Let's go." I gently pry her arms from around my waist, taking her hand in mine and intertwining our fingers together. We walk into the kitchen together, and there's something about having her by my side, something about the way she squeezes my hand in hers, that gives me a burst of confidence. Her dad looks up from his bible, then grins at us and gestures for us to take our seats.

Sarah's mom walks in bearing a steaming bowl of potatoes. "Alrighty," she says. "I've got mashed potatoes, noodles, meat loaf, and gravy." She places the last bowl on the table, then sits down beside Sarah's dad. "Honey, are you going to say grace?"

He smiles and takes her hand, then takes Sarah's hand as well. Sarah grabs my hand too, and I stare at it in confusion. What's happening?

"Zander, did you hear me?" I jerk my attention back up to Mrs. Jones. As I glance around the table, I notice that they're all staring at me expectantly. I frantically look over to Mrs. Jones again. She reaches across the table, taking my hand in hers. "It's alright, we're going to pray. You don't have to join in if you don't feel comfortable with it, okay?" I nod cautiously, my palms becoming awkwardly sweaty. *I hope they don't notice that.*

She smiles and nods toward Mr. Jones to start. He bows his head and closes his eyes, Sarah and Mrs. Jones following his lead. I sit awkwardly as they start to say their prayers, then bow my head as well to say my own little prayer.

Uh, dear God, I say. *Let this go smoothly. I wouldn't mind living a little longer, so, um, thanks?*

"Amen! Let's eat!" Mr. Jones smiles cheerfully, breaking the circle by reaching for the potatoes. Sarah gives my hand a little squeeze and smiles over at me.

After a few minutes, Mrs. Jones finally looks up at me with a smile, her eyes glinting with what I know are a bundle of questions waiting. *God, I hope you're with me...*

"So, Zander, let's start off with some simple questions."

I gulp nervously but nod in agreement, internally preparing myself for the onslaught. Sarah stares at her potatoes awkwardly.

"How did you two start dating, exactly?"

"We were friends for a while, and I just kinda started liking her more as a friend then asked her..." I smile awkwardly, my eyes flickering over to Sarah for her approval. She's hiding behind her hand, laughing at my predicament. .

"Next question," says Mr. Jones. "What do you like to do for fun?"

I frown and look down at my plate. Everyone falls silent, waiting for my reply. *I hardly get to do anything for myself anymore, I don't even know...*

"Well, um, I like to go out and watch the birds and such. I also like mechanic work." A broken smile tugs at the corner of my lips, remembering the work I put into my bike.

"I've always wanted to learn how to fix cars," says Mr. Jones. "But Lord knows I don't have that skill! What do you do for work?"

I straighten up a bit and grip my fork a little tighter. "I work at the local grocery store as a shelf stocker." *And part-time where you have to clean up after your mess of a father.* I shove the thought away. "Down near Gateway Street. It pays well for now until I can get a full-time job after school."

"What are your parents like?"

Sarah drops her fork loudly, drawing everyone's attention toward her. "Sorry," she mumbles. Her parents look back at me. I grimace at my plate. Clenching my jaw, I look up again with a tight smile. "Well, my mother died, and my dad is an alcoholic. Next question, please?"

Mrs. Jones stares at me with shock and Mr. Jones smiles at me with sympathy. *Great, just what I didn't want.* We fall into an awkward silence again, Sarah stuffing food in her mouth and Mr. Jones loading more potatoes onto his plate to avoid further poking at the subject. Mrs. Jones clears her throat and smiles at me.

"Why do you want to date our daughter?"

I look down at my plate and smile softly before I face them again. "I want to date your daughter because she makes me happy, and she makes me feel wanted and important. She's a blessing in disguise, really. She's sweet, caring, loyal, beautiful, and all around a great person to be with. I can't help but to want to call her mine."

Mrs. Jones smiles widely at that, nodding her head in approval. I glance over at Sarah to see she also has a big grin on her face, her cheeks tinted with a blush. I feel a gentle pat on my knee under the table, causing me to jerk in surprise and slam it against the table. I look back up with wide eyes and look towards Sarah to see her silently giggling to herself. Mrs. Jones smiles over at us knowingly, and for some reason I feel like everything's going to be okay. *I could get used to this.*

I settle down on Sarah's soft bed, stretching my legs out across it. She sits down beside me, her shoulders slumped as she gives me eyes that say, "I know you won't like this." I have a bad feeling that she's right. "I, um, I'm sorry they brought up your mom." She looks down hesitantly.

I squeeze my eyes shut as a million and one emotions rush through me, none of which are good. Sighing softly, I sit up straight and gently pull her towards me. She moves willingly, resting her head against my chest while I hold her. These thoughts of my mom always burden me, pulling me into this loop of sadness and feeling of worthlessness. I think back to my date with Sarah, the words she said to me then. And she's right, I shouldn't let what happened weigh on me. It wasn't my fault that she died, and we did what we could to bring my father back from the edge. But in the end, that was his choice to make. His family, or his liquor.

Ultimately, we weren't enough for him.

A broken sound claws up my throat, and it comes out like a whimper. She gently pulls me to her chest, running her fingers through my hair while whispering sweet nothings in my ear. I wrap my arms around her tightly and bury my head against her shoulder. She plants a soft kiss on the top of my hair, then rests her cheek there.

"Your mom would want you to be happy, Zander."

And somehow, that's all I needed to hear.

__chapter thirty-two__
Sarah

I don't understand any of this.

More people cheer in victory when one of our players goes sprinting off down the field, a football clutched tightly to his chest while the opposing team chases after him. *That just looks terrifying.*

"Does anyone else not understand what's going on?" I ask.

Gina snorts and shakes her head. "I have no clue what's going on." She stops abruptly and jumps up in her seat. "Oh! That guy just got hit!"

Zander laughs loudly. "For someone who didn't even want to come, you seem pretty excited."

Gina shrugs indifferently and sits back down, "I can't help it. I enjoy the slight undertones of violence."

"Of course you do, you violent chipmunk," I say. We all fall back into watching the game. So far, our team is losing by two points with only a few more minutes till half time. I search the field for Keagen's number, but draw a blank. *What number was he again?* I frown and pull out my phone.

Game starts at 6:30 p.m. and admissions are five dollars per person. My number is 49, hope to see you there!

Zander rests his chin on my shoulder, his arm snaking around me and pulling my body against his chest. "What's that?" he says into my cheek. His lips press small kisses against my skin. I smile softly and turn off my phone, looking back out into the field and leaning into his hold.

"Keagen's text. I still can't seem to find him on the field."

"I think I see him?" Gina squints her eyes and points towards the middle of the field, "He's number thirty-nine, right?"

I let out a small laugh. "No, forty-nine. Maybe he's just on the sidelines right now?"

Zander sighs, causing chills to rise across my skin as his cool breath fans across it. "Don't worry about it. He'll be on the field soon enough."

I can't help the giggle that passes my lips. Turning slightly, I look back at him with a grin. "Sounds like you're jealous, Froot Loop."

Zander grumbles in response, hiding his face in the crook of my neck and tightening his hold around me, so I can't turn around again. I catch Gina's eyes and we share knowing looks. I reach back and pat his head. "Don't worry, I only have eyes for you."

Something pinches my shoulder, and I squeak in surprise. Zander laughs and pulls away from my neck, his eyes shining in victory. I gape at him as the wind blows over a chilly wet spot on my neck.

"Did you just bite me?" I ask.

He looks away innocently. "I don't know what you're talking about." I turn to Gina for help, only to get a wide grin before she looks away as well. I turn back towards Zander and smack his shoulder playfully.

"Just because you call me 'Buttercup' doesn't make me edible."

"Well, technically, humans are edible," Gina adds. "It's just called cannibalism." I give her a deadpan look.

Zander turns back around, looking deep in thought. Gina and I raise an eyebrow at him while he stares off into the distance. He gets up suddenly, a few people behind us giving their protests.

"Speaking of edible," Zander says. "I'm gonna go get some food. Do you want anything?"

Gina gets up too, earning us some more unwanted attention from other students. She stretches slightly and grabs her bag.

"I think I'm gonna go, too. I'll meet you at the stand!" She jogs down the bleachers, disappearing into the crowd of people.

I look back up to Zander with a small smile. "Could you get me some nachos, extra cheese?"

He nods and smiles softly, leaning down to lightly kiss my forehead. Then he's off down the bleachers. Without their presence, I suddenly feel very self-conscious. Shifting in my seat to wrap my jacket tighter around my frame, my eyes scan the field and bleachers in front of me. The cheer team begins lining up along the fence row, some already practicing their routine and some of the others standing in a circle talking. My eyes snag on her blond hair, ducked down to stare at her phone, her eyes glancing up every few minutes to check her surroundings. She almost looks nervous, as if she's waiting for someone to show up. I don't know what comes over me, whether it's the fact that I'm finally feeling better about myself this year or just plain pettiness, but I take out my phone and scroll down through the contacts list. I hover over her name, biting my lip as I contemplate what I'm about to do. Before I overthink it, I shoot the message.

Good luck, Samantha.

I tuck my phone back in my pocket, huffing a breath of relief. Despite the fact that she has been nothing but terrible to me, I can't help but want to understand what happened between us. Perhaps being the bigger person and saying something nice is the first step towards that. Samantha's head darts up, her eyes narrowing suspiciously at the crowd before her. I doubt she still had my number saved, so I don't expect her to know it was me. I relax back into my seat, smiling at the small win. It may not have been much, but it's a start.

Minutes pass by before they finally come back. It's halftime and the players are running off the field to their respective sides. The cheer team fills the vacated spots.

"What'd we miss?" Gina plops down on the bleacher beside me, and Zander takes his seat on the opposite side of me. I look over at the outstretched bowl of nachos excitedly, my mouth watering at the sight. I reach out to take them, but Gina pulls them away from me with a suspicious look on her face, before breaking into a grin and handing them to me.

I cradle the bowl possessively against my chest. "To answer the question you asked before trying to withhold my nachos, you didn't miss much. I believe they're about to start the halftime thingy." I gesture towards the field before shoving a bunch of chips in my mouth, my eyes fluttering closed at the wonderful taste.

"That is going to make for a wonderful wallpaper." Zander presses some buttons on his phone, then puts the picture on display. I struggle not to choke on the chips still stuffed in my mouth. In the picture, my eyes are half-open, and chips and cheese poke out of my mouth as I hunch like a goblin over the tray.

"Oh my gosh, that's gold! Send that to me!" Gina says. I glare at Zander darkly and swallow my mouthful, grabbing at his phone.

"Delete it!" I whisper-shout.

"Never!" He holds his phone out of reach.

"Oh hey! There's Jenny!" Gina says, interrupting our argument. I glower at Zander, who gives me a victorious grin before stuffing his phone back in his pocket.

I scan the field, spotting Jenny in the center getting ready for their cheer routine. She searches the crowd for a second then spots us, her face lighting up as she waves up at us. Gina and I grin and wave back, then settle back down in our seats. My eyes roam the field a little, locking onto Samantha again. She barks out orders at the whole team, pointing each girl into place and making corrections as she goes. Once she reaches Jenny, she physically readjusts her arms, causing Jenny to glower at her.

"Who shoved the stick up her butt?" Gina scoffs. I shrug and look away, forcing my nerves to calm down. *You did nothing wrong, Sarah, it's fine.* The band starts playing and the cheerleaders start their routines. Jenny quickly takes over the show, smiling wide and leading the rest in perfection. Samantha glowers her way every chance she gets, even trying to knock Jenny out of her routine by jumping in front of her to take over. Samantha smiles wide and proud as she continues to stand in Jenny's way, both girls shouting so loud their voices are heard over everything else.

"Someone's salty." I mutter under my breath, rolling my eyes and looking back down at my food, no longer interested in the show.

"Whoa, did she actually just do that?" Zander gawks down at the field. Jenny sprawls on her back on the ground, wincing. She sits up and grabs her ankle. My hands fly up to cover my mouth. Samantha steps to the side, and I catch her horrified expression before she quickly covers it up with feigned disinterest. People rush down to the field to help, and eventually the EMTs arrive with a stretcher. Jenny limps and grimaces with every step they take. She sends a deadly glare to Samantha before the EMTs load her into the ambulance.

Our principal, Mr. Tennison, comes onto the field. "Alright, due to the unfortunate circumstances, we will be starting the game again now. Good luck, players!" Our principal awkwardly waves to the crowd then jogs off the field, all the players rushing back to take his place. I wonder if Jenny will be okay.

"Oh hey, now I see Keagen." I point towards the center field where Keagen is huddled with the rest of the team. The timer goes off and the players start crashing into one another. I cringe back into my seat for more rounds of the game.

"I'll see you tomorrow, Buttercup." I smile back up at him, my heart melting in my chest. He kisses my cheek again before jogging to his bike. He waves at us and pulls out of the parking lot. Gina sighs softly from beside me, her eyes trained on something in the distance. I stand on my tip-toes to see over the mass of people and finally spot what, or I should say who, she's looking at. Kyle Cunningham gives a low-five to one of his teammates before wrapping his arm around him in a bro-hug.

"Why don't you just go talk to him?" I ask.

She spins around with an appalled look on her face. "No way!" She blushes brightly and looks at her boots. "Besides, I highly doubt he likes me back. No use getting my hopes up too high, right?"

I shake my head and grab hold of her shoulders. "Listen." I duck my head to catch her eyes. "You are beautiful and have a wonderful personality. Any guy would be lucky to have you."

Her eyes search my face before she pulls me into a tight hug. "Shut up, you sap." She mumbles against my shoulder.

Keagen jogs up to us. "I hope I'm not interrupting anything?" he teases. Gina lets me go and steps back, her blush returning.

"Nah, you're not. I'll go get the car, okay?" She turns away, waving goodbye to Keagen, and disappears into the crowd. I turn back to him with a small smile, nodding towards the now semi-empty field.

"You guys did great out there."

He smiles and actually blushes slightly, awkwardly rubbing the back of his neck. "Thanks. It was pretty tough, but we did it." He averts his eyes for a second. I awkwardly shift on my feet, looking for Gina's car.

"I was wondering..." he says. I turn back to him and he continues. "My birthday is coming up and I was wondering if you, and of course the others, would want to come to my house for, like, a mini-party?"

I think about it for a second. I've never been to a party, and from what I've read, they can sometimes be a bad idea... Gina's car pulls up beside us, her windows down and music blasting. But then again, he said it would be small. I glance back at her, then smile at Keagen. "Yeah, sure. Just text me the details!" I shout over the music as I run to the car. He smiles widely and nods, giving me a thumbs up before I hop in the car. I sit back into my seat and buckle up, pulling out my phone to send a quick text to Zander.

On my way home now. Goodnight, Froot Loop.

Gina sings loudly as she drives away, drumming along on the steering wheel. I rest my head back against the seat, closing my eyes happily. My phone buzzes in my hand, and the text back melts me into a little puddle.

Goodnight, my beautiful Buttercup.

__chapter thirty-three__
Sarah

I sigh heavily and rub my forehead, a small headache slowly forming. The math book mocks me as the words seemingly blur together. I groan and slam the book shut, pushing it off my bed and onto the floor. I grab my phone off my headboard to check the time.

"Crap!" I roll off my bed and rush to my closet to change out of my school clothes. Stopping for a second, I dial Gina's number, then put her on speaker while I try to find a different pair of jeans.

"Y'ello?" Gina answers cheerily, the sound of chewing filling up the silence.

"Gina! Thank fudge! Are you ready to go?" I spot the pair of jeans in the corner and grab them.

"Wha-? No?"

I pause. "Gina! Zander is going to be there any minute to pick you up, why aren't you ready?" I button my jeans and start looking for a nice shirt.

"Geez, woman, chill! I thought Zander would've told you himself, but I guess the lil' turd didn't."

"Tell me what?"

She goes silent for a minute, then finally speaks. "I can't go tonight. I opted to stay home with Mom." She sighs. "I'm sorry, S. I wanted to go, but she needs me right now."

My heart aches for her. "No need to apologize, G, I get it. And hey, maybe I could come over sometime and we can all hang out, maybe even make her favorite cake?"

"Yeah, I'm sure she'd like that." The chewing starts again. "But I don't think she would like it if we made a big mess like last time."

I snort back a laugh. Gina and I had a massive food fight in her kitchen one day. The floor, walls, and even the ceiling were covered in flour and cake batter. Gina's mom found us giggling on the floor with the ingredients all over our faces, and one cake in the oven. She sighed and shook her head at us, then smiled and told us to get cleaned up while she started cleaning the kitchen. "She didn't even get mad at us then!" I say.

Gina snorts loudly. "Yeah, until you left. Then I got an earful about it!"

I shake my head. "Well, maybe you shouldn't have thrown that first handful of flour."

"I did not! That was you!"

"That's your word against mine, but we both know who your mom would believe." I smile devilishly and put my shirt on.

"You're impossible."

"I thought you said it was just a few friends?" Zander grumbles as he tries to find a parking spot near the house. Dozens of cars line the road. People are dancing in the yard and filing into the house as lights spill out from the doorway.

I fiddle with my sweater sleeves uneasily, my nerves bubbling up inside me. "I thought it was..." My eyes drop down to kick an empty soda bottle away from my toes. The litter on the floor of his dad's car is nothing compared to what I expect inside, *at least basing off of what I've read before.*

Zander parks near the end of the street, sending me a sympathetic look. "We don't have to go in if you don't want to."

I shake my head, wiping my clammy palms on my jeans. "No, let's at least go in and say hi, and then we can leave."

He nods and shuts off his dad's car. I hop out, pulling my coat tighter around me to block out the cold wind. Zander rounds the vehicle and takes my hand, pulling us towards the front door. I glance around at all the different people, some I recognize.

Such as James from class, who is currently leaning against a counter flirting with two girls on the cheer team. Jenny, who is using crutches leaning against the wall as she plays a game of cup pong with Kyle. There are others I've never seen before. *Maybe they're from another school?*

"Don't let go of my hand." Zander tightens his grip on my hand before pushing through the front door. Bodies are tightly packed together in the house. The music pounds so loud that the house shakes. Some teens grind against one another on the makeshift dance floor. Some couples make out on the couch in the living room. I catch sight of Claire tangled together with one of the football players. Zander glances back at me with a grin. I glare back at him, and he lets out a small bark of laughter. We push through the mass of teens before finally reaching a less crowded area in the kitchen. I sigh gratefully, leaning against the counter as Zander digs around in the fridge.

"Hey! You guys made it!" An overly excited Keagen stumbles over to us, a huge grin plastered across his face. He pats Zander on the shoulder then turns to me, pulling me into a sloppy hug. I smile and awkwardly pat his back, pushing his shoulders back.

Zander laughs. "Looks like you already started partying without us, Buddy." I give Keagen a once over. His body slightly sways while he stands. His shirt looks rumpled, his shoulders slumped down.

He grins widely again, "Only a few beers is all. I had to get the party started somehow!"

A few random guys show up then, hollering at Keagen to join them while they start pouring out more drinks. He gives a thumbs up, then turns back to us. He points over his shoulder at his friends and opens his mouth to speak. We motion for him to go ahead. He nods and waves before staggering over to them.

"Happy birthday!" I shout after him. I slump down against the counter and sigh. Not even here for ten minutes and I'm already worn out. Zander throws his arm over my shoulder and pulls my body into his. I smile up at him softly, getting on my tip-toes to press a soft kiss against his lips. He kisses back gingerly, his lips curving up into a smile through the kiss.

He breaks the kiss to pull back slightly, his eyes shining down at me with something new. He drops his arm down to grab my hand, nodding towards the group of people dancing together. "Wanna go dance?"

I look over my shoulder to the crowd of people, then back up at Zander. "I don't think that's a very good idea..."

"Nonsense, I think it's a great idea." He grips my hand and pulls us into the crowd. We stop somewhere in the middle, a small clear patch in the room. Zander slides into his groove easily, but I stand awkwardly as everyone dances to the music, the occasional person bumping into me. I turn to Zander, my hands starting to sweat nervously. I'd rather be home under a pile of blankets right now.

He yells over the music. "Just dance!" He shimmies his shoulders to the beat, doing a little spin. I grimace when another person bumps against me, my skin getting sticky with nervous sweat. I raise my hands slowly, glancing around at the other dancers. I look back at Zander, who repeats his shimmy and spin, and does jazz hands, grinning awkwardly. I try to mimic his dance, almost tripping and falling into someone else when I attempt the spin. He just stares at me for a second before bursting out into laughter, drawing attention from the girls beside us. I blush and grab his arm, pulling us back towards the kitchen. Zander laughs all the way back, using my shoulder as support. We stop beside the fridge again and lean against the counter. I cross my arms and glare at him darkly, which quickly develops into a pout.

"Stop laughing at me!" I whine softly, my cheeks burning.

He wipes the tears from his eyes as he slowly stops laughing, until he looks at me and bursts into another laughing fit. I roll my eyes and turn away, spotting a table sporting Solo cups at each end. A few girls stand at the other end, tossing ping-pong balls onto the table and landing them into the cups at my end. My hands twitch. It looks like fun. They notice my staring, and a tall brunette smiles widely at me, waving me over. I walk over to them, my hands clasped tightly in front of me.

"Hey, ever played Beer Pong before?" She gestures to the table.

"No." My muscles relax. "But I think I get the gist? What happens when you score?"

The girl laughs, "The losing side has to drink the cup, of course!"

My eyes dart up to Zander, who is oblivious as he inspects the fridge, breaking into conversation with Jenny. I bite my lip, looking back at the brunette beside me, "Do I have to drink anything if I don't want to?"

She shrugs. "I don't think there's a rule that says you have to."

A shorter blonde girl nods excitedly. "Let's get a few more people, then we'll have a full game!" She waves some people over, and another girl and two guys come to join us. She directs everyone to their respective sides, splitting us into two even teams.

"Whatcha playing?" Zander wraps his arms around me from behind, his chin resting on the top of my head. I grin as the game starts, my hands reaching down to intertwine with his.

"Beer Pong," I say, watching his reaction closely. He raises an eyebrow at me in question, to which I quickly add, "I won't be drinking anything though. I have no interest in that."

His shoulders relax a bit and he chuckles softly above me as he kisses the top of my hair, "Well, good luck."

The two girls, whose names I learned were Eve (the brunette), and Veronica (the blonde), pull over two more guys to join our teams. "Guys! This is Sarah, she's going to play with us." Eve smiles at me and motions to the two guys, "This is Stan," she motions to the guy on her left, a tall boy with shaggy brown hair. He waves happily before walking over to stand beside Jenny. "And Fred." Fred waves and joins our side of the table.

Jenny pushes off the counter behind her and nods. "I'll play too." Shooting me a smirk from the other side of the table she says, "Be prepared to lose, Jones!"

"Bring it!" Fred calls back, looping his arm around Eve's and my shoulders. He pulls us into a team huddle, "Alright, ladies, here's the plan." He points to me first, "We'll try to teach you this first round, but then you'll have to hold your own." I nod in agreement as he continues to Eve, "You'll have to help distract them while I make the winning shots." He shoots a halfhearted glare across the table. "I can't have Stan distracting me again like last time."

Eve snorts back a laugh, "Okay, got it." We break apart and line up at the end of the table, ping pong balls in hand.

Our game begins with a rough learning curve from me. I struggle to get the balls in the cup, only accomplishing it once within the first round. Eve and Fred make up the loss by drinking for me, which soon leaves me to make the winning shots. We're down to one cup on each side, with Jenny shooting for the opposite team and I for ours. My hands feel clammy around the ping pong ball in hand, the lone cup on the other side feeling miles away. Jenny smirks from across the table, giving me a subtle thumbs up. Fred pats my back roughly as he leans in, his breath smelling of the cheap beer on the table. "You've got this, Sarah!" He says, a goofy grin on his face. I glance off to the side to find Zander leaning against the wall, an encouraging smile on his face. I nod to myself, taking a deep breath. *You've got this, just do it!*

I toss the ball onto the table. It bounces, then lands perfectly in the cup.

I shout in victory, fist pumping with Fred and Eve. Zander swoops me up into his arms, grinning down at me before planting a huge kiss on my lips. I grin widely and bounce in his hold, the thrill of winning lingering over me. Fred waves us over, our team huddled together.

"Sarah, come get a pic with us!" he says.

I run over to them, posing in the picture with a goofy grin across my face. Zander stands off to the side, his eyes shining with the same look as before. He nods towards the nearby steps and takes a few steps back in that direction. I nod in understanding and quickly exchange numbers with them, then rush over to the bottom of the steps where Zander stands and waits for me. I take his hand.

He gently tugs on my hand and leads us up the steps, the music fading into a soft background noise. "Where're we going?" I ask.

He stops at the top of the steps. "I needed to go to the bathroom. I wasn't very comfortable leaving you down there with friendly Fred." I roll my eyes. He grins widely, then goes down the hall to the bathroom. My phone buzzes in my pocket, and I look at the photo Fred sent. I save the photo and send it to Gina.

"There you are." I look up to see Keagen at the top of the steps. "I was wondering where you guys disappeared to, I thought you might've left."

I shake my head. "Nah, we stuck around for a bit. Who knew beer pong could be so fun?"

He laughs, then points to a closed door across the hall. "Dude, you've got to see this awesome painting I got from my parents. You'll love it!" He skips down the hallway, actually skips, and grabs a pair of keys from his pocket to unlock the door.

Confused, I frown and point at the doorknob. "Why'd you have it locked?"

He looks back at me sheepishly. "I didn't want anyone breaking into my room."

A light blush covers my cheeks. "Right...That'd be awkward."

He chuckles, then pushes open the door and waves me forward. I step into the room and look around curiously, my eyes stopping on a jaw dropping painting of the night sky. I gasp softly and walk closer. The constellations painted within are so vivid. Trees line the sides of the painting, giving it the illusion of gazing up at the stars. It draws me in, and I reach out to it. But I can't bring myself to touch it. It reminds me of the night on the roof with Zander, a small smile forming at the memory of our first kiss.

He sighs behind me. "Beautiful, isn't it?"

I nod, still in awe. "It's breathtaking." I face him, only to find he's standing a little too close. I stumble back. His eyes stay glued to the painting, his hands pushed deep into his pockets.

"It's only half as beautiful as you." His eyes fall from the painting to my face, his smile sad. "Too bad you're already spoken for."

A sense of foreboding slams into me. I blink up at him in disbelief and take another step back again. I clear my throat. "I should go..." I brush past him. He grabs my arm, and he grabs on tight.

"No! Please—I—Sarah, I need you." He squeezes my arm, digging his fingers into my skin. "Please don't go."

"No, Keagen, let go of me," I say firmly, jerking my arm out of his grasp.

He lunges forward, pulling me flush against his chest, and wraps his arms around me tightly. I faintly hear two knocks on the door before Keagen slams his lips against mine. I cry out and try to push him away, but his hold on me is too strong. I can't move. He shoves his tongue in my mouth, wriggling like a worm and leaving the bitter taste of alcohol in its wake. All I want is to be out of his grasp.

He moans loudly against my lips, his hand tangling in my hair. I pound on his chest, but it's no use. He doesn't let me go. My lips already feel bruised. The door flies open behind me so fast that it hits against the wall. Keagen finally pulls away from the kiss, but does not release his hold on me. I swear my heart stops beating in my chest when I hear Zander's voice crack.

"Sarah?"

__chapter thirty-four__
Zander

I dry my hands on the small towel by the sink, staring into the mirror at my reflection and fixing a few hairs that strayed from their place. My thoughts drift back to the beer pong game, and I remember Sarah's breathtakingly beautiful smile when they won.

I head back down the hall. Instead of Sarah, I find Samantha leaning on the door across from where Sarah was standing. She smiles up at me, her arms crossing over her chest.

"Where's Sarah?" I ask her.

She blinks up at me innocently. "What?"

I roll my eyes and clench my fists. "Cut the crap, Samantha. Where is she?" I growl, scanning the hallway. Samantha straightens up, a frown forming across her lips.

"Zander, that's no way to talk to a lady, is it?" she chides, crossing her arms over her chest as she glowers at me.

I sneer at her. "No, but to talk to a bully? I think it'll work." I step forward, her eyes widening. I take another step forward. She huffs loudly before stomping off down the hall. I roll my eyes at her retreating figure and turn to the ajar door across the hall. I shove it open roughtly, and it bangs against the wall. A loud, and rather obnoxious, moan draws my attention to the center of the room. My heart stops beating at the sight before me. Someone else has his fingers tangled in a girl's red hair. *My* girl's hair.

"Sarah?" That someone else leans back from the kiss and looks up at me with a giant smirk. Anger flares in my chest. His hands are wrapped around her tightly, and her hands weakly trying to push him off. She tries to turn around but he halts her, dipping his head back down to lock lips with her again.

Oh, hell no.

I pluck her from his grip and lunge at Keagen, hitting with an uppercut to the jaw. He shouts out in pain, his hand flying up to cradle his jaw. I knock him in the jaw again, sending him stumbling. I smirk, pleased by the loud cracking. His blood smears across my knuckles, his small gasps of pain egging me on. I shove him roughly, he falls back against the bed and then onto the floor. As I stand over him menacingly, my breathing comes out in short, ragged breaths.

A soft touch on my shoulder draws me out of my glare fest at Keagen laying on the floor. I close my eyes tightly, pushing all my anger down. I glance over my shoulder at her, my heart aching when I see how upset she is. I turn back to Keagen and kick him in the stomach sharply, my anger satisfied for the time being. *I'll go after him again later.* I take Sarah's arm and pull her out the door so we can get out of this house. I stare blankly ahead, the rage clawing at my chest as the scene replays in my head. I get to the bottom of the steps quickly, growling in annoyance at the amount of people everywhere. It's going to be rough getting out of here.

I pull Sarah closer and tightly wrap my arm around her waist as I push through the people. The need to get out overwhelms me.

She asks me to stop. I look down at her. She squeezes her eyes closed and grips her forehead. I place a hand on her shoulder. She whimpers, my heart breaking all over again.

"What hurts?" I ask quietly.

"I'm so sorry, Zander, I—" She falls forward. I barely catch her just in time and hold her against my chest tighter than before. She struggles to keep her eyes open as I hold her.

"C'mon, stay awake. Tell me what hurts," I plead with her, gently shaking her.

"Head...dresser..." She mumbles weakly, her eyes staring off unfocused. I reach around and gently touch her head. Her blood stains my fingers when I pull them back. *No no no!*

I let go of her waist and pick her up bridal style, careful not to hurt her again. I sprint to the car and place her down in the seat, my fingers moving to cradle her face as she starts to nod off.

"I wanna sleep..." She whispers softly as her eyes start to close more. I frantically pat her cheeks to keep her awake. How am I going to get to the hospital without her falling asleep?

"No, no, no, c'mon, baby, stay awake for me. Don't fall asleep!" I call out to her in a panic, my heart beating wildly in my chest.

She opens her eyes again to look at me, barely able to stay awake. "You're bossy." If the situation wasn't so dire, I would've laughed. I grip her hand, sending her a small smile to cover up the amount of panic I'm in. *C'mon, keep it together man, she needs you to!* I run so many stop signs and red lights, it's a wonder we make it in one piece. Once parked I scoop her up in my arms then walk quickly to the door.

"Stay awake, baby." I plead, my legs shaking in fear as I run through the main door. A nurse sees us and runs over to me, directing us to another room. I lay Sarah on the bed. The nurse asks about a million questions while we walk. I can barely get the answers out before she asks another. A doctor shows up and they shove me out of her room as another nurse leads me to the waiting room.

I pace the room as I tremble, tears starting to fall down my cheeks. *No, no, no, this can't be happening. I did this!* I kick a chair over, breathing rapidly as my heart clenches in my chest. I shakily search for the number on my phone before dialing.

"Zander?" Gina asks, confused. "Zander, what's going on?"

"Sarah's in the hospital. Come quick. I picked a fight with Keagen. Call her parents." *I'm no better, I'm no better than him...*

"What?" she asks. "What happen-" I hang up. I grip at my hair, my legs carrying me back to the car. The old engine heaves to a start, but I don't pay it any mind as I speed off into the night, my eyes blurry and unfocused.

I park the car and shut it off, dumping my keys into my pocket. I stumble out to the tree line in a daze. My knees give out when I reach the spot and the stones dig into my legs. Curling up into a ball with a sob, my chest heaves as I gasp for air. *I hurt her. I'm no better than my father, I hurt her...it's all my fault!* The once-forgotten voices come back to scream at me. I squeeze my eyes shut tightly, my fingers gripping the dirt underneath me. *I'm no better.*

__chapter thirty-five__
Sarah

A soft beeping noise jars me awake, my mind still fuzzy. The smell of sterile cleaner stings my nose. I open my eyes with a groan and I move to cover them, only to be halted by a cord attached to my arm. *What the...?*

"Sarah! You're awake. Oh, thank goodness." Gina's voice draws my attention towards the other side of the room, the sight of my disheveled best friend like a shock to my heart. I try to sit up quickly, wincing at the sharp pain shooting through my head. *What the heck happened? Where am I?* I choke back a gasp when it all rushes back to me. The party, Keagen, the blood...

Gina rushes to my side and gently stops me from moving anymore, a slight scowl on her face. "Quit trying to move; you hit your head pretty bad. The doctor needs to come check on you now." She spots the help button. She brushes a strand of hair off my forehead, "What happened, Sarah?"

My eyes dart up to meet hers, my lip quivering as I start to retell the story, "Keagen….he—" A sob escapes me, and within a second Gina has her arms wrapped around me.

"It's okay, Sarah." She holds on tight. "Just tell me what happened."

I begin telling her what happened between sobs. My head aches the more I cry, like hammers pounding on every corner. Gina sits in shock, her mouth opening and closing every few moments as she struggles to find words to say.

I groan again, squeezing my eyes shut tightly. "Where's Zander?"

I open my eyes again. She turns back to me and bites her lip nervously. I squint at her suspiciously as she fidgets.

"He called and told me you were here, but when I arrived, he was nowhere to be found," she whispers timidly. She fiddles with my bed sheets, not meeting my eyes. Something's up.

"What aren't you telling me, Gina?"

She sighs, her shoulders slumped. She keeps her eyes down. "I asked one of the nurses if she had seen him, and the nurse said she saw someone matching his description storming out of here with bloodied knuckles. That was the last anyone saw of him."

I look down at the blankets as I absorb what she said. *Why would he leave?* I meet her worried stare. "Did anyone call my parents?"

"I tried calling them, but they never answered."

The doctor bursts into the room, a gigantic smile plastered across his face. "Glad to see you awake, Sarah! Now, let's check those bandages."

A few hours later, I'm standing by Gina's car outside my house. "Thanks for bringing me home, G," I say through the open window.

"Of course. Are you sure you don't need me inside with you?" She looks over at me worriedly, her hand hovering over the ignition key in her car.

I pat her shoulder. "Nah, I'll be alright. You heard the doc. As long as I don't do anything strenuous or too loud, I'll be better soon enough. Besides, you gotta get back to your mom."

"Okay. If you say so." She places her hand back on the wheel, only to turn and point an accusing finger at me. "Don't you dare do anything to hurt yourself, and call me as soon as you need something, you hear?"

I laugh and nod. "Yes, Mom. I understand."

She settles back into her seat. "Okay, good. Love you, loser."

I step away from her car. "Love you, too." She waves at me then takes off down the road, heading right back to the hospital. I sigh heavily and walk up to my house, my nerves eating away at me. *Why would he just leave like that?*

__chapter thirty-six__
Zander

I wake up with a start and sit up, my body screaming in pain. *What time is it?* My phone buzzes in my pocket. I groan and push myself up against the head board, sniffling and wiping at my face. I dig around in my pocket and grab my phone.

"Hello?"

"Zander! Where the heck are you? I've been calling for like an hour now!"

I draw the phone away from my face to look at the time. 10:35 a.m. *I slept for that long?*

"Zander?"

I shiver and curl into myself some more, pulling my blankets up over my head. "Yeah. Yeah, I'm here. I'm alright."

Her breathing is the only thing I can hear for a few minutes. *I really messed this up. I messed this all up.* "Zander, where were you?" She sounds exhausted. I squeeze my eyes shut, forcing back the fresh set of tears as the night replays in my head.

"I'm at home now, I was in the woods—"

She gasps. "Oh, my fudge. Zander, did you sleep out there?"

I open my eyes and look around, my fingers tightening around my blanket. Glancing out the window I watch as the wind blows the tree branches back and forth. I can't help but smile sheepishly. "No...?" I reply. A shiver rakes through my body.

"—Hurry up!"

I rub my forehead. "What was that?"

"I said: Get your butt back on that bike before you get even more sick. Come to my house, and hurry up!" She sighs softly. "I'd much rather talk to you in person than over the phone, please."

"Okay, I'm on my way."

I hang up and lean my head back against the headboard, my mind spinning as the different possibilities of what's to come play in my head. *She probably hates me.* I get up and quickly make my way to the front door. My feet stop short. It is awfully cold outside to drive my bike now. I glance over my shoulder to find my dad still asleep on the couch, then back out the window. Without a second thought, I grab his car keys off the table beside the door then head out. Once settled in his car, I blast the heat up to calm my shivering nerves. The drive to her house doesn't take long, yet it feels like an eternity as I think of the different ways to apologize, of the different ways to get her to stay. I pull into her driveway and run to the door. I raise my fist to knock, but Sarah rips open the door before I can touch it. I open my mouth to start my list of apologies, but they die on my tongue when her eyes start tearing up.

"Zander, you had me worried sick!" Sarah pulls me into her arms, stunning me into silence as she holds me tightly. Suddenly, she pushes me back at arms length, "Why did you leave me like that?" She demands, her eyes heated.

"I'm so sorry, Sarah." I squeeze my eyes shut and wrap my arms around her, burying my face in the crook of her neck. She runs her fingers through my hair and presses a quick kiss against my cheek. My words are mumbled as I bury my face into her strawberry scent, "I was so scared I hurt you. I should have never run, and I'm so sorry that I did."

"C'mon, let's get you inside." She sniffles and pulls away, wiping her tears off on her shoulder as she pulls us inside. I follow her to the couch obediently. Her hands move up to my face and push away the stray hairs, her bottom lip wobbling as she juts out.

"I'm so sorry—" We both speak at the same time, our eyes locking as we stare at each other shocked. She continues. "I'm so sorry that all of this happened, that you were reduced down to that." She winces at her words. "I never thought something like that would have happened…"

"What do you have to be sorry for?" I cringe back at my own words, quickly realizing how harsh they sound. "I mean, you didn't even do anything wrong. I was the one who hurt you. This is all my fault...I was so afraid of what I did," I look away as tears start pooling in my eyes again, my heart constricting painfully in my chest. "I couldn't face you knowing what I did— just like him." This is where my happiness dies isn't it?

"You're an idiot."

I look back up at her with wide eyes as my mouth drops open. She shifts so she's now on my lap, and she grabs my face so I can't look away. Her stare pierces me.

"You're an idiot. A total idiot, you hear me?" she says.

I watch her with wide eyes, my heart pounding wildly. What is she going on about?

"You saved me, Zander. Sure, I hit my head pretty bad and I forgive you for that. But you *saved* me." She takes a deep breath, her eyes closing as she composes herself. Her tears slide down her cheeks and drop onto my shirt. She opens her eyes again and stares at me with something I can't decipher, a small smile forming across her lips. "You're my hero, Zander, but I don't understand why you still feel like the bad guy here."

I look down and close my eyes, "I hurt you. Whether or not it was to help, I still hurt you." I whisper, the tears from before now quickly spilling down my cheeks. I look back up at her and choke back a sob. "How am I any better than him? I'm just the same."

She quickly pulls me into her, her arms wrapping around me. "You are nothing like him, Zander. You're better than him." She pushes me back so I can face her again, her eyes red with tears. "You are such a sweet, loving, and caring man." She cradles my face in her hands. "You didn't hurt me intentionally. Don't you ever think that you did, you hear?" She gently shakes me, her voice coming out strong but trembling. I sniffle and nod, my heart flooding with adoration and something else, something I haven't felt in years. It takes everything in me to stop myself from jumping up and screaming it at the top of my lungs.

I love this girl. I love her so much.

"I don't deserve you," I whisper with wonder, my heart doing backflips. She shakes her head, her lips tilting up into a small smile. The small smile that I know ruined me for anyone else.

"You deserve the world, Froot Loop," she says. "You just gotta let me give it to you."

I choke back a laugh, her sweet words instantly melting me. I move my hands up to her face, gently pulling her down to meet her lips in a soft kiss. She kisses back slowly, her warm hands sliding around the back of my neck. I close my eyes and revel in the feeling, my heart swelling with love for the small redheaded beauty in my arms.

She pulls away from the kiss with a small giggle. "You're gonna make me sick, too."

I open my eyes and grin up at her. "It'll be twice the fun." I plant a sloppy kiss on her lips, laughing loudly when she pulls away with a squeal. I hold onto her tightly, my laughter dying down into a small smile. She leans down to rest her head against my chest, a sigh passing her lips.

"Are we good?" she whispers, her arms wrapped tightly around my waist.

I pull her closer and plant a soft kiss on the top of her head. "Yeah, we're more than good, Buttercup." I rest my head on top of hers and close my eyes. I can't help but chuckle when a new thought occurs to me. "I'm still going to beat Keagen, though."

__chapter thirty-seven__
Sarah

I hold the spoon up and glare at him. "Eat. Your. Soup."

He narrows his eyes at me and shakes his head. "I don't want soup."

I huff, setting down the bowl of chicken noodle soup I made from my mom's recipe. "Zander, you *cannot* eat three cheeseburgers while sick. You'll only feel worse!" I close my eyes, pinching the bridge of my nose. "Will you please eat your soup, for me?" I look back up at him and hold the soup out for him.

He stares at me blankly, then bursts out into a fit of laughter, which quickly turns into a coughing fit. I gently rub his back as he coughs, giving him a flat look when he smiles over at me sheepishly. "You're insufferable." I smile softly, my heart warming despite my annoyance. I look down at the soup and stir it up again, biting my lip to hold back a smile.

He sighs loudly, drawing my attention back up to his face. I raise an expectant eyebrow and he groans. "Yes, I'll eat the soup. Only because you asked so nicely." He pokes my side, and I jump.

I swat at his hand. "Quit it!"

"So demanding." He shakes his head. "Too bad it only makes me want to rebel even more." He reaches out and latches onto my hips, abruptly pulling me towards him. I gasp loudly when the soup sloshes forward, spilling all over the front of his shirt. I cover my mouth and stare down at the mess, then look back up to him. He stares down at his shirt with surprise and pokes at a noodle on his stomach. Slowly, his eyes make their way up to meet mine.

"Well, that didn't go as planned, did it?" I place the now empty bowl on the table and turn back to Zander. My eyes almost fall out of my head when I see him. *What is breathing?* His toned abs and arms look so strong, like he could take on anything that was thrown at him...

"No, it didn't." He shakes his head at himself. "Do you have any shirts for me?" He rolls up his shirt in his hand and looks back up at me. "What?"

'I—I,uh...Yeah, just let me..." I rush up to my parents' room as a blush blazes over my cheeks, shutting the door behind me. I lean against the door and shut my eyes tightly. Images of Zander's naked chest start floating around my head again. *Oh my fudge, woman. Get a grip!* I take a deep breath and open my eyes. I rummage through my dad's shirt drawer. It mostly contains business shirts and flannels; I push them all aside. *It's gotta be in here somewhere...*

I pull out the faded Led Zeppelin shirt from the back of his drawer. I slam the drawer shut and spin around, walking back downstairs to find Zander rinsing his shirt under the sink. He turns around slightly *and oh boy those abs, I can't. I'm going to die.*

I force myself to look up at his face, keeping my smile intact. "Here you go. Trade?"

He smiles gratefully and reaches out to take the shirt. "Thanks, Buttercup."

"Ah, ah, ah." I pull the shirt back. "Hurt this shirt, I'll hurt you. Please, return it as soon as you can."

He nods and flashes a cheeky grin. "I wouldn't dream of it. Now." He wrings out his shirt and turns back to me, holding the damp shirt in his hand. "Got a way of washing this?"

"You got me sick, you jerk!"

Zander grins widely and shrugs. "Like I told you, it'd be twice the fun. Now, scoot over!" He gently pushes my blanket-covered feet out of the way before sitting down on the couch with me. I grumble in response, defiantly moving my feet back to lay in his lap as I twist around on the couch and get comfortable.

I sniffle and grab a tissue, cradling the box to my chest. "Ugh, why is being sick so miserable?"

"Because you're sick. Duh." He grabs the remote, turning up the volume as *The Avengers* starts. This is his way of nurturing me back to health. Halfway through the movie, he disappears into the kitchen. I stay focused on Chris Evans's beautiful face.

I hear a loud crash and Zander hisses out a curse. I run to the kitchen and stop at the door frame. Pieces of glass are scattered everywhere. Zander smiles sheepishly and points to the broken mess on the floor. "I can explain that..."

I lean against the door frame as a cough racks through my body. "What ha-happened?" I clear my throat after the last cough.

"No, stop!" He motions towards the floor. "You might step on one. Stay where you are and I'll clean up." He grabs the broom from beside the hallway entrance and sweeps up the mess till he's beside me.

I lightly touch his shoulder. "What happened?" The shards on the floor remind me so much of the first day he was here. It's amazing how far we've come from that first day.

"I didn't realize I grabbed two bowls, so the second ended up on the floor before I could catch it. I guess you'll have to wait a bit until I can make you soup."

I grin stupidly. "You were going to make me soup?"

He looks back over at me with an eyebrow raised, a small smile on his lips. "Yes...? Is that a big deal?"

I blush, but nod anyway. "Yes, it's a very big deal in my book." I pretend to pull a small book out of my back pocket and make a check mark.

He stares at me with a huge grin on his face now, "Are you serious?" He sweeps the last of the glass into the dust pan, disposing of it in the trash can. I purse my lips thoughtfully as he takes my hands in his.

"Well, yeah, this is a very serious matter." He chuckles as I begin to explain. "There's a book I like where making soup is a symbolic gesture of love."

He stops laughing almost immediately, a blush rising across his cheeks. He looks down at our hands and back up into my eyes again. His eyes look so sincere, my breath catches in the back of my throat. I search his eyes frantically, looking for anything to tell me what's going on. He smiles widely as tears form in his eyes, and he cradles my face with a blend of urgency and tenderness that has my mind spinning in circles.

"I do." He lets out a breathy laugh. "Sarah, I love you."

Tears blur his face in front of me as I clutch at his arms. "Really?"

He nods and kisses me with a fiery passion. I can't help the happy tears that fall down my cheeks. He pulls away and rests his forehead against mine, entwining my fingers with his. He opens his eyes. "I do, I really do."

I press some more soft kisses against his lips, pulling away to say, "I love you, too."

He scoops me up into his arms and spins us around as I squeal. When he sets me on the ground, my eyes struggle to focus.

"That probably wasn't such a good idea while I'm sick..."

__chapter thirty-eight__
Sarah

I shove the papers back into my locker for the fifth time and slam the door. Gina sighs softly from beside me, staring off at the end of the hallway. I glance down as well, rolling my eyes when I see Kyle with Keagen. Gina looks half sad, half disgusted with the sight before her. I lean against the locker and leaf through my science homework. I sigh loudly and shove the papers into my bag, my annoyance levels rising by the second.

"You know, just looking at him won't lead up to much," I muse softly. She groans and leans back against the lockers with me, a sour expression painted across her face.

"I know," she says. "But it's all the further I can get. I'm too chicken to do anything about it."

I pat her shoulder. "Just go over and say hi. You don't know what'll happen."

She snorts loudly. "I *do* know what'll happen. Total embarrassment." We both look back down the hall at Kyle, who laughs at something Keagen said, "Besides, he likes Susan Hartly. It's just a matter of time before they start dating." Her shoulders slump as she looks away.

I throw my arm around her shoulder. "You'll find someone, G. Kyle isn't the only nice guy here."

She looks up at me and smiles weakly. "Yeah, you're right." Her gaze slips back down the hallway. I think hard for a second, mentally scanning all the kids in my classes, then grin widely when I think of him.

"What about Stan?"

She squints. "Who?"

"Stan. He was at the party. He's super nice!" I pull my phone out of my pocket and show her the picture of my beer pong team. She stares at it for a second, then lights up in recognition.

"Oh, Stan, I know him. He's in one of my classes, I think, but isn't he supposed to be moving to Wisconsin or something?"

I deflate slightly. "Oh." I close the picture and shove my phone back in my pocket. *Well forget that idea.*

"Sarah!"

I look up towards the voice calling me. Keagen makes his way down the hall. Gina straightens up and grabs my arm. I hold onto her tightly as we both turn around and sprint the other way, almost bumping into other students passing by.

"Sarah, wait up!"

No, thanks. I choose life.

We dart into the bathroom, leaning against the sinks as we try to catch our breath. Gina glances down at her watch, groaning loudly as she drops her head back. "Class starts in ten minutes." She looks over at me, "Are you gonna be okay to walk to your next class?"

I glance up to the clock by the door, crossing my arms over myself. "Yeah, I have to go to Home Ec next, and it's right next door." The warning bell rings, and Gina sighs as she gives my shoulder a reassuring squeeze before she disappears out the door. A sigh leaves me as I turn to face the mirrors. My reflection is not pretty. Dark circles hang under my eyes from restless nights of sleep over the weekend. A big bruise covers the left side of my forehead, disappearing into my hairline where I hit my head. My hair is tied back in a loose bun, strands fraying out in every direction. The bathroom door swings open, but I ignore it as I continue to stare at the ever so visible scar.

"You look like crap." The voice sounds out behind me, making my veins run cold.

My eyes squeeze shut, "I can't do this right now, Samantha." I open my eyes again to find her hesitating by the door, her brows furrowed with the same look she had that night at the party. I frown as well. "What do you want?" My voice is harsher than intended, but all the same. I don't have it in me to deal with another of her verbal beatings, not after what I went through over the weekend.

"I, uh…" Her hesitance surprises me. She fidgets with her fingers, finally taking a step closer so I can see her more clearly in the mirror behind me. She huffs and drops her hands. "I wanted to ask if you were okay." She looks away, her gaze settling onto the stalls beside us.

I frown immediately. "Is this a joke?" She winces at my words, her gaze dropping to her shoes as her face hardens. "Since when do you care?" I ask in disbelief.

She balls her hands into fists. "Forget it." she spins on her heels, fully intent on leaving.

"No, wait!" I spin around too, calling after her. Perhaps this is my chance to finally understand this thing between us. I may never get this moment again. She stops, slowly turning to face me. Her eyes are rimmed red, like she's been crying before she came in here. I slouch against the sink again, tired of this constant fight between us. She waits for me to continue, still afraid to meet my eyes. I decide to start small. My voice comes out wobbly. "I just don't get it. Why are you asking?"

Her lips press into a thin line before she says, "I saw what Keagen did to you. I just—" She closes her eyes and takes a deep breath. "I was worried." Finally, her blue eyes flicker up to mine, wide and vulnerable. My breath catches at the sight before me. This is the girl I used to be friends with, the girl who allowed herself to be completely real to me before she shut me out. Why, after all these years, would she finally change her mind? She winces, as if she read my mind, and walks to lean on the sink furthest from me. "I know that's weird coming from me…"

"Very." The words tumble out before I can stop them.

She glances over, her lips forming the smallest smile before it turns into a frown again. "I'm sorry, Sarah." She looks up at me again, tears shining in her eyes. "I don't have a valid reason as to why I did the things I did." She wipes away her tears bitterly. "It's just so hard when your parents expect so much from you, and criticize every little thing you do as to not being good enough. Comparing you to every kid around you, using their accomplishments to bring you down." She shakes her head, dropping her gaze to the floor. I knew her parents were hard on her growing up, but I never knew it was so severe.

"Is that why you turned on me?" Years and years of events start to make sense. Her constant need to be better than me, than everyone. Nights of staying at her house, her constant mood swings as we got older the more I stayed over. It got so bad that Samantha had stopped inviting me over, then soon after the art class ordeal had happened.

She hangs her head in shame. "You were a constant reminder of my parents' disappointment. I thought if I could prove to them that I could do better than you, they would show their love more than their disappointment." She shakes her head again, reaching up to run a hand over her face. "I've realized what a fool I was for thinking that."

I stare at her in astonishment before looking at the floor, trying to make sense of what she's telling me.

"I realized how much I've missed you." My eyes dart back over to her. Her voice wobbles as she continues. "I know you texted me at the football game. I still have your number saved." My eyes widen and my cheeks heat up. She shrugs her shoulders. "I thought if you could still be kind despite everything I've put you through, I could salvage a piece of what we used to have…Change a part of myself…" She trails off.

"I–" I stop as soon as I start, at a loss for words. What do you say to someone who is the sole reason you've hated yourself for so many years? Who wants to be friends again? I swallow past the lump in my throat.

She smiles sadly. "I don't expect you to forgive me, Sarah. I just wanted to tell you how I felt." She shrugs again, absentmindedly brushing her hand along the sink basin. "I know we probably will never be as close as we once were, but…" She looks at me again "I would like to work towards that if you would be willing to try that someday."

I contemplate her words for a moment. Our friendship has felt like a missing hole in my life, a constant question as to why. Can I trust her to not turn on me again? Can I forgive and forget everything that has happened all these years? I search her face, staring back at me with sadness and hope. I find my answer almost immediately.

"I would like to try."

She smiles, genuine and surprised, before she nods. "Okay," She pushes off the sink, wringing her hands together before nodding again. "Okay, well…I'll let you to it." She makes it to the door before turning back to me again. "Thank you." With that, she walks out the door. I release my breath, slumping against the sink.

The bell rings overhead, jarring me. Pushing off the sink, I turn back around to face the mirror once more. I really hope I didn't make the wrong choice...

"He tried talking to you again?" Zander fumes beside me in Home Ec, his voice an angry whisper beneath Mr. Barnes's lecture.

I nod solemnly. "Yeah. I don't know what he expects, though."

Zander scoffs a little too loudly. "He's expecting to get knocked out again, that's what."

"Mr. Mills, is there something you'd like to share, since you seem so adamant about talking?" Mr. Barnes raises his eyebrow at Zander.

Zander looks to the front of the room and smiles tightly. "No, sir."

He nods and points at both of us. "Good. Keep it that way." He turns back to the whiteboard and Zander turns back towards me with a worried frown.

"Are you okay?" he asks.

I shrug. "I don't know." My mind races when I think about what happened. I can't believe Keagen would do something like that. I glance over at Zander. "I just don't understand why he did it."

Zander frowns, before he pulls his phone out of pocket to shoot a text. I try to peek over his shoulder, but can't tell what he said. He looks over at me with a smile. "We're going to figure that out."

"I don't know about this, guys." I whisper towards the rows of bookshelves around me. I shift from foot to foot, my hands shaking.

"It'll be alright, Sarah, I won't let him hurt you." Zander peeks through a stack of books, smiling softly in reassurance.

I nod back and take a deep breath, looking back down the length of shelves as I wait. My phone buzzes in my hand. I draw in another deep breath as I read Gina's text.

He's coming.

I exhale sharply, and straighten up when I see him round the corner. He smiles at me and walks towards me with his arms outstretched for a hug. I take a step to the side, dodging his hands quickly.

"What do you want, Keagen?" I ask, a glare fixed onto my face. His smile drops as guilt takes over his features.

"Sarah, I–" He reaches out for me again, but I slap his hand away, hyper-aware of the small space we're in.

"Keagen, what happened to you? Why would you do that to me?" I cross my arms over my chest to put some extra distance between us.

"Me?" He exclaims bitterly, staring at me with astonishment. "You were the one who led me on." He accusingly points at me, "We had the start of something special until *you* threw it all away."

My mouth drops open in shock. "I told you I wasn't interested!" Tears threaten to fall down my cheeks, but I refuse to let him have the satisfaction. "We could have been friends, Keagen."

He shakes his head, reaching up to run his fingers through his hair. "I wanted more than that!" He shouts, his eyes pleading with me. "Why can't you see that?"

I lift my chin up high, blinking back the tears. I refuse to let another person walk all over me just to get what *they* want. "Why can't *you* see the flaw in your thinking?" His eyes search mine frantically, at a loss for words. I scoff, shaking my head. "It's over, Keagen. Don't talk to me anymore." I move to brush past him. He catches my arm and pulls me back, my body slamming into the bookcase behind me as he crowds my space. I squeak in shock, my eyes wide as I stare into his pleading gaze. My head pounds as my gaze blurs.

Suddenly, Zander rips Keagen off me and shoves him to the floor. He towers over Keagen, and he turns over his shoulder to look at me. "Go to Gina," he says softly. He turns back to

Keagen, who slowly rises from the floor. I run past him, barely hearing him push Keagen back again before shouting, "Stay away from her, man."

Gina catches me by the library doors, her eyes frantic as she checks me over. "Are you okay?" I shake my head no, my tears from earlier now freely falling.

Zander comes up beside me, pulling me into his embrace. "Let's get you to the nurse."

Once we make it to the nurse, she checks me over and gives me some pain meds to help with my headache. Zander gently rubs my back. I rest my head on his shoulder, closing my eyes. "That was a terrible plan."

He chuckles softly, using his finger to lift my head, "Yes, but you were able to stand up for yourself." I nod in agreement, forcing a smile. He places a gentle, barely-there kiss on my lips. He stays close, his forehead leaning on mine. He kisses me again. "I love you."

I smile again and pull him closer, resting my head right over his racing heart. "I love you, too."

__chapter thirty-nine__
Sarah

"This is huge, okay? Huge! Are you sure you want to do this right now?"

I roll my eyes and glare at the floor. "Yes, I'm sure." I grab a bag of Skittles off my desk and start chewing away. "Besides, it's better now than never, right?"

"Right." He sighs softly on the other line of the phone. "I don't even know if he'll remember." He scoffs bitterly and mutters something else under his breath.

"If he does or doesn't, it's going to happen either way." I plop down on my bed and throw a Skittle up into the air, trying to catch it in my mouth. It hits the side of my mouth and bounces across the floor. *Dang it, it was an orange one, too.*

"Yeah, you're right." He shuffles around a bit. I hear him start the car through the phone. "Alright. Well, I'm on my way now, Buttercup."

I smile and jump off my bed to pick up the Skittle. "Okay. See you soon, Froot Loop." I giggle when he snorts, and then I hang up. I wander over to my closet to look at my shoe choices.

My phone rings loudly in my hand. I look at the caller I.D. and don't recognize the number. *Who could this be?*

"Hello?"

"Sweetie!" My Dad's excited voice answers back. "How're you?"

"I'm fine, Dad, but what's this all about? Why're you calling on an unknown number?"

He laughs brightly and seems to speak away from the phone. I press the phone closer to my ear to try to understand him, my mom's laugh floating through the speakers as she continues to talk with dad. He finally returns, his laughter barely controlled while he speaks. "Your dear mother decided it'd be hilarious to chuck my phone into a nearby pond, so I had to get a new one."

My mouth drops open in shock. "She what?!"

Her voice interjects in the background. "I didn't chuck it into the pond. I was trying to take a picture of the fish and dropped it!"

He laughs again. "Yeah, she did that. Anyways, save this number. We'll be home soon—" He stops midway and mumbles something to Mom. "Your mother wants to know how things are going between you and Zander. Something about making sure the ship is still afloat?" There's loud shuffling before Mom shouts into the phone.

"ZARAH ALL THE WAY!"

I snort back a laugh, a wide smile making its way across my face while my parents bicker about how insufferable Mom is. A loud honk sounds outside my window. I pull the phone away from my ear and walk over to look out to find Zander waving up at me. I wave back and bound down the steps and out the door.

"Hey." Zander meets me halfway across the driveway and kisses my cheek. I blush slightly and point towards the phone, indicating we're definitely not alone and being listened to. "Oh," he mouths.

I put my phone on speaker, rolling my eyes when their bickering continues.

"Mom, Dad, shut up for a second, would ya?" They both stop talking immediately. "Things are fine, great actually. Zander is even here now." I glance up at him quickly.

"Hi, Mr. and Mrs. Jones," he says politely, a soft smile on his lips. I stare up at him happily, my heart doing little somersaults in my chest.

"Hey there, son," my dad says cheerfully.

Zander's smile falters for a second before it expands. "How're you, Mr. Jones?"

Dad laughs softly. "Considering my wife is a lunatic…" A loud smack sounds through the phone accompanied by a little shriek of pain from him. "Ouch! Anyways, I'm doing alright. How're you, son? Are you taking care of our daughter?"

I blush brightly and look up at Zander. He looks back down and replies, "I'm great, we're getting along just fine, but uh…" He clears his throat, then continues. "Are you sure some of the lunatic genes didn't get passed down?"

I swat his arm, and he bursts out laughing. Mom's voice quickly pushes through. "That's it! I'm actually going to throw this one in the pond!" There's some shuffling and a lot of grunting before Mom speaks again while breathing heavily. "Bye, sweetie, have fun," she says. "We'll be home soon. I love you!" The line goes dead and we both stare down at the phone in shocked silence. We stand there for a second until a laugh bubbles out of my chest.

Zander taps on the steering wheel, his lip caught between his teeth as he stares blankly ahead. I look between him and the shabby house in front of us. There's a light on inside. I look back over at him and rest my hand over his white knuckles. He jumps slightly and his eyes dart over to me before his body relaxes again.

"We don't have to do this now if you're not ready," I whisper. He shuts his eyes tightly for a minute and takes a deep breath, wraps his fingers around mine, and squeezes my hand.

He opens his eyes to look at me. "No, it's now or never." He gets out, jogging to my side to open the door and reach his hand out for me. "Let's go." I thread my fingers through his, standing up on my tip-toes to kiss his lips.

I pull away and gaze up at him. "I'm here. We've got this."

He stares down at me gratefully, then smashes his lips to mine for another kiss. I kiss back just as hard, my eyes fluttering closed. His hand cups my jaw, his tongue gently pushing past my lips and brushing over mine. My fingers tighten around his.

He reluctantly pulls away and my eyes flutter open again. I'm in a daze, my mind reeling. He grins down at me and kisses my nose. "I love you so much," he whispers softly. He drops his hand from my jaw and takes my hand as we walk to the house.

He tentatively opens the door and steps inside, and I follow closely behind. He knocks a bottle to the side, and it rolls to the other side of the little room. A stirring comes from the room to the left. Zander steps forward, his eyes darkening. I squeeze his hand and wait for his cue to continue forward.

"Dad," he barks, his cold tone surprising me.

"Son. Where've you been?" The man's words come out hoarse, but his voice still booms across the walls. I shiver and grip Zander's hand.

"I brought Sarah over, like we talked about." He gently pulls me forward, bringing me into view of Mr. Mills. He's a rather tall man, with stubble and black hair that desperately needs a cut. His clothes are crumpled as if he's been wearing them for a few days. Beer bottles litter the floor and he clutches another in his hand. My eyes meet his, and a gasp escapes me. He has Zander's piercing green eyes. Mr. Mills glares down at me, and his eyes snap over to Zander.

"So you brought her home. Want a medal?" He snaps his gaze back over to me, causing me to jump in fright. "Don't get yourself pregnant. We don't need any more low-lifes running around here." He downs the rest of his drink and throws the bottle to the side. The bottle shatters when it hits the wall. Zander flinches, his shoulders tense. Anger fills me. How dare he say that to his own son? To the man who has been taking care of him this whole time? Zander tries to step in front of me, but I tug on his hand and he stops immediately. I drop his hand and walk up to Mr. Mills.

"Quite frankly, sir..." I look up at him and square my shoulders, fixing my eyes on him. He raises his eyebrow, his mouth formed into a snarl. "You're the only low-life here. Good day." I grab Zander's hand and pull him out the door. A bottle hits the wall beside the door and shatters, barely missing Zander's head. We run down the driveway before he can hit us and get in the car. Zander starts the engine and pulls out of the driveway as Mr. Mills stumbles out the door. In the side view mirror, I see him throwing another bottle in our direction.

Ten minutes pass in total silence, both of us still too shocked to say anything. Zander slows down and pulls into a little dirt parking area surrounded by trees. I look around, totally lost as to where we are. I look back at him. He grips the steering wheel and stares down the greenery around us.

"Zander?" I ask. He shakes out of his daze and turns towards me, his expression filled with awe. I frown. "Zander, where are we?"

He blinks a few times, then shakes his head, a small smile forming on his lips. "I want to show you something. C'mon." He jumps out of the car and starts down a little dirt path. I chase after him until we stop at a little creek in the middle of a small clearing. Light filters through the leaves, dappling the ground and the creek. The trees wave their leaves at us. The creek is so clear that I can see the little fish swimming about. I look around with wonder, trying to mentally take pictures of the beautiful place so I don't forget. I eventually look back over at Zander, and he stares at me with the same awe as before.

"Where are we?" I ask. "Why are we here?"

He smiles and gently takes my hands in his and staring down at me lovingly. "Thank you," he whispers, his eyes glistening with unshed tears.

I blush brightly and shrug, my eyes dropping down to my toes. "I just couldn't take him talking to you like that. I—"

He dips down to kiss me, long and passionate. He pulls away, a large smile on his lips. "This is where I went when I wanted to get away from him, from the world." He chuckles softly as his eyes drop to the dirt beneath us. "I actually haven't been here as often."

"Why not? It's beautiful here."

"Because..." He smiles down at me lovingly, pulling my body closer to him until our chests brush against each other. "You're my happy place now. You're all I ever needed. Your love is enough."

I gasp, happy tears pooling in my eyes. He looks at me as if I held all the stars in the world. I jump into his arms and bury my head in his shoulder. He laughs and picks me up off the ground. I wrap my legs around his waist, the tears slowly rolling down my cheeks. He sits us against a tree. He gently kisses my cheek and his lips slide to whisper into my ear. "You're my home."

__chapter forty__

Sarah

Six Months Later

I bounce my leg in my seat, earning a look of annoyance from the girl beside me, but I'm too excited to care. This is one step closer to following my dream. I feel like I've done so much to get here.

I look up and glance to the row behind me, smiling gratefully when my eyes meet Zander's. *God, I love that boy.*

Mr. Tennison calls out another name, and Susan Hartley walks onto the stage proudly with a gigantic smile on her face. She grabs her diploma and holds it up in the air. The audience cheers even louder as she turns and walks back off the stage. I stare after her with wonder, my gut clenching. *If I were to try that, I'd fall flat on my face. And it's even a vertical motion!*

Soon, half the students have been called up to the stage and it's getting closer and closer to being my turn next. They're currently at the H stage, with only a few more students to go before they hit my section. *Lord, help me.*

"Sarah Jones!"

I jump up, waving at the people clapping and cheering as I make my way onstage, putting my best Converse forward as I remind myself to smile. My gown sways as I walk, barely brushing across the floor.

"Woo, Sarah!" I glance out at the audience, my cheeks burning wildly at the sight of my parents standing in their seats cheering loudly. I walk up to Mr. Tennison and grin widely.

He smiles at me fondly and hands me my diploma. "Well done, Sarah." He reaches out to shake my hand, but I raise my hand up for a high five instead. He chuckles and high fives me, then ushers me to the other side of the stage. I wobble down the steps, waving at my parents as I go by to sit in the student seating. There are only a few students left before Zander. I glance over at him, his leg is bouncing with nerves as he stares up at the stage. I grin widely and shake my head. *And he thought I was being ridiculous.*

"Zander Mills!" the principal calls out.

With a soft squeal, I turn my camera on and start recording. He walks up onto the stage with a soft smile, shaking hands with the principal and exchanging a few other words.

"I love you, Froot Loop!" I scream at the top of my lungs, gathering a few laughs from the crowd. Zander grins and blows me a kiss. I giggle and pretend to catch it in the air. My heart races with adrenaline. But I don't find myself glancing around to see who is staring, all I am focused on is the handsome boy on the stage. He walks off the stage, joining me in the seats with a large smile. He leans down to plant a kiss on my lips before sitting down. Soon, Gina's name is called as well and she is rushing down the steps to sit beside me.

"We made it!" She whisper-yells, gripping her hands in mine. She yanks me forward, wrapping her arms around me in a tight hug.

"We made it." I sniffle against her shoulder. "I couldn't have done it without you."

"You're stronger than you know." She says. She smiles through her tears and pulls me back into the hug. She giggles softly, "Of course, I'll take some of the credit."

Mr. Tennison continues calling names until there is only one student left. She nervously walks across the stage, her eyes roaming the crowd for her parents. The auditorium is silent as she walks, her face dropping. I jump up in my seat.

"Yay, Samantha!" I scream, scaring Gina beside me. Samantha releases a breath, a small smile forming as she stares at me, then turns to take her diploma. The crowd starts clapping as I settle back into my seat, looking over to find Zander smiling at me. He leans over to kiss my forehead, wrapping his arm around my shoulder and pulling me into his side.

"Class of 2022!" Fred shouts and takes his cap off. The rest of us graduates stand up and take our caps off as well before we all throw them in the air, the audience erupting into even louder cheering. We start pushing towards the exit, filing out to get pictures done with our friends and families. Somehow, the three of us get mixed up into the group, unable to get out of the crowd until we're outside.

"Oh my gosh, they're still animals!" Gina huffs heavily, glaring at the people scattered everywhere. "Animals!"

Jenny laughs and places a hand on her shoulder. "Gina, chill. Our families are right there anyways." She points towards the doors where our parents are pushing their way to us. I relax slightly when I see them, my grin returning when my dad runs up and engulfs me in a huge hug, with Mom joining in soon after.

"We're so proud of you, Sweetheart." My mom kisses my forehead, her eyes tearing up slightly. I smile up at her brightly, turning to look at my dad, my eyes widening in surprise to see him full-on crying. Mom rubs his shoulder, her eyes soft.

"My little princess is all grown up," Dad says, pulling me into another hug. I close my eyes and force down my small laugh, wrapping my arms around him. Slowly, he pulls away and wipes away his tears. "Okay, okay, I'm good. Go see that boyfriend of yours and bring him over here." I kiss my dad on the cheek before running off to see Zander.

At first, he doesn't see me coming, but when I shout his name, he spots me and opens his arms to catch me. I jump into his arms and wrap myself around him, giggling when he starts spinning us in circles. I lean forward and capture his lips in a kiss, my hands sliding up to run my fingers through the baby hairs at the nape of his neck.

He pecks my lips a few more times before resting his forehead against mine. "I love you too, Buttercup." I grin and kiss him once more before dropping my legs down, forcing him to set me back on the ground.

I pull away and grab his hand. "C'mon," I say. "Our family is waiting for us."

And in that moment, I swear his smile was brighter than the sun.

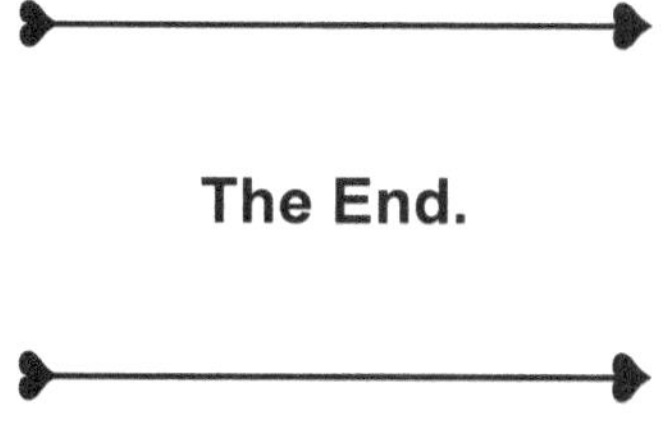

The End.

__bonus chapter__
Sarah

Five Years later.

"Millie, no! Drop it!" Zander runs across our living room with his arms outstretched towards our small tabby cat, who is currently holding his shoelaces hostage. Millie darts in front of the TV, where the Macy's Thanksgiving Parade is playing.

I giggle from my spot on the couch, watching with amusement as Millie runs right between his legs and back into the kitchen. Zander groans in and makes his way to me, dropping to his knees in front of me and resting his forehead on my stomach. I smile and run my fingers through his hair.

"I could always buy you new shoelaces," I say.

He shakes his head. "What? So that devil cat can steal them again?" He sighs and rests his head on my stomach, his hands splaying protectively along my sides. "I won't let that devil cat hurt you, buddy." He gently kisses my stomach, a happy smile floating across his face as he runs his hands over me.

I narrow my eyes down at him and place my hand on top of my stomach, "You refer to our baby as a he, but I'm certain *she* will surprise you in six months."

He challenges me with a smirk firmly planted across his lips. "Or *he* will be surprising you." He looks back down to my stomach and his expression melts into one of pure happiness. He leans forward again and rests his forehead there gently. "Ain't that right, little guy? But I'm thankful for you no matter what you turn out to be," he whispers softly, making my heart stutter in my chest. Beaming, I run my fingers through his hair as he rests there.

The moment is ruined, however, by the shrill sound of the door bell. Millie tears off immediately and hides underneath the couch.

Zander sits up and sighs, standing up with my hands now in his. He smiles and leans back down, capturing my lips in a sweet kiss.

"I gotta go get the door, Buttercup." He smiles into the kiss, his words nothing but a soft murmur. I hum in response and press my lips firmly against his again. He finally pulls away, and I follow him to the door.

"I brought desserts!" Gina exclaims when we open the door, a huge tray filled with different assortments of sugary delights. My eyes roam the plate filled with brownies, lemon bars, buckeyes, and caramel pecan tarts. My mouth waters at the sight of them and my stomach rumbles loudly.

"Those look heavenly," I say, gesturing for Gina to come in. My eyes don't leave the tray.

"Yeah, but it was a mess when she tried to make them." Zach, Gina's husband, joins us in the hallway, a container in his hands. "She wouldn't even let me in the kitchen." She lightly punches his shoulder, and he laughs. I smile at him warmly.

"I bet," I say. "I've seen Gina in the kitchen. It's definitely a nightmare." I lean forward and shield my mouth as I whisper, "Even worse than Zander when it comes to desserts."

"Hey!" Zander exclaims, shooting me a playful glare.

Zach laughs and glances at Zander, who is leaning against the door jamb to the living room. Gina sighs and takes my arm, grabbing the container from Zach. "I'm stealing Sarah. Don't come into the kitchen unless called!"

I roll my eyes at her. "It's not like we're hiding something in here, G."

She hushes me with a simple look. "Sit, I don't want you overworking yourself." She smiles down at my stomach, her eyes shining with love.

I repress another eye roll and give her a pointed look. "I'm not immobilized, you know. I'm barely even three months along!"

She points a finger at me. "I don't care. I don't want my little nephew getting hurt." This time, I snort back a laugh. She claps her hands. "Okay! So I brought you in here today to try this secret dessert." She leans forward and whispers, "Don't tell them. I want to see their reactions when they accidentally eat one."

I frown at the tray. "What're you...Oh my cheese balls, did you really make them?"

She nods as she unwraps the plastic covering. She turns it so the chocolatey desserts are facing us. "I still don't understand how this even remotely sounds appealing to you, but yeah, I made them."

I stare down at the tray, my mouth watering in anticipation. Mini chocolate cupcakes with buttercream frosting, topped with a chocolate-covered pickle chip. I pick the cupcake up and pop it in my mouth, my eyes fluttering closed in pure delight. The sweet flavor of chocolate and buttercream clashes perfectly with the tang of the pickle. Gagging noises pull me out of my dream world. I open my eyes. Gina holds a piece with a bite taken out of it, a grimace on her face. I lean back and laugh loudly.

"That is the worst combination ever!" She throws away her piece, wiping her hands off on her jeans.

I giggle softly and rub a hand over my stomach. "She doesn't seem to mind at all."

She shudders, then throws a disgusted look towards my baby bump. "He's gonna come out as weird as you then."

Zander chooses that moment to walk into the room. "Sarah, your parents are here." He walks over and gently takes my hands in his, pulling me up to my feet. I roll my eyes again and swat him away, walking towards the front door with ease.

I smile when I see them. I pull them each into a hug and usher them into the dining room where everyone is already seated. After we all say grace, Zander is the first to dig into the food. He stacks his plate full of mashed potatoes, filling, and turkey. I watch him and smile with amusement, then begin to fill my own plate with little helpings of each item.

Soon, we're all leaning back in our seats, happily full when Gina decides to bring out the tray of chocolate. My mouth waters again. Gina throws me a sly grin, then sets them down in front of Zach and Zander.

"Oh, what're these?" Zander goes for one of my "special" desserts. He sticks the whole thing in his mouth with a giant grin, which quickly turns to a scowl as he spits it out onto his plate.

Zach stares at him with wide eyes and quickly reaches out, popping one into his mouth as well only to spit it out all the same. "What the heck, why would you make chocolate-covered *pickle chips?*"

Gina points an accusing finger towards me. "Ask the pregnant lady over there."

My dad chuckles softly from his seat and looks at Zander with amusement. "Get used to it, son," he says. He glances over at my mom fondly. "This one really seemed to like bananas and rice together. Who would've thought?"

I scrunch my nose up in disgust. "That just sounds nasty."

Zander whirls back around to face me. "Says the girl eating chocolate-covered pickles!"

"What's wrong with them?" I ask, nonplussed. Everyone, except my mom, cringes at the question. I hold back a satisfied grin.

"I could give you about a million different reasons as to why those are not a good combination." Zach scrunches his nose up and looks over at Gina. "And you made these?"

She shrugs her shoulders and smiles over at him. "Sure did, and the little guy seems to love 'em!"

"That's assuming *she* is a *he*, again!" I say.

My mom grins and reaches across the table to grip my hand. "I'm sure it's her too, sweetie."

Zander snorts from beside me and shakes his head. "Wanna bet?"

"Yeah, how much?" Dad asks.

They all start to haggle over the bet. I run my hand over my baby bump and smile down at it, my heart warming at the thought of what's to come. I gaze at the people surrounding the table.

"Hey, Buttercup," Zander whispers in my ear. "Are you alright?"

"I'm absolutely perfect," I say, my heart booming with all the love in the world for this man I can call my own.

He kisses my cheek and whispers in my ear, "I love you."

"I love you, too." I wrap my arm around my baby bump and stare up at him, tearing up as well. He turns his attention back to the bet, instantly jumping in to add his two cents on the matter.

This is my family, my own little family, and I couldn't be happier.

___contact the author___

Now that you've finished reading *The Secret Ingredient to Falling in Love*, I'd love to hear what you thought of it! Please share what you liked, disliked, or how this book has helped you. You can do this by writing a review on *The Secret Ingredient to Falling in Love* Amazon listing to help other readers find the best book for them. If you'd like to start a conversation, email me directly at authormollyk@gmail.com.

You can also follow me on:

Facebook: Author Molly K.

Instagram: author_molly_k

Pinterest: Author Molly K.

Wattpad: Word_Addict_5976

Goodreads: Molly Kendall

Website: authormollyk.com

Read on for a sneak peek at *Amazon*

bestselling author Molly Kendall's next novel.

Saving Ariel

She can't move on to her future if she keeps living in the past…

Available on *Amazon* and *authormollyk.com*

• *Saving Ariel* •

It's winter in the middle of the state of Wisconsin. In a small coffee shop at the corner of town sits 18-year-old Ariel Matthews holding a small cup of hot chocolate. Her sweater is a tad too big, but still comfortable. Her long black hair is thrown up into a messy bun, just the way she likes it.

She sits behind the counter, every now and then getting up to help the one or two customers that walk in for an evening drink to warm themselves from the freezing wind. The sleeves of her sweater cover half of her hands, keeping all but her fingertips warm. With a sweet smile and a light wave, she bids the customers farewell and relaxes back into her chair where her book awaits her, getting lost in the world of fantasy and romance once again.

That is, until he walks into the store. He came in to apply for the newly opened spot as an employee, the spot she was hoping wouldn't be filled, even though that meant double the work for her. She enjoys helping the customers and watching the happy smiles on their faces as they drink their coffees and laugh with friends. She enjoys the free moments she has to sit and wait for the next customer, to just bask in the overwhelming smell of fresh coffee brewing behind her. It has always been peaceful.

But when 19-year-old Axel Stone came in, her world changed completely.

~•~

"Why do you always wear sweaters?"

"They make me feel safe."

"I could do that for you instead."

The night is colder than most. I wrap my coat tighter around me as I walk toward the coffee shop. My dear brothers took my car to go to hockey practice, leaving me to walk to work this evening since we all have to share a vehicle. We share it because Matti wrecked their first car when he was seventeen, and it has just been easier for us to only have two cars for now. Sounds crazy, but considering we also don't have the parking space, it just works better. They're all older than me. Brody, Zach, Matti, and I have always been close.

Despite them being triplets, they're polar opposites of each other. Brody is interested in mechanical engineering, Zach is focused on his hockey career, and Matti is studying to be a history professor. Matti has a knack for reading, just like I do, and also dabbles a little in writing. Zach is the goofball of the family. If at any time we're laughing our guts out, Zach is usually the cause of it. Along with his goofy personality, he is also very serious when it comes to his hockey career and taking care of the family. Brody, who takes pride in the fact that he was born first, takes on a leadership role within the house. He's always there for us when needed, and he knows just what to do when things go wrong. He's the most similar to our dad, and we love him dearly for it.

As for looks, the four of us are fairly similar. I have long, black hair and auburn brown eyes to match my dad, and the boys all have black hair like mine, but blue-green eyes to match our mother's. The boys inherited our father's height, each reaching as tall as 6'0", while I stand at 5'6"—just like our mother.

I don't usually come to work on Wednesday nights, only a little in the morning, but Steve asked me to take the second shift so he could go to the hospital with his wife. She's currently eight months pregnant with their fifth child. *How one can have five kids, I will never know.* The little bit of snow on the ground crunches beneath my feet, collecting on the sides of my black ankle boots.

Today I had on my normal work attire, leggings with an oversized sweater and a pair of boots. Steve is pretty lenient with work attire. As long as we at least have our name tag visible on the side of our shirts, we can pretty much wear whatever we want. Some days I wear the black sweater he had specifically made for me. *I know, I know. I'm special.* Other days I just wear one of my regular sweaters with my name tag.

I see the bright Stevie's Coffee sign before I even see the building itself. I quicken my pace to get there faster. Nobody is there, and the lights are on, but thankfully the door is locked. I take out my keys and unlock the door, stepping into the warmth. Steve told me I only had to stay until at least twelve, eleven-thirty if nobody continued to show up.

Five minutes later, I'm finishing wiping the counter and all the other tables with fresh coffee brewing behind me. The door opens, and in steps a boy who looks between eighteen and twenty years old. His shoulders are slumped as he walks, his hands shoved deep in his pockets and his mouth curled down in a frown like he hates the world—or as if he believes the world hates him. A black hoodie is draped over his head, with hair slightly sticking out at the top, and since he is staring at the floor I can't quite see his face.

My heart starts to race as I think about how sketchy this stranger looks right now. *Not to judge, but dude, you look like you're about to rob someone.*

He goes to a seat in the back, not even glancing over at me. *Maybe I should check to see if he wants anything.* I watch him for a few more minutes, contemplating if I should approach him or not, but end up starting towards him anyways.

He's huddled over his phone, tapping away but not appearing to talk to anyone. I get closer and slightly peek over his shoulder. *Flappy Bird. Nice.* For some reason the fact that he's simply playing a game on his phone makes me feel more relaxed. Although it doesn't say much about him, I can sense that he's just a normal guy. My shoulders relax, and I'm able to step forward with a little bit of confidence now that he seems a little less intimidating.

"Hello. Would you like to order anything?" I grab my pen and paper from my apron, something Steve got me because Lord knows I can't remember things, and smile down at him. His fingers stop tapping, and then he turns to face me. His brown eyes seem to pierce right through me, and my smile dies down a notch. The feeling of intimidation washes over me again. He notices and frowns, turning back to his phone.

"No."

Well alrighty then. I nervously fiddle with the sleeves of my sweater and take a step back, nodding softly, but then realize he probably didn't see it. I gather up all the courage I have left and speak,

"Okay, well if you need anything I'll be at the counter." I wait a few seconds for a response, even a slight nod or look in my direction, but nothing. Nothing at all. It's like he doesn't even know I'm still here. I shake my head and turn away, walking back to the front. I take a look around. The shop is empty except for Hoodie Boy over in the corner.

Smiling, I grab my book and plop down onto the stool by the register. *I have been waiting all day to read this again.* My smile turns into a grin as I slowly run my fingers across the pages, listening to the soft ruffle as they flip across my fingers. The smell of the book's old pages wafts up to my nose, making me close my eyes as I breathe it in. Call me crazy—heck, call me whatever you want. But the smell of an old book's pages is nothing I've ever experienced before. It's something special. To think that so many words were written, all printed onto these pages and left behind as someone's life work, or maybe even a small hobby—either way, it's amazing. The same euphoria comes to me through new books as well.

"You going to get me something or are you going to sit there and sniff your book all night?" His voice is unexpected, causing me to jump in my seat and drop my book onto the counter. I blush, closing my book and placing it back on the shelf under the register. Hoodie Boy, whose name I still haven't asked for yet, is staring at me with eyebrows raised and a small amused smile on his lips, his hands resting on the counter and a couple dollar bills between his fingers.

"Oh, uh yeah, um right. What can I get you?" I stutter awkwardly and slide off the stool, my cheeks still slightly pink from getting caught. Although I'm not ashamed, it's still kind of embarrassing.

He points toward the coffee machine and says, "One coffee. Black." Nodding, I type in his order and tell him the amount. He mutters a low "Thanks," and tosses his money onto the counter before walking back over to his seat. I eye up the dollar bills and sigh, putting them into the register even though I feel like chucking them right back at him. *Would it kill him to be a little nicer?* I brew his coffee and pour it into one of the standard mugs, considering he didn't seem to want to elaborate on what size cup he wanted, or if he even wanted it for here or to go. *He didn't even tell me his name so I could call him back up here!*

He's hunched over the table again, looking lost in the world on his phone screen. His broad shoulders look intrusive compared to the small back side of the chair he's seated on.

Grumbling under my breath, I walk over to his table and place the cup down. Not even bothering to plaster the fake smile onto my face. To my surprise, he actually looks up at the cup when I set it down. He reaches forward and pulls it towards him, bringing the cup up to his lips to take a sip of the steamy liquid. I didn't realize I was staring until he stopped mid-way and turned his gaze up to me.

"You can go now." Despite his rude reply, I still saw the corner of his mouth twitch up into a short but small smile, as if he thought I was amusing.

I awkwardly pat my hands on my thighs and clear my throat. "Oh, right." I rush back over to the counter and busy myself with cleaning up, keeping my back turned toward Hoodie Boy until I hear his seat squeak from sliding across the floor and the doorbell jingle when he leaves. I run my hand down my face, sighing in relief that he's gone.

"I grab a dish towel and head over to his table, grumbling and mentally slapping myself for acting so stupid. His coffee cup was completely empty, not even a drop left behind. And under the cup saucer was a crumpled up ten dollar bill. Lifting the bill between my fingers, I can't help but feel intrigued by this interesting character. Shrugging off the odd encounter, I continue about my night. *Another day, another dollar.*

__about the author__

Molly Kendall is a kind, quick-witted, quiet twenty-year-old Christian girl who appreciates dramatic stories, adores nature, and loves to inspire others. When she isn't spending time with her family, friends, and cats, she's either working at her full-time job as an assistant manager, part time at Rebel Queen Books, or dreaming up her next big idea. Molly strives to bring hope to her readers in everything she writes. You can visit her online at authormollyk.com, or email her at authormollyk@gmail.com.

rebel queen

We hope you loved Molly's book as much as we have loved partnering with her in preparing it for you! Her voice and perspective are fresh and the future of fiction.

With a combined 20+ years in publishing, we know how to help *anyone* write, launch, and market a book. So if a book is on your bucket list? We're the team to take it from brain dump to bestseller.

RebelQueen.co
marti@rebelqueen.co
Facebook and Instagram @rebelqueenbooks